## ABOUT THI

Dionne Haynes spent most of her childhood in Plymouth, England. She graduated from medical school in London and enjoyed a career as a doctor for over twenty years. After returning to Plymouth, she traded medicine for a career writing historical fiction.

### BY DIONNE HAYNES

*The Second Mrs Thistlewood*

The Roseland Collection
*Mawde of Roseland*
*Mistress of Carrick*

The Mayflower Collection
*Winds of Change*
*Running With The Wind*
*The Winter Years*

For more information and updates:
www.dionnehaynes.com

# MISTRESS OF CARRICK

## THE ROSELAND COLLECTION
### BOOK TWO

## DIONNE HAYNES

Allium

Published by Allium Books 2024
22 Victoria Road, St Austell, Cornwall, PL25 4QD

Copyright © Dionne Haynes 2024

Dionne Haynes asserts her right under the Copyright, Designs and
Patents Act 1988 to be identified as the author of this work.

This story is a work of fiction. The names, characters and incidents
portrayed in it either are products of the author's imagination or are used
fictitiously. Any resemblance to actual persons, living or dead, events or
localities is entirely coincidental.

First published by Allium Books in 2024
Allium Books is a publishing imprint for
Dionne Haynes, Author

A CIP catalogue record for this book is available from the British Library

Paperback ISBN: 978 1 915696 05 2
Hardback ISBN:978 1 915696 04 5
Ebook ISBN: 978 1 915696 06 9

Book cover design by Dee Dee Book Covers

*For my family*

# A NOTE FROM THE AUTHOR

The pages you are about to read are a work of fiction. The characters are products of my imagination or fictionalised versions of real people. I have meddled a little with the coastline and layout of the village, and have altered the name of the very steep hill where the Holy Well is located.

Now let me take you back in time to a tale set in Tudor Cornwall…

# CHAPTER ONE

1537

The River Fal glistened in the distance, every ripple sparkling like a jewel in the June sunlight. The air was still, the heat intense. Beads of sweat melded together on the back of Mawde's neck and between her breasts. Tiny rivulets tickled her skin and dampened the linen of her shift. She dabbed her brow and neck with a square of linen, silently cursing Nicholas for insisting they walk through the fields while the sun was at its zenith.

'Can you believe this is all mine?' Nicholas waved his arm in a grand sweeping gesture. 'Everything from here to almost the headland where King Henry will build his castle.'

A bubble of pride rose from Mawde's stomach, but dispersed as quickly as it came. Nicholas had said 'mine' rather than 'ours', and not for the first time.

'How will we manage all this land? We know nothing about farming.' Mawde bent to pluck a stem of a corn-flower, its blue petals faded and dried by the sun.

'We won't work this land. I told you before we wed, I

would look to your family members for their guidance and expertise.' Nicholas removed his doublet and blotted his forehead with his shirtsleeve. 'I thought your cousin might have negotiated harder, but I can't deny my pleasure at agreeing terms favourable to me. I'll earn a decent income without wielding an axe or a scythe.'

'Cousin Henry's a farmer, not a businessman.' Mawde stumbled on a patch of rubble. She reached to the ground to pick up a pebble and turned it over in her hand. The pebble was hot against her palm and worn smooth with time and weather. She tightened her fingers around it, squeezing hard to distract herself from the tears misting her eyes. She knew where the pebble had come from.

'There's a wall here,' said Nicholas, brushing earth and dust from the uppermost stones before sitting and twisting to look towards the river. 'The King took so long to grant this land to me, I feared he had changed his mind.' He fixed Mawde with a mean stare. 'I feared he might have discovered something that caused me to fall from his favour. Something not of my making.'

A breath caught in Mawde's throat. 'He's probably had other things on his mind since he wed Jane Seymour, and especially now she's heavy with child.'

'Perhaps.' Nicholas patted the crumbling stones beside him. 'Come, sit with me and share my joy. By God's grace, the owner of this land died without leaving an heir, and now it will be me and my heir who will benefit.'

Mawde perched beside Nicholas and scanned the wild-flowers and grass, seeking more traces of the past. In the twelve months since her return to St Mawes, it was the first time she had walked in this meadow.

Nicholas continued speaking. 'I see a glorious future, Mawde. My share of the fruits of this land, and other ventures I have in mind, will bring significant wealth. We'll enjoy a lifestyle that would have been mine sooner had my mother not married beneath her.'

'She married for love,' Mawde said, guarding her tone and searching her husband's eyes for the warmth they had held before they were married. 'You told me that yourself and even seemed to admire her for it.'

Nicholas loosened the laces of his shirt. 'That I did. But, alas, love does not put food on the table nor dress a person in fine clothes. We, however, will never lack for comfort. I will see to that.'

While Nicholas enthused about making his fortune and working his way into minor gentry, Mawde held her silence. She tightened her grip around her pebble, imagining she was clinging to her father's hand. Grief ripped through her, leaving a deep ache in her chest. She would trade everything she had to go back in time and correct her childhood mistakes. She would not forget to pass on the important message to her father, and he would not fall from his horse in his rush to catch the Penryn ferry. Their home would not be little more than scattered patches of rubble, and her family would not send her away to work in another county. And she would make very different choices as an adult.

'Why so solemn?' Nicholas held Mawde's chin between his finger and thumb and forced her to meet his gaze. 'You will be the envy of every wife in the village. Does the prospect not thrill you?'

'Of course it does.' Tears welled in the corners of Mawde's eyes. She tried to blink them away.

'Why must you ruin a glorious day with despondency?'

Mawde swallowed a sob. 'We're sitting on the ruin of my father's workshop.'

'Is that so?' Nicholas released her chin. He rose from the wall and brushed dirt from his breeches. 'This land will serve us well, Mawde. Henry said it's ideal for growing wheat. I'm also thinking about buying sheep. I hear there's good money to be made from wool.'

'Sheep.' The word slipped from Mawde's lips in little more than a breath. She stared at a patch of parched grass where her chickens had strutted about. Once upon a time, the air had been filled with sounds from her father's workshop: sawing, scraping, banging and shouting, and wheels creaking across the courtyard, groaning beneath the weight of his cart.

A ragged blackbird brought Mawde back to the present, the soft flurry of his wings creating a small but welcome draught. Mawde opened her fingers and stared at the fragment of her childhood. She had thought that returning to St Mawes would lay old ghosts to rest, but instead she was plagued by nightmares. Every dream was filled with screams and choking clouds of smoke. God was punishing her for a sin committed as a young girl and for every poor decision she had made since that day.

Mawde tossed the pebble towards a nearby pile of rubble. If only she had raised the alarm as soon as she saw the flames. If only she had tried to help instead of watching her grandmother burn.

# CHAPTER TWO

MAWDE WOKE WITH A START. Her heart pounded against her ribs. Her skin was slick with sweat. She tried to swallow, but her tongue was dry, as if dusted with ash. The same nightmare again. The intense heat of a house fire. Suffocating smoke. Hands too slippery to grasp her grandmother's arms and drag her to the safety of the courtyard. Mawde screaming for someone to help until her throat was raw. The scenes were as vivid as a well-held memory. But her attempt at a rescue hadn't happened at all.

The silvery light of a half-moon slipped through the open window, reaching across the bedchamber in pearlescent bands. Mawde watched the rise and fall of Nicholas's chest, the slow cadence confirming he was in a deep sleep. She slipped out of bed. Silent as a shadow, she moved about the room. She peeled off her shift and replaced it with a clean one, followed by a lightweight summer kirtle. She tiptoed from the bedchamber, crept down the stairs, then held her breath while opening and closing the front door, praying it would not squeal on its hinges. Today was the day she would become mistress of her own home. She felt so ill-prepared.

The air outside was already warm despite the early hour. Mawde walked along the deserted street, then turned down a slipway and stepped onto the beach. The ebbing tide lapped at the shore, shimmering and whispering and dragging tiny stones. The soft crunch of shingle traced Mawde's steps towards a large crop of rocks. She picked her way between pools and crags and settled on a ledge. Barnacles pressed against her palms, their sharp edges leaving indentations in her skin. Small circles of animosity. Her thoughts drifted to the women of the village. Since her return, they had been wary of her, casting sidelong glances or muttering when she passed. They treated her as an outsider, never as a friend. Every woman had judged her and found her guilty, punishing her without knowing how she had sinned.

The sky shifted from grey to pale orange. The soft light of dawn and the tranquillity of the morning were balms to Mawde's jangling nerves. Most women of twenty-four years would be eager to run a home. But Mawde knew little about household accounts, or when to plant vegetables and herbs. For twelve years, until marrying Nicholas, she had worked as a kitchen servant. She understood the seasonality of foods but lacked knowledge of planting and gardening. Her mother had shown great patience over the last twelve months, with Mawde shadowing her from dawn until dusk. But there had seemed so much for Mawde to learn, the domestic routines forgotten since she had left them behind in her childhood.

The sun crept higher in the sky and bathed the village's stone jetty in warm, golden light. Mawde's gaze drifted towards the higgledy-piggledy houses hugging the waterfront, an untidy mix of tired three-storey merchants' houses and small ramshackle cottages. St Mawes had altered during her absence. Merchants had moved away to lucrative towns such as Fowey and Penryn, while the families left behind struggled to exist on meagre earnings and a shortage of food. Mawde closed her eyes and prayed for rain. Another hot, dry summer would ruin the crops again.

A cockerel's crow wafted across the harbour. Mawde stood and took a few steadying breaths. It was time to return to her mother's home and load furniture onto carts. It was time to show Nicholas she was a worthy choice of wife.

When the first loaded cart was preparing to depart, Mawde went indoors to find Agnes and Beth. 'Will you two oversee the rest of the loading? Mamm's already on her way to the house and I'd like to be there too when the first cart arrives.'

Beth shooed her away with a smile.

Mawde hurried through the village and along the track towards the house. She found her mother in the middle of the courtyard, staring at the building.

''Tis a fine home, Mawde. It's almost as grand as the manor.' She nodded towards an open door that led into the kitchen. 'Your husband's inside but wants us to wait until everything's been unloaded.'

'He said he wants to surprise me.' Mawde allowed herself a fleeting moment of delight. Never had she imagined she would live in a house so grand. There were even four stables and sheltered animal pens to house her mother's chickens and goats. Mawde linked her arm through her mother's. 'King Henry holds Nicholas in high regard,' she said, 'and rewarded him well for his service. This is your home too, Mamm. Yours and Agnes's.' She smiled. 'If not for your furniture, we'd have to sit on cold flagstones and sleep on wooden floors.'

Mamm made a strange noise in her throat but said nothing. Mawde noted a dimming of her mother's eyes and deep furrows in her brow. She gave her mother's arm a gentle squeeze. 'We were apart for too long, Mamm. I treasure our time together now.'

Two youths from the village arrived with the first load of furniture. Mawde watched them struggle in the heat as they unloaded a settle, a trestle and two elegant chairs. Sweat glistened on their florid faces, and they cursed and groaned as they buckled under the weight of a large bookcase.

'We should keep some of this furniture for Agnes's dowry.' Mawde ran her hand over the carving on a large oak chest. 'How about this?'

Mamm's eyes narrowed. 'Agnes can be sickly. No man will want her for a wife. And as for a dowry, none of this furniture is mine to give.'

Blood ran cold in Mawde's veins. 'What do you mean? These items became yours after the vintner died.'

'They did. My husband, God rest his soul, left a decent sum of money, too, but much of it disappeared on rent, food and apothecary bills for Agnes. Your husband said we could move into this house if I gave him everything I had left.' She placed one hand on Mawde's cheek and looked deep into her eyes. 'Cousin Henry would have taken us in if I had asked. But dearest Mawde, I'd have given Nicholas my soul in return for sharing your home.'

A sob caught in Mawde's throat. 'Oh, Mamm, I promise I'll do whatever I can to care for you and Agnes.'

Mamm sighed. 'I know.'

Nicholas came out of the kitchen as another cart

rumbled into the courtyard. He called to Mawde and beck-oned for her to join him. Mawde hesitated.

'Go.' Mamm placed her hand on Mawde's back and nudged her forward. 'Your husband is not a man who likes to be kept waiting.'

Mawde forced a smile and walked towards Nicholas. She touched the flower pendant dangling from her neck. The enamel flowers of his old love token burned like ice against her skin.

The kitchen was a large, spacious area equipped with shelves, spit racks, two large cupboards, a table and an array of ironmongery. Mawde pictured herself elbow deep in flour while baking tarts, bread and biscuits. They moved into the hall and admired the neat plasterwork on the ceiling and the wood panelling on the walls. There was a new trestle table with benches pushed underneath it, a carved oak sideboard and a large hearth. Mamm's settle was opposite the hearth, and there were two cushioned chairs.

Nicolas opened a door leading to a small parlour. 'My sister will use this as a bedchamber, for now. Beth will enjoy the view of the estuary.'

There was a larger parlour at the opposite end of the hall that was set up for Nicholas to use as a study. Mamm's old bookcase filled one wall, and there was already a pile of new ledgers on one shelf. Two large chests sat side by side, both secured with thick leather straps and sturdy iron locks. Mawde wondered what might be inside.

Nicholas called her to the staircase. She followed him to the upper floor and onto a small landing with three doors.

'This room is for your mother and Agnes,' Nicholas said, opening one door. He opened another and smiled. 'And this room is reserved for our children, although it has no furniture yet.' He opened the last door and gestured for Mawde to enter. She caught her breath. The room was half the length of the house and furnished with a new wooden bedstead. Thick drapes framed the windows, the fabric embroidered with leaves and yellow flowers.

'This house is perfect, Nicholas. I love it!'

Nicholas's deep brown eyes glowed like the polished newel posts on the bed. He drew Mawde towards him and peppered her lips with delicate kisses. A warm flush rushed through Mawde's body, chasing away her mother's shocking revelation. Nicholas's fervour pressed against her through the weave of his breeches and the layers of her skirts. It reminded her of the affectionate days early in their courtship. She had feared she had lost his love since their wedding the previous year. Nicholas had spent many weeks away since then, on the King's and Cromwell's business. He always returned in a sullen mood and snapped at her mother and Agnes. But his boyish charm was back again now he was master of his house, and Mawde convinced herself that was what he had been missing. How hard it must have been for him lodging in her mother's home! Mawde's heart swelled with love as she returned his kisses. Nicholas lifted her skirts, lighting a fire deep inside her when his fingertips touched her skin.

'Mawde? Nicholas?' Mamm's excited shouts drifted up the stairs. 'Where are you?'

Mawde withdrew from Nicholas's embrace and gave a mischievous smile. 'We'll continue this when we retire for the night.'

Mamm called to them both again, causing Nicholas to

scowl. 'Go. Your mother's need for attention clearly outweighs mine.'

'That's a foolish thing to say.' Mawde reached for his arm, but Nicholas knocked her hand away. 'It couldn't have been easy for Mamm to give up her home.' She paid a high price, Mawde thought, by giving you everything she had. 'We must make Mamm feel welcome and see what gives her great excitement.'

Mawde hurried down the stairs and stepped into the courtyard.

'Look, Mawde,' Mamm said, beaming. 'Cousin Henry is here.'

Henry was grinning beside a fully laden cart. 'I have two sacks of flour, a boiled ham, cheese, butter and two dozen eggs.' He lifted a crate and placed it on the sun-baked ground. 'Three piglets that will fatten well.' Reaching for another crate, he added, 'And five reliable hens.'

Mawde flung her arms around his neck and kissed him on the cheek. 'Such generous gifts. Thank you, dear cousin.'

'There's one more thing.' Henry delved into the cart with both hands and lifted out a large cockerel. The bird gave a loud squawk and an agitated flurry of feathers. Henry chuckled and lowered the bird to the ground. 'As mistress of such a magnificent house, you'll run out of hours in the day. This handsome fellow will be sure to wake you early.'

'Hail fellow!' Nicholas gave Henry a friendly slap on the back. 'Welcome to our home. Come inside for a refreshing cup of ale.'

Relieved to see Nicholas had shed his petulance, Mawde exchanged smiles with her mother. They herded Mamm's goats and the chickens into one pen and Henry's piglets into the other. Mawde secured the gates and watched the animals explore their new home.

'I'm sure everything will work out well for us, Mamm.'

Mamm linked her arm through Mawde's. 'I hope so, daughter. For all our sakes.'

# CHAPTER THREE

'Mawde?' Nicholas's deep voice carried into the kitchen.

'Coming.'

Nicholas ushered her into his parlour and gestured for her to sit. Mawde shivered despite the autumn sunlight streaming through the window and a fire burning in the grate.

Nicholas settled at his large writing desk and reached for a rolled parchment. 'The builders will return next week.'

Mawde frowned. 'Why?'

'I have instructed them to build two rooms against the far wall of the courtyard. One will serve as a laundry room, and I want you to employ a laundress.'

'A laundress!' No more plunging her hands into lye or climbing into the bucktub to pummel linens with her feet. Mawde wiggled her fingers. They were still cracked and sore from washing clothes two days earlier. 'Thank you, Nicholas.'

Nicholas gave Mawde a fleeting smile. 'A house of this

size should have a separate laundry room. And I can only imagine what guests might think of your unsightly hands.'

Mawde tucked her hands under her skirt. 'Guests?'

Nicholas straightened in his chair. 'I intend to elevate our social status to at least minor gentry. I can't have my wife resembling a common washerwoman.' He unrolled the parchment. 'These are the building plans. You will also have a still room, and a large one at that.'

Mawde clapped her hands together. 'That is the best news!' She pictured herself in the still room with Mamm, learning recipes for perfumes, ointments and balms. 'I'll have somewhere to dry herbs,' she said, 'and I'll make tinctures for Agnes.'

'And brew ale and berry wines,' Nicholas said.

'Yes! I'll also make essences to sell at the market. A still room will free up space in the kitchen, and I'll have room to make confections.' Mawde imagined surprising Nicholas's guests with comfits and subtleties worthy of a place on a royal table. 'Perhaps the builders might build a bread oven too? The one in the kitchen is far too small if we are to entertain guests.'

'Very well.' Nicholas rose from his chair and moved towards the window. 'This house will become the envy of the village. We must live to a certain standard if I'm to shed my label of yeoman farmer – a term better suited to your cousin than an educated man like me. I wish to be considered a gentleman.' Nicholas turned to face Mawde. Conceit hardened his eyes. 'I worked hard and took risks. I deserve more than this.' His expression softened. 'One day we'll own a larger house.'

Mawde tried to imagine living a life of privilege such as she had witnessed while working at Powderham Manor, then for Thomas Cromwell and at the Greenwich royal court. Fine clothes and sumptuous food would be easy to enjoy, but the thought of entertaining knights and lords filled her with dread.

Nicholas returned to his seat and rolled up the building plans. He shuffled papers on his desk before unfolding a letter. He smoothed the paper with his palm. 'Cromwell has sent a summons. I leave tomorrow morning.'

'To London?' Mawde asked. It would be his first absence since they had moved into their house, and a respite from his moods. One day he was cheerful and loving, the next he was criticising her or insulting Mamm and Agnes.

Nicholas hesitated before giving his reply. 'Yes.'

'May I request a few items for the still room and ingredients for comfits?'

Nicholas raised an eyebrow. 'My wife is already preparing to impress. Tell me, what do you need?'

'Cinnamon, gum dragon, almonds and sugar cones.' How the local children would enjoy her sweet comfits! 'Oh, and I'll need a large pestle and mortar too.' Mawde's thoughts raced as she pictured all the confections she would create. Sweet treats that would draw smiles from adults and children alike. 'I'd like bottles of rose water and olive oil, a supply of preserved ginger and a few storage pots.' She would enjoy many an hour creating marchpane decorations and delicate shapes from sugar work, and she would bake spicy biscuits and little fancy cakes.

Nicholas unlocked a wooden coffer and lifted the lid just high enough to slip his hand inside. He pulled out a leather pouch and gave it to Mawde. The pouch was small but full of coins.

'Be sure to make that money last. I'll be away for at least a month or two, but I hope to be back for Christmastide. There are sufficient funds to pay a laundress and to buy provisions and firewood.'

Christmastide was three months away. 'And if there isn't enough?' Mawde asked.

Nicholas locked the coffer and tucked the key inside his doublet. He fixed Mawde with stern eyes and said, 'It's up to you to see that it is.'

# CHAPTER FOUR

Queen Jane was dead. A hush fell inside the village chapel as members of the congregation absorbed the news. Mawde bowed her head and offered a silent prayer for her soul. Only two weeks earlier, they had rejoiced at the news she had given birth to King Henry's heir. Now her body lay stiff in a casket, waiting to be laid to rest. A wave of regret rushed over Mawde. If she had not exaggerated and lied to Cromwell, Anne Boleyn might still have her head. She might have given King Henry a son, which would spared Jane Seymour her tragic fate. Mawde clenched her fingers. Her nails dug into her palms. What cruelty had she inflicted on these women because of her eagerness for coins? Mawde reached into the pocket tied at her waist and pulled out a penny. She crossed herself and bowed to God, then left the chapel with the penny clasped in her hand.

Grey clouds hovered above, threatening to drench the village. The men and women dispersed and walked towards their homes, their ragged cloaks a paltry barrier against the late October chill.

Mawde urged Mamm, Agnes and Beth to go on ahead

without her. She waited for them to reach the bottom of the hill before turning in the opposite direction and hurrying to the Holy Well of Saint Maudez.

Mawde crouched beside the small stone arch and threw her penny into the water. 'Help me atone for my sins,' she pleaded. 'Guide me with your wisdom and teach me to shun poor choices.'

''Tis good to pray to the saints for guidance as well to our Good Lord.'

Mawde scrambled to her feet. 'Father Ambrose.'

Father Ambrose dipped his head. 'Mistress Sherman.'

'Father Ambrose, I overheard two women gossiping during this morning's service. They said Place Priory will close. Is it true?'

The prior lowered his gaze. 'Inevitable, I fear.'

'But why? The village needs the priory. Who will nurse the sick? Who will take services at the chapel? And what will happen to the men you employ to work the priory land?'

'So many questions with uncertain answers.' Father Ambrose gazed towards the bottom of the hill where cottages nestled side by side and faced the water's edge. 'The King desires for us to convert to his Church of England. We are fortunate the priory survived this long.'

'Is there nothing we can do?'

The prior's eyes darted towards her. ''Tis odd that you, of all people, should ask that question.'

Mawde searched his face for the meaning behind his statement. 'Forgive me, Father Ambrose, but I don't understand.'

The prior's rheumy eyes clouded with sadness. 'Few men dare to go against the King. Religious houses are closing and feast days are disappearing. Life is changing to a more sombre affair with his new Church of England.'

The prior shivered and pulled his sleeves down to cover his wrists and hands. 'I suspect he'll have closed the priory by the time winter has passed. Cromwell's men have already robbed our gold and taken our altar plate. They'll come again for the building and arrest anyone who tries to stop them.'

'Who will take the services here if you and the Brothers leave?'

Father Ambrose shrugged his shoulders. 'That will be for the rector of St Just to decide seeing as this village is part of his parish.'

A flame of anger burned in Mawde's chest. She was certain that King Henry would continue to indulge in pleasures at court. He'd strip his commoners of all things joyful while impressing his courtiers with feasts, dancing, jesters and sport.

'We should resist,' Mawde said in a moment of defiance.

The prior's expression turned serious. 'I would caution you against that, Mistress Sherman. The King has gifted St Mawes Manor to his loyal servant Sir Hugh Trevanion, a man who will not hesitate to prove his allegiance.'

The sky turned black. Spits of rain struck the ground. Mawde raised the hood of her cloak.

'Mistress Sherman, if you wish to oppose the changes, you could start closer to home. Your husband has been quite the instrument of the King's religious desecrations.'

'My husband?' Mawde felt her knees weaken and placed her hand against a wall to steady herself. 'What has he done?'

The prior gave her a pitying look before bidding her a farewell and returning to the chapel.

Heavy rain fell in sheets and soon drenched Mawde's cloak. She picked up her skirts and hurried towards home, stumbling on stones and slipping on mud. Her mind raced as she tried to determine the meaning of the prior's words. How could Nicholas be involved with closing the priory? His work took him to London, not houses of religion. Mawde shook her head and quickened her pace. Father Ambrose must be mistaken.

# CHAPTER FIVE

Advent arrived and Mawde's shelves were stacked high with apples, bowls of cranberries, a sugar cone, almonds and spices. Agnes wrote Christmas menus in her neatest hand and Mawde sketched elegant subtleties she would make to decorate her festive feast. How Nicholas would praise her for the opulence of their Christmas table, the first of many they would enjoy in their new home.

Mawde spent most of Christmas Eve chopping, kneading and baking. The advent fast had left her longing for rich sauces, roasted meats and sweet, spicy biscuits. Every time she heard a noise from outside, her eyes darted towards the door. Every time, she was disappointed to find Nicholas was still not home.

Late in the afternoon, Agnes and Beth burst into the kitchen.

'May we bring in the green now?' Agnes said, her eyes dancing with joy. 'If we don't go soon, it will be too dark.'

'Had you forgotten, Mawde?' Beth smiled. 'Was your mind filled with thoughts of Nicholas? Any time now, he'll come striding through the door. He'll want to be home for Christmas.'

'I hope you're right,' Mawde said, scouring the kitchen for her pattens.

Wrapped in her thick woollen cloak, Mawde relished the bracing air of the woodland. Frost-coated leaves crunched underfoot and the chill made her cheeks tingle. They cut sprigs of holly with dark glossy leaves and vibrant clusters of berries, and found a log large enough to burn for the twelve days of Christmas.

The three women spent the evening decorating the hall with wreaths and garlands of greenery. Mawde and Mamm made a kissing bough of holly and rich green ivy, then added apples, dried oranges and a large sprig of mistletoe. Mawde envisaged kissing Nicholas beneath it and felt a flutter in her chest.

But on Christmas Day there was still no sign of Nicholas. Mawde had no appetite for the spiced mince pies, the roasted turkey and the sweet sauce of orange and cranberry. Everything dried in her mouth and left the bitter taste of disappointment. She forced a smile for every person at her table, but even Henry's jesting failed to lift her mood. While her family members danced and sang on each of the twelve days of Christmas, Mawde sat quietly and stared into the fire, fretting about her husband.

'It will soon be February,' Mawde said to Beth one morning, as they kneaded dough for bread. 'He should be here by now.'

Beth twirled a lock of flame-coloured hair around her index finger. Mawde could see from the set of Beth's jaw that she, too, was worried.

'You know what he's like, Mawde. Nicholas can disappear for months or years and not send word to us.'

'I know.' Mawde had waited two years to hear from Nicholas after he left her behind at Powderham Manor, but since their wedding, he'd been away for weeks at a time, not months. 'What if someone attacked him and he's rotting in a ditch?' Mawde clutched her apron with both hands, scrunching it up as she did so. Despite Nicholas's unpredictable moods, she struggled with his absence. She missed his praise for her pies and sauces, and his late-night amorous advances. She missed hearing his views after each Sunday sermon and his opinions on matters of politics.

Mawde moved to the window and pressed her forehead against a frigid pane of glass. 'I need to clear my head of these thoughts. I'm going to the market.'

By the time Mawde reached the village, wet mud engulfed her pattens and her toes were numb with cold. She felt a twinge of disappointment – there were fewer stalls than usual. The seamstress with the second-hand kirtles was missing, and so was the blacksmith's wife, who sold dishes, cups and spoons. Mawde searched the scanty stalls for a little pot of honey to make a soothing syrup for Agnes's cough, but there was no sign of the Brothers from the priory.

Mawde rested her forearms on the sea wall and stared across the water towards Place Priory. The grey stone buildings had lost their lustre and turned severe beneath a darkening sky.

A young woman lifted a small girl onto the wall.

Mawde smiled at the child and then at the woman. 'Good morrow to you.'

The woman studied Mawde for a moment before replying. 'I'm afraid there's nothing good about it.' Her eyes dimmed as she looked towards the priory. 'I turned up

there for work this morning and I was home again by
noon. Cromwell's men – or so they claimed – were taking
over the house and church.'

Mawde thought of Father Ambrose.

'They said it's the King's property now,' the woman
continued. 'And there ain't no call for a laundress.' Her lips
twitched as if she might cry. 'Ain't no call for a laundress
here neither. Folks can't afford to buy bread, let alone pay
me to wash linens.' She lowered her voice. 'Me 'usband's
out of work now, too. No longer needed in the priory
gardens and orchards. Lord knows how we'll get by.'

Mawde's heart melted at the little girl's rosy cheeks and
shy gap-toothed smile. 'I can help.'

The woman shrank away from her. 'I wasn't asking for
charity.'

'Forgive me. I didn't mean to offend you. It's just that I
have a new laundry room at home, and I need someone to
work in it. I'll pay ten pennies a week for laundry services
and daily household chores.'

'You will?' The woman hesitated. 'May I bring my
daughter? She's only in her seventh year but already a
good worker.'

'Of course.' Mawde leaned towards the little girl. 'I'll
pay you half a penny a week to care for my animals and
collect the eggs. Tell me, what is your name?'

'Jenet.' The little girl beamed at her mother and then at
Mawde.

'It's a pleasure to meet you, Jenet.' Mawde straightened
and turned to her mother. 'Do you accept my terms?'

'I do.' The woman smiled. 'Clare Bennett at your
service.'

'It's a pleasure to meet you, Clare. I live in the house
near the headland.'

Clare's smile vanished. 'You're Mistress Sherman?'

'I am.' What had the village gossips said for Clare's smile to fade so fast? Whatever it was, Mawde needed to prove them wrong. She took a coin from her purse and pressed it into Jenet's palm. 'The baker's frying pancakes. I can smell them from here. That should be enough to buy one each for you and your mamm.'

Clare's expression softened. 'Thank you, Mistress Sherman. We'll see you tomorrow morning, a little after dawn.'

Mawde returned to the market. There were no stalls selling fowl and only one stall selling fish. Mawde settled on a cod and ling for salting, and two flounders for that day's dinner.

The sliver of sun disappeared behind the clouds. Shouts from the priory carried on the wintry air but were soon lost among the cries of hawkers eager to sell their wares.

Sleety rain saturated the muddy road already churned up by footsteps and cartwheels. By the time Mawde reached her front door, the sleet had turned to snow. Her muscles were tired from trying not to slip, and her bones ached with cold. A malodorous slop coated her pattens and her kirtle was filthy and soaked. But Mawde felt a glow deep inside her chest as she opened the door to the kitchen.

'You're a different woman to the one who left this morning,' Beth said, helping Mawde out of her pattens.

Mawde indulged in a moment of pride. She had saved a family from ruin.

Mawde wiped condensation from her bedchamber windows and peered outside. The snow had stopped falling and had left a thin blanket covering the ground. A movement caught Mawde's eye. A black shadow grew in the distance and took the form of a man wrapped in a cloak and hunched against the cold. Mawde's stomach lurched. The black cloak reminded her of Thomas Cromwell. Was he here to relay bad news? She felt for the pendant dangling from her neck. Please God, don't let me be a widow. She pressed her palms to the icy glass and watched the stranger approach. He was shorter than Cromwell and lacked his uneven gait. This man walked with slow stiff steps like a man who needed help.

Mawde hurried down the stairs and opened the door before the visitor knocked. The man's skin was pale, his lips were blue, and worry lines ruffled his brow.

Mawde saw him shiver. 'It's freezing today,' she said. 'Please come inside and warm yourself by the fire.'

Beth emerged from the kitchen. 'I heard a man's voice. Has Nicholas returned?'

'Not yet, Beth.'

Mawde gestured for her visitor to approach the hearth. 'Come. Sit. Beth will fetch a bowl of pottage while you tell me what brings you to our door.'

The man made himself comfortable on the settle and lowered the hood of his cloak.

Mawde recognised him and smiled. 'You're Brother Matthew, aren't you?'

Her visitor furrowed his brow. 'Have we met before?'

'Many years ago. You showed me a kindness I've never forgotten. A gift of a jar of honey.' Mawde's smile faded. 'I heard Place Priory has closed.'

The friar nodded. Tears trickled onto his cheeks. 'God is punishing me for my selfish dreams.' He rested his palms on his knees. 'I often struggled with my vows and dreamed of a secular life, but this is not how I wished to leave.'

Mawde knew the price of selfish dreams – Queen Anne had died for hers. She knelt on the cold flagstones and held the friar's icy hands. 'God knows that, Brother, and He does not punish you. The priory closure was not of your making.' Mawde searched her mind for words that might ease his anguish. 'God granted you this opportunity to change your way of life. He brought you to my door for a reason, and I will not turn you away. My home is your home for as long as you need or want it.'

A log shifted in the hearth and sent up a flume of orange sparks. It reminded Mawde she had put off splitting more logs because she struggled to wield the axe. There was also a wall that needed building and a large kitchen garden to plant and maintain. 'There's plenty of work here for you to earn your keep.' Mawde's smile returned. 'And we all enjoy your honey.'

Brother Matthew lowered his head. 'The bees are still in the priory skeps. I fear for the future of my little angels while they have no beekeeper to care for them.'

Mawde chose her words carefully before speaking again. 'Perhaps, in time, the bees will find you here. You will keep bees again.'

Brother Matthew's eyes misted. 'Thank you for your kindness. In return, I will do whatever you ask of me, no matter how hard the labour.' He paused, then added, 'For-give me, but I have another favour to ask. My religious life is over and I'm no longer Brother Matthew. Please call me Perry. I'm Peregrine Carew.'

Mawde widened her eyes. 'Carew? Of the Antony Carews who grew their fortune from Cornwall's tin mines?'

'The very ones.' Perry gave a sad shake of his head. 'Although I bear the family's name, I do not have their affection. I haven't seen my family in over twenty years.'

'It pains me to hear that, Perry. With God's blessing, you'll find comfort here.'

Beth emerged from the kitchen with a bowl of steaming pottage and a large hunk of bread. Mawde watched Perry break off a piece of bread and soak it in the pottage. He closed his eyes as he relished the morsel, then swallowed and licked his lips.

Mawde stoked the fire and reflected on her day. She had saved a family from an uncertain future and given refuge to Perry. She hoped God had witnessed her good deeds and that He knew she was trying to atone.

# CHAPTER SIX

THE DAYS LENGTHENED and spring arrived with sunshine and gentle winds.

Mawde picked daffodils to decorate the hall and found Mamm sitting at the table, sorting through a pile of bills. 'Henry's owed money for seed,' she said. She picked up a small piece of paper and held it out to Mawde. 'The miller needs paying too.'

Mawde took the miller's bill and stared at the handwriting. She could make out the numbers, but the letters danced and merged. 'Four shillings and sixpence. What are his terms?'

'By the end of the week.' Mamm took the paper from Mawde's hand. 'Can you settle?'

'I can.' Mawde felt a pressure building in her temples and massaged it away with her fingertips. Settling the miller's bill would leave her just enough to pay Clare's wage, but she would have to ask Henry to wait for the money he was owed. 'What's this?' she asked, picking up another piece of paper.

'Items we need for the still room,' Mamm replied. 'None of them are urgent.'

Mamm's handwriting was neater than the miller's but Mawde still couldn't make out the words. She could sketch intricate designs for subtleties and marchpane but could only read her name. Even Agnes could read and write a little, having learned from her stepfather. Mawde's lack of education left her feeling vulnerable. Anyone could present a document for her to sign and keep her ignorant of the content. She slapped the list on to the table. She was in a serious muddle. If Nicholas did not return soon, she would have to sell furniture to raise money. What would he think of her then? She retreated to the kitchen to make a batch of dough and regain her composure.

The sound of a rake dragging stones across the courtyard grated on Mawde's nerves. She could hear Perry huffing and puffing, and she yelled at him to stop.

'Forgive me, Perry,' Mawde said, when he joined her in the kitchen. 'Today is not a good day.'

Perry was flushed and sweating. Mawde poured him a cup of ale.

'Agnes asked if I would teach her about beekeeping.' Perry raised the cup to his lips and took several gulps. 'It would be my pleasure to teach her if you give your consent.'

'Please do. I'm sure Agnes will make an excellent pupil.' An idea took root in Mawde's mind. 'Perry, there's something else I'd like you to do.'

'Yes, mistress?' Perry refused to use her name, no matter how often she encouraged it.

Mawde swallowed her embarrassment. 'Will you teach me to read and write?'

Mawde was a fast learner and looked forward to her daily lessons. She studied with Perry every afternoon and practised writing late into the evenings. After six weeks of Perry's patient instruction, Mawde could sound out unfamiliar words and write lists and letters and recipes for dinners, cakes and balms. She was updating the household ledger with the money owed to Clare when Beth burst into the hall.

'Mawde! There's a horse and cart approaching!'

'Nicholas?' Mawde blotted ink from the tip of her quill and rested it on the table.

Beth smiled. 'I think so.'

'At last!' Mawde rose to her feet. She tucked a loose lock of hair beneath her coif and then removed her apron. She rushed through the kitchen and into the courtyard, eager to welcome Nicholas. The chickens squawked and scattered across the yard as a youth from the village drew the horse to a halt. Nicholas jumped down from the cart looking radiant and handsome in a new doublet and hose. He held his arms open to embrace Mawde.

'This is a joyful welcome home,' he said, as Mawde ran to him and kissed his cool cheek. 'It warms my heart to know you missed me.'

'You were away for so long,' Mawde said. 'I feared something dreadful had happened. Why didn't you write?'

A look of puzzlement flickered on his face. 'I sent a letter before Christmas. Cromwell sent me to Northern England so I wrote to say I'd return in the spring.' His expression brightened and his eyes seemed to sparkle. 'My time away was fruitful, Mawde. I received handsome rewards. But first, tell me how you fared during my absence.' Nicholas stroked the back of her hand with a warm and gentle touch.

'I employed a laundress, like you said. She cleans for us,

too.' Mawde smiled. 'I did something wonderful while you were away. I learned to read and write. Come into the hall with me and meet my wonderful teacher.'

As soon as they stepped into the hall, Nicholas released Mawde's hand. 'What is he doing here?'

'This is the man who is teaching me to read. Peregrine Carew.'

Nicholas scowled at Perry and pointed to the door. 'Get out of my house!'

Confused, Mawde looked from Nicholas to Perry. Perry's face had paled.

'But Perry is so much more than my teacher. He looks after our garden and does all the heavy tasks outdoors. He's already built a skep enclosure and a garden wall.'

'I said get out of my house!' Nicholas was clenching and unclenching his fingers like a man eager for a fight.

Perry stood and dipped his head. 'Yes, sir. As you wish.'

'No! He can't leave!'

Mawde flinched as Nicholas spun towards her.

'Am I not the master of this house?' he demanded.

'Yes,' she said meekly, shrinking beneath his glare. 'Why does Perry's presence anger you so?' She looked from one man to the other. 'Have you met before and had a disagreement?'

'The man is a papist!' Nicholas's face was puce. 'How dare you harbour a recalcitrant Catholic while the King turns this country to his true faith? What if someone finds out?'

'Perry's not a Catholic now! And he's not recalcitrant!' Mawde softened her tone. 'Tell him what happened, Perry.'

Perry lowered his head. 'Your husband does not want me here. I thank you for your kindness, mistress. I will gather my things and go.'

'No!' Mawde fought back tears. 'Look at him, Nicholas. He has no tonsure or clerical robes, and he has no desire to resume that way of life. Even King Henry would admire such a radical change of heart.' Mawde tried to grasp Nicholas's hand, but he stepped out of her reach. 'Let Perry stay, I beg you. Is it not our Christian duty to offer food and shelter to a man in need? Perry works without complaint and has proven himself an excellent tutor.' Mawde cringed at her wheedling tone and forced confidence into her voice. 'Are you not thrilled to have a wife competent at reading and writing?'

The fire in Nicholas's eyes dimmed. He fiddled with the lace on his cuff. 'I agree it is fitting for my wife to have some education. And I suppose it wouldn't hurt to keep him as a servant.'

Mawde disliked Perry being called a servant, but Nicholas's acquiescence lifted her spirits. 'Perry may stay?'

'For now.' Nicholas gave Perry a hawk-eyed stare. 'If you displease me, you will find yourself homeless.'

Perry gave Mawde a thin smile. 'It's my honour to serve and teach you, mistress, and I will continue for as long as your husband permits.' Perry bowed to Nicholas and left the hall.

'Let me show you what I've achieved so far.' Mawde picked up a ledger to show Nicholas her handwriting but received cool praise for efforts. She kissed her husband's taut cheek. 'I'm so pleased to have you home again. Let us find my spices and sugar. The boy will have unloaded the chests by now.'

'You will leave those chests alone.' Nicholas's voice was cold and brittle. 'I had important matters to attend to while away, and no time to myself. I remembered none of your items.'

Mawde swallowed her retort. She scrutinised the fine

lines etched on Nicholas's face and the arrogant set of his jaw. Gone was the kind and affable man to whom Mawde had given her heart. This man was taut and lacked compassion. A man she would struggle to love.

✿

The April sunshine had done little to warm the bedchamber. Goosebumps covered Mawde's arms as she untied her flower pendant and stowed it in a wooden box. In the mirror, she watched Nicholas creep towards her. He smiled at her reflection and planted kisses on her neck.

'I thought of you while I was away. In fact, I bought you a gift.' Nicholas reached inside his jacket and withdrew a green velvet pouch. 'Close your eyes,' he said.

Something cold settled against Mawde's breastbone.

'Now open them.'

Nicholas was staring at her reflection. Mawde ran her fingertips along the delicate gold chain Nicholas had draped around her neck. Tiny, neat links supported a golden snowflake which had a diamond at the centre the size of a wheat seed. Small diamond chips sparkled on each arm.

Mawde paled. 'It's the most beautiful piece of jewellery I have ever seen, but I can't wear it. We're not of the right social status.' She twisted on her stool to face Nicholas. 'If I wear it in public, someone might report me for flouting the sumptuary laws.'

'My dear wife, you worry too much, and anyway, my social standing is on the rise. I might have arrived here as a yeoman, but now I'm almost gentry. And don't forget the noble blood I inherited from my mother's line.'

'But what will the villagers think if they see me wearing this? They already treat me like an outcast.' Mawde had seen lords and ladies dressed in jewels and opulent gowns, but never imagined a day when she would own such trappings of wealth. The gold chain and pendant were warming against her skin. 'Perhaps I can wear it concealed beneath my clothes.'

'That's more like it.' Nicholas reached for Mawde's hand and raised her from her stool. He loosened the laces of her sleeves and bodice and watched her take them off. He drew her towards him and held her close. Passion ignited inside her and burned against the heat of his desire. Nicholas freed Mawde from her skirts and eased her out of her shift. He appraised her with roving eyes while she shivered in the candlelight. His gaze settled on the jewels. 'Now you may thank me,' he said, his voice heavy with lust. 'And in return for my generosity, you will give me an heir.'

Mawde's passion fizzled and died. Something akin to a business deal had displaced a romantic gesture. She went through the motions of pleasing her husband while begging God to bless her with a boy child. His appetite sated, Nicholas yawned and drifted off to sleep. Mawde lay still and stared into the darkness, wondering what had happened to the man who had captured her heart. The snowflake pendant was pretty but he had bought it as a mark of social standing, not as a token of his love. Silent tears slipped onto her cheeks. What type of business was her husband involved with? Clearly something lucrative if he could buy expensive jewels.

# CHAPTER SEVEN

Mawde rose long before the cockerel's crow. She wrapped herself in a shawl and tiptoed down the stairs. Since Nicholas had returned home, nightmares had broken her sleep four or five times a night. Her limbs ached, her eyes felt dry and fatigue slowed her thoughts. She sat in the kitchen and nibbled a piece of bread crust, wondering if God was punishing her for Nicholas's mistakes.

A blackbird trilled somewhere in the courtyard, breaking the silence that preceded the cacophony of dawn. Mawde opened the kitchen window and threw the crust into the courtyard. If the blackbird didn't eat it, the chickens surely would. She needed to discover how Nicholas made his money and hoped the answer lay somewhere in his parlour.

Mawde lit a candle and crept through the hall so as not to wake Perry. She stepped into Nicholas's parlour and closed the door behind her, grimacing at the creak of the latch. She placed her candle on a shelf and wrinkled her nose with disgust. Letters, books and papers lay strewn across every surface. The two large chests still hugged a wall, and one had two coffers stacked on top. A large oak trunk filled a corner, documents spread across its lid. Mawde identified receipts for wine and clothes including a doublet, a set of hose and two new pairs of boots. A letter referred to the sale of silverware, but the scrawled handwriting hid the details in a forest of swirls and loops. Mawde selected one of the coffers. The box rattled when she shook it, suggesting it harboured a trinket or a coin. There were two small locks on the coffer, but neither held a key. Mawde swapped it for the second coffer, but it too was locked. There was no rattle when she shook it, but she detected a soft scrape of paper against wood. Next, Mawde turned her attention to the new oak trunk with its two wide leather straps and a central iron lock. She wrestled with the stiff leather straps and eventually worked one free. But with no sign of a key for the lock, she had no choice but to secure the strap as tight as she had found it.

'What are you doing?'

Mawde's heart rose into her mouth. Nicholas was standing behind her.

'Why are you in my parlour?'

'I was only… Mawde's stomach clenched. 'I… I thought… I mislaid the household ledger and thought it might be in here.'

'It isn't.' Nicholas loomed over her and raised his right hand. Mawde cowered beneath him. She closed her eyes and tensed her muscles, expecting him to strike her. Instead, she heard a swish of fabric as he yanked the drapes apart. Nicholas turned and strode into the hall. When he returned, he had the ledger in his hand.

'This was on the sideboard where you left it.'

Mawde hands trembled as she took it from him.

He glared at her and flicked his wrist. 'Go. Don't let me find you prying in here again.'

❀

By the time spring warmed to summer, Nicholas had grown more volatile. He snapped at Mamm and Agnes and rarely spoke to Perry. Even Beth fell victim to his spiteful remarks.

Mawde washed the window in Nicholas's parlour, watching two jackdaws bicker like a mismatched married couple. Her task finished, she sat on Nicholas's chair and fanned herself with a letter. Sweat cooled and dried on her brow as she looked around the room. The parlour was tidier than usual, with folded letters stacked on the desk. The chests and trunk were in their usual places, but the coffers were on a shelf. The more Mawde stared at the trunk, the more she grew determined to find out what it contained. Nicholas was with Henry discussing matters concerning his land. At least a couple of hours would pass before he returned.

The ripples and twists of rush matting pressed against Mawde's knees. Puffing and panting, she wrestled with the straps of the trunk until she worked them free. All that remained between her and the contents was the heavy iron lock. Mawde searched every nook and cranny of the room but could not find a key. Her gaze flicked to the two small coffers, both of which were locked. She selected the one that did not rattle when shaken and went in search of Perry.

Mawde entered the skep enclosure. The gentle hum of bees drifted through the air.

'Perry?'

'Here, mistress.' Perry walked towards her carrying a bundle of willow. He dropped it beside a half-built skep. 'Is all well?'

Mawde held out the coffer. 'I've lost the key.' She

touched the chain of the pendant hanging from her neck. 'I don't want to wear this while working in the house and thought it best to lock it away. But without the key…'

Perry smiled. 'I can help with that. The cofferer locked himself out of his room before we lost the priory. A traveller staying overnight taught us how to pick the lock.' Perry chuckled. 'I hate to think why the traveller knew how to do it. I need two thin pieces of metal. Perhaps a couple of hairpins?'

Mawde withdrew two pins from beneath her coif. After Perry succeeded at opening the lock, she asked him to show her how to lock it.

'But mistress, we've only just opened it!'

'I want to lock the necklace inside,' she said. 'I still need to find the key.'

After Perry showed her how to use the pins, Mawde returned to Nicholas's parlour. She swapped the coffer for the one that rattled and repeated what Perry had shown her. It was more difficult than she expected, and she almost gave up. But then the bolt shifted and Mawde raised the lid. The box contained a key. Mawde tried the key in the trunk's lock. It glided in easily, but she could not make it turn.

'Hairpins won't work in a lock this size,' she said under her breath. She tried the key again and something shifted a little before meeting stiff resistance. Mawde feared the key might snap if she forced it too hard. She tried one last time and the bolt shot across. Mawde's heart hammered against her chest. She listened for footsteps coming towards the door but could only hear Clare and Agnes singing in the kitchen and a pigeon cooing outside. Mawde lifted the trunk lid, shuddering at the screeching hinges. When she looked inside, her heart rose into her throat. Silver and gold altar plates reflected her astonishment, and jewel-encrusted chalices glinted in the light. The items belonged in a church, not in Nicholas's trunk. Mawde was certain they related to the tension between Nicholas and Perry. She spent a fretful minute or two re-securing the trunk. Checking everything was as she had found it, she returned to the skeps and marched towards Perry.

'I insist you tell me how you met my husband.'

Perry removed his veil and gloves. 'Very well.' He gestured to a seat outside the enclosure. 'May we sit together while I tell you my version of events?'

Mawde clamped her lips together and nodded.

'Dear Lord, forgive me for telling tales,' Perry said when they were seated. 'I first encountered your husband during the summer. He arrived at the priory with a group of Cromwell's men.'

'Last summer?' Mawde puckered her brow. 'That can't be. We had moved away from London by then and we were living in St Mawes.'

'But was your husband always at home, or did he travel for matters of business?'

Blood turned to ice in Mawde's veins. 'Continue,' she said.

'I remember the day clearly. It was early. The sun was warm and the bees were emerging to forage for nectar. That's something I'll never forget, how your husband mocked my love of bees. I called them my angels and he taunted me for it.' Perry looked at Mawde. 'Your husband kicked two skeps to the ground. I urged him to stop his attack but he refused to heed my warning and lifted another to smash it. It broke apart in his hands. My angels reacted and swarmed his face, neck and arms.'

Mawde gasped. 'Nicholas must have been terrified.'

Perry gazed into the distance. 'He was. He panicked. I urged him to stop screaming and told him to run through a cluster of bushes to dislodge the bees from his skin. But by the time he did as I suggested, the bees had stung him hundreds of times. Angry welts covered every patch of his exposed skin.'

A ladybird crawled on to Mawde's hand. She gently blew on it and watched it fly away. 'What happened after that?'

'I scraped every sting from his skin and nursed him while he was unwell.' Perry shook his head. 'Not once did he thank me for the countless hours I sat with him. Instead, he blamed me for his foolish actions and said I set the bees upon him. That's why he dislikes my presence in his house.'

Mawde's heart ached. 'You said he was with Cromwell's men, but they didn't close the priory until the day you came here. So why were they there last summer?'

Perry sighed. 'To take the priory's valuables and give them to the King.'

Mawde's mouth turned dry as she thought of the gold and silver locked away in her house. She chose not to mention it to Perry.

'We dared to hope the priory wouldn't close once the King took possession of our valuables,' Perry added. 'But a few months later, soldiers arrived and threw us out of our home. A few Brothers pledged to convert to the new religion and even to preach in the King's new churches. Others, like me, chose to leave the religious life and attempt to navigate a new path in this world.'

'What happened to Father Ambrose?' Mawde asked.

Perry flinched. 'He resisted the King's directive. I believe he was arrested. I would have been too if I hadn't left when I did. My support for the prior cost me a pension. That's why I left the priory with so little to my name.'

'I'm so sorry, Perry. I can't imagine what you've been

through.' Mawde stood. 'I need a little time alone to make sense of what you've told me.'

Mawde left Perry sitting on the bench and walked through the fields and woods to the wreckage of her childhood home. She perched on the wall she had shared with Nicholas when he had bragged about his plans. She reached into her pocket and clasped the small wooden carving of Madonna and Child while praying for guidance from her father's spirit. From the quantity of valuables hidden in her house, it was clear Nicholas had robbed Place Priory and other religious houses. In effect, he had stolen from the King. If caught, he would be executed, and that would bring misery to them all. She had no choice but to keep her knowledge to herself. Mawde stared at the cloudless sky and cursed her curiosity. Her knowledge of the secret hoard made her as guilty as Nicholas. Another sin to add to her list. Something else for which to atone.

# CHAPTER EIGHT

Mawde fluttered a square of linen beneath her nose, but the subtle lavender scent did little to displace the stench of rotting fish.

'The smell worsens every day,' Beth said, covering her mouth and nose with her hand.

Mawde looked towards the fishing boats anchored in the harbour. Deckhands pushed coarse brushes back and forth, pausing intermittently to sit back on their haunches and wipe sweat from their brows. 'It must be the nets,' she said. 'Anything trapped will spoil so fast in this heat. Their clothes must reek too.' Her gaze drifted towards Place Priory, where men were clambering over scaffolding. Half of the main building was already in pieces, reduced to piles of rubble spread across the grounds. Mawde frowned. 'Why are they destroying the priory? It would have made a beautiful home.'

'Few folks have the money for a grand home like that.' The baker's wife elbowed her way between Mawde and Beth. She gave Mawde a look of contempt. 'I'm surprised your 'usband didn't buy it. Everyone knows 'e fancies 'eself as a lord of the manor.' She stared towards the priory and slowly shook her head. 'Word is the King wants the priory stone to build a castle somewhere near 'ere. Must be expecting someone to invade us.' The sound of the baker shouting his wife's name caused her to roll her eyes. 'Never lets me 'ave a minute to meself,' she said. 'I'd best get on.'

Mawde watched her merge with a crowd of men, women and children milling about in the village square. Almost everyone looked gaunt and weighed down with worry. A young mother emerged from the doorway to her small, dilapidated house and sat to watch her two little daughters play with stones in the dirt. They were all dressed in threadbare clothes. Neither child wore shoes.

Mawde linked her arm through Beth's and spoke in a whisper. 'We'll cook extra food today. Clare can take the leftovers to that home. No child should go to bed hungry.'

'What about that family?' Beth nodded towards another woman and child who also looked undernourished. 'You can't save them all, Mawde.'

'Maybe not, but I can help one family at a time.' Mawde smiled. 'Perhaps Cousin Henry's new baby has arrived. I propose we visit the farm before we return home.'

They climbed the hill out of the village and stopped by the Holy Well of St Maudez. Mawde threw a half-penny into the water and prayed for a good harvest. By the time they reached the top of the hill, both women were breathless. They sat in the shade of an ash tree looking towards the shimmering harbour while they recovered their breath.

A commotion sounded behind them. Mawde turned to see a brawny man yelling at a young boy and flapping his arms to shoo away a goat. She scrambled to her feet and strode towards him. 'Stop shouting at that child!'

'This is Trevanion land, and he's trespassing.' The man

had a narrow face with a hooked nose and an unsettling piercing gaze. His rolled-up sleeves revealed taut muscles and skin bronzed by the sun. He stared down at the boy like a buzzard eyeing a shrew.

'This pasture has been common grazing land since I was a young child.' Mawde rested her hand on the boy's bony shoulder. 'The common land is overgrazed, and the heat has parched what remains of the grass. You must allow the child to feed his goat here.'

'I must do no such thing.' The man moved closer and towered above her.

Mawde took two steps back.

'This might have been grazing land once, miss, but I assure you it's never been common. Sir Hugh wants this pasture fenced off for sheep so your scruffy little goatherd must go elsewhere.'

'Sir Hugh's land stretches as far as the Percuil,' Mawde said, waving her arm in the general direction of the priory and adjacent river. 'Surely he can spare this small patch for grazing?'

'I have my instructions.' The man smacked the goat hard on its rump and sniggered when it jumped and bleated.

Mawde turned to the child and pointed to a narrow track heading west. 'Take your animal to the headland. It's further to walk, but there's fair grass for your goat.' She glared at the man as the boy moved away. 'I'll speak to Sir Hugh about this tomorrow.'

The man gave a shrug of indifference. 'I'll tell his steward to expect you.'

❁

Mawde stood in the grand hall of the manor and gazed at the portraits on the walls. Sir Hugh's ancestors stared back at her. Their haughty expressions and fine clothes reminded her she was not of their class. One austere gentleman sat in a regal pose with a ship in one hand and a golden orb in the other. He looked like a man who owned the world. The portraits bragged about Sir Hugh's wealthy ancestry. Surely he could spare the small field at the top of Chapel Hill!

'Sir Hugh will see you now.' Sir Hugh's steward turned away from her. 'Follow me.'

Mawde wiped her moist palms on her skirt as she followed the steward into Sir Hugh's impressive library. More paintings adorned the walls, including one of Sir Hugh from his younger days. He was posing in a haughty stance and had three hunting dogs by his side. He held a sword dripping blood from its tip and stood with one foot on the belly of a stag with a large gaping wound in its neck.

'What's this about then?' Sir Hugh's face was florid, and he wheezed as he talked. He stood behind a grand writing desk and instructed Mawde to sit in a high-backed chair. What Sir Hugh lacked in stature he made up for in girth. His chair creaked as he settled his bulk on the seat.

'Thank you for seeing me, Sir Hugh.' Mawde's mouth was dry and the words seemed to stick in her throat. She took a deep breath and savoured the scent of old leather-bound books and the musky woody fragrance of their pages.

'What was that? Speak up, woman!' Sir Hugh's thick bottom lip wobbled as he spoke. He stared at Mawde with piggy eyes and looked her up and down.

A wave of nausea carried bile into Mawde's mouth. She swallowed.

Sir Hugh reached for a goblet filled with wine. He gulped a couple of mouthfuls, then dabbed his lips with a white handkerchief, unbothered by the creeping purple stain. 'Well?' He folded the ruined handkerchief and tucked it inside his doublet.

'It's about grazing land, Sir Hugh, and your pasture at the top of Chapel Hill.'

'What of it?'

Mawde fixed her gaze on the ripples of his neck. 'The villagers need to use it. The common land has been over-grazed, and what little grass remains is too dry, even for goats and pigs.'

'Not my concern.'

'Please, Sir Hugh. Villagers have used that top pasture for as long as I can remember. Although it's not common land, your predecessor turned a blind eye whenever villagers were desperate.'

'My predecessor was a weak man. I, however, am not. The answer is no. I need that land for sheep.' Sir Hugh pressed his forearms on his desk and hoisted himself from his chair. 'The pasture is private land and henceforth out of bounds to every villager.'

Sir Hugh's chubby fingers fumbled with the laces of his doublet in a manner that seemed familiar.

'Please, sir, will you reconsider?' Mawde could not shake the feeling she had met Sir Hugh before, perhaps at Greenwich Palace when she worked there as a confectioner.

Sir Hugh waddled towards the door with his palms clasped to his rotund belly. He held Mawde's gaze for a few long seconds and then bellowed for his steward.

Mawde stepped into the sunlight and paused to steady her breathing, but the steward was quick to close the door and knocked the back of her shoe, causing her to stumble forward. A raven took off from the stony path in front of her. She felt a draught from the flurry of feathers and smiled at the sound of its disgruntled croak.

The manor commanded a spectacular view across the harbour and Percuil River. If Sir Hugh would only take a moment to study the view from his window! He would see the dilapidated rooftops huddled in the village below. He would see strip farms with meagre crops that should be more bountiful this close to autumn. Mawde adjusted her bonnet to shield her eyes from the searing sun. She set off for home, finding shade where she could, determined to remain hopeful.

# CHAPTER NINE

NICHOLAS WAS LATE JOINING the household at the dinner table. Mawde felt the atmosphere shift with his arrival and conversations dwindled. She speared a piece of ham and let it drop onto her trencher. A dry summer followed by torrential autumn downpours had turned meagre crops to mush. While she relied on salted meat and pickles to fill the trenchers for her household, men, women and children scavenged the beaches for mussels, cockles and limpets. 'More than half of the villagers have turned to parish relief,' she said. 'We should do something to help them.'

Nicholas gulped a mouthful of wine and peered at Mawde over the rim of his cup. 'It's all very well proclaiming we should help, but what do you propose we do? We're already generous with alms and I know you give away food.'

Mawde ripped a piece of crust from a loaf still warm from the oven. She held it between her finger and thumb and furrowed her brow. 'I could bake extra loaves and gift them with pots of honey. Perhaps after Sunday service?'

'A kind gesture, Mawde,' Mamm said in a gentle voice, 'but it might offend the baker.'

'Your mother's right.' Nicholas handed his cup to Agnes and gestured for her to refill it.

Mawde imagined Sir Hugh sitting at his dining table, gorging on roasted meats and hearty stews. Lady Trevanion was charitable whenever she stayed at the manor, but Sir Hugh still refused to spare precious blades of grass even though he had no sheep on his pasture. She stared at the uneaten food on her trencher. A glistening dollop of apple relish smelled of spices, honey and vinegar. The bread had a golden crust and the ham was pink and succulent. But guilt had stolen Mawde's appetite. How could she eat a filling meal while children starved in the village?

'May we buy a pig from Cousin Henry? I can use some of the meat in small pies and salt the rest for pottages.'

Nicholas turned his bloodshot eyes towards Mawde. He swirled the contents of his cup, slopping red wine onto the table. It glistened like spilt blood before soaking into the wood. 'Yes, you may ask Henry for a pig.'

'I may?' Mawde had not expected him to agree without a fuss.

'Why not?' Nicholas swallowed more mouthfuls of wine. 'No doubt God will reward us for our charity.'

Perry tutted. Mawde tensed, but Nicholas appeared not to have heard him.

Mawde steered the conversation in a different direction before Nicholas changed his mind. 'You were at the farm today, Beth. Tell us about the antics of Henry's children.'

'The baby is adorable,' Beth said, with a look of wistful longing. 'And I swear he knows my face.'

Nicholas threw his empty cup on to the table. Mawde's

heart skipped a beat. She saw his temples twitch and braced herself for an outburst.

'Please excuse me,' Perry said, rising from the bench. 'I'll take the leftovers to the village.'

'Come, Agnes,' Beth said. 'Help me tidy the kitchen.'

Mamm went to excuse herself too.

'Stay,' Nicholas said. He leaned across the table. 'It must have crossed your mind by now that your daughter is probably barren?'

Mamm cast a sympathetic gaze towards Mawde. 'The Lord will bless you both with a babe when He believes the time is right.'

Nicholas jabbed the tabletop with his index finger. 'Or punish us in perpetuity for your daughter's sinful past.'

A knot tightened in Mawde's stomach. 'No one lives a sin-free life, Nicholas. I pray every day for God's forgiveness and I'm trying to atone for my mistakes. Our turn for a child will come.'

Nicholas contorted his face into an ugly sneer. 'I take it your mother knows nothing about your goosey ways?'

The colour drained from Mamm's face. Cavities appeared in her cheeks as she drew them between her teeth. 'What goosey ways?'

Nicholas threw his head back and laughed. 'Your beloved daughter played bedfellow to her master. Cromwell's favourite, by all accounts.'

Heat crept from Mawde's chest to her forehead. She stared at her lap and fidgeted with her fingers, steeling herself for Mamm's reaction.

'Mawde? Is it true?' Mamm's voice cracked. 'Did you lay with your master?'

'She did a lot more than lay with him. Your daughter entertained him with every whore's trick. She has performed them for me, too, and I won't deny I enjoyed them, although it's not the behaviour I expected from my wife.'

'Nicholas!' Mawde pleaded. 'Don't say such things!'

But Nicholas refused to be silenced. He kept his eyes fixed on Mamm. 'One of my acquaintances saw Mawde in the Greenwich stews when she was a harlot in a house of ill repute!'

Mawde stared at him. 'Who told you that?'

'It does not matter who. The fact is you were there.' Nicholas fastened the buttons on his doublet. 'I'm going into the village to show my support for the alehouse. I'll leave you to confess your past to your disappointed mother.'

Nicholas slammed the door when he left the house, causing trenchers and cups to rattle on the table.

'Did he speak the truth, Mawde?' Mamm's voice sounded hollow.

Mawde ran her fingertip over a scratch on the table. 'In part.'

'How could you?' Tears glistened in Mamm's eyes. 'If word gets out in the village, it will destroy your reputation.'

Mawde did not feel she had much of a reputation to protect. The village women tolerated her, but no one treated her as a friend. 'Nicholas won't say anything. He won't risk besmirching his own name. And anyway, Mamm, I swear before God, apart from Nicholas, I have lain with only one other man – Thomas Cromwell.'

Mamm crossed herself. 'May our dear Lord forgive you. Why, Mawde?'

'I was desperate to come home to you, Mamm, and could never have achieved it on a servant's wage.' Mawde lowered her head. 'It was the only way I could earn extra money.'

'And the brothel Nicholas mentioned? Is that where Cromwell found you?'

'Goodness, no!' Mawde struggled to swallow. 'But one of Cromwell's men did. I was prepared to do anything to leave Greenwich and return to Roseland, but by God's grace, he rescued me before I raised my skirts.'

Mawde fell silent for a few minutes to give her mother time to think. A stiff breeze blew outside and sent a draught through the nearest window. Mawde shivered.

'Please, Mamm, forgive me?'

Mamm used her sleeve to dab tears from her eyes. 'Come here,' she said, patting the bench beside her. Mawde moved to the other side of the table and settled next to her mother. Mamm put her arm around her and kissed the top of her coif. 'It's not for me to judge your sins, but for our beloved Lord. May He see the woman you are now, Mawde, full of kindness, devotion and love. Mistakes from the past cannot be undone, and therefore I propose we never mention them again.'

Mawde reached for her mother's gnarled fingers and gently entwined them with her own. The sweet fragrance of rose oil wafted from Mamm's skin and triggered a vivid memory that stole Mawde's next breath. She had seen Sir Hugh Trevanion at Mistress Walker's brothel in Greenwich.

# CHAPTER TEN

ON A WINDY DAY IN JANUARY, Mawde was preparing eggs and ham for breakfast when the kitchen door flew open and crashed against the wall. She dropped the carving knife she was holding and jumped backwards to avoid the blade as it plummeted to the floor. Nicholas stumbled towards the kitchen table. His hat was skew-whiff and his soft leather boots were stained with salty tidemarks. The flames in the hearth wobbled and flickered as a gust followed him indoors.

'Where's the monk?' he said, leaning on the table to catch his breath.

'I'm here.' Perry entered the kitchen, laden with pots of pickles and preserves he had collected from the pantry.

'Fetch your cloak,' Nicholas said. 'And be quick about it.'

'Where are you going?' Mawde asked.

Nicholas lifted his head. His expression turned serious. 'A ship foundered on the headland last night. If we hurry, we can salvage cargo and claim it as our own before word reaches the village.'

Mawde recognised the glint of greed in his eyes. 'You can't claim salvaged cargo if there are survivors.'

Nicholas looked away and fiddled with the laces on his thick winter doublet. 'The wreckage is bad. The ship broke apart. I doubt there will be survivors.'

Mawde pulled her cape from a peg. 'I'll go with you.'

'There's no need.'

'If there are survivors, they will need help,' Mawde replied. 'If not, I'll help you salvage the cargo.'

'Very well, but hurry. Word will soon get out.'

The air was fresh after the violent winds of the night, and debris littered the coastline. Seaweed covered much of the beach and clung to branches wrenched from trees. A small section of a ship's hull hugged a craggy rock, but the rest of the ship had been rent apart and scattered by the storm. Two sailors lay motionless on the rocks, their limbs splayed at odd angles. A third man lay sprawled face down on a clear patch of shingle. The back of his jacket had a rip on one side, and it was wet with blood. Mawde pressed her fingers to his neck. His skin was cold and waxy, and she could not feel a pulse.

'Leave him!' Nicholas shouted. 'He's dead.'

Mawde offered a quick prayer for the souls of the deceased men before picking her way across the rocks, buffeted by the wind. Crates and casks had broken open and spewed out their contents. Mawde reached for a bolt of fabric, but it was heavy with sea water and difficult to lift. Her arm muscles burned as she scooped up lengths of worsted wool, linen and lawn, hoping it might all be usable after a careful rinse. Nicholas and Perry were stacking small crates that were splintered but intact. Nicholas sent Mawde to fetch a handcart. By the time she returned, Nicholas and Perry had a haul of caskets containing sugar cones, almonds and more bolts of cloth. They had also collected four undamaged barrels which Nicholas declared contained fine Portuguese wine.

Nicholas and Perry took turns to wheel the loaded handcart from the beach to the top of a steep narrow track, then ferried their haul of salvaged goods to the house with Nicholas's horse and cart. Mawde kept a vigil over the three dead men until Nicholas and Perry returned for them and carried them off the beach. They laid them out on the back of the cart and Mawde covered them with spoiled cloth.

'Will you take them to the chapel, Perry?' Mawde shouted across the wind.

Perry gave her a solemn smile. 'Of course, mistress.'

Nicholas reached up to Mawde to lift her down from the cart. As he did so, his doublet opened, revealing blood on his shirt.

'Nicholas, you're hurt!' As soon as Mawde felt the ground beneath her feet, she pulled his jerkin open.

Nicholas knocked her hands away. 'It's nothing,' he said, tightening the laces. 'Scratches from a stumble on the rocks.'

'It looks worse than that.' A prickling sensation crept across Mawde's skin. She had seen no rips in Nicholas's shirt, only the livid blood stains. And he had a hunting knife sheathed at his side. 'Nicholas,' Mawde hissed, checking no one was within earshot. 'Promise me you didn't kill a man so you could claim your salvage rights?'

Nicholas gave Mawde a withering stare. 'What do you think?'

'This morning's excitement gave me a hearty appetite,' Nicholas said, helping himself to a generous serving of succulent beef and drowning it in onion gravy. He brandished his knife at Perry. 'You haven't eaten a mouthful of food. What's wrong with you?'

Perry pushed a piece of carrot around his trencher. 'I'm wondering if the ship would have foundered if St Anthony's fire still burned. No one has tended to that fire since the day the priory closed.'

Mawde shook her head. 'The ship couldn't have been anywhere near St Anthony's headland to have wrecked where it did on our shore. Black Rock is closer and the more likely cause. It's impossible to see Black Rock in the dark, let alone in a storm.'

'I agree with you, Mawde, but the monk might be on to something.' Nicholas reached for the loaf of bread sitting on the table. He ripped off a large chunk and used it to soak up some gravy. 'Relighting that fire would make us some money. I should look into it before someone else has a similar idea.'

'How would a fire make money?' Mawde asked, wishing Nicholas would address Perry by name.

Nicholas refilled his goblet. 'If we light that fire every night, we can charge a toll for every ship entering the Carrick Roads and docking in Penryn. Think of it as a fee for the benefit of a light that keeps them out of danger. It's a busy waterway with ships coming and going late into the night, so it need only be a modest sum for us to make a profit. Captains could pay the dues at the same office that collects Customs and Excise duties.' Nicholas stroked the point of his neatly trimmed beard. 'The King owns the old priory now and all the surrounding land. He also receives the excise duties. I'm sure he'd agree to sharing the spoils from the fire provided the terms are fair. I might suggest a third of the fire dues for him, and two-thirds for me. It's only right I take the larger share because I'll have to pay men to light the fire and stay all night to guard it. Even with such a generous split, I would do well from it.'

Mawde's thoughts drifted to the local fishermen. A fire would benefit them too, and they would not have to pay dues for it. 'I think it's a good idea,' she said.

'I'm glad you approve, wife.' Nicholas's tone was thick with sarcasm. 'Perry, I appoint you as leader of the fire team.'

Mawde felt her spirits lift at Nicholas using Perry's name. A gust of wind rattled the windows. Orange flames buckled in the hearth but soon leapt up again. Mawde raised her goblet to her lips and savoured the taste of fruity Portuguese wine.

Nicholas pushed his empty trencher away and wiped his knife clean before sheathing it. 'I depart for London four days from now to attend to a matter for Cromwell. I'll draft a proposal and present it to the King. Then, when I have the King's approval, Perry can attend to the fire every third night in return for his board and lodging.'

'Perry doesn't have time for that!' Mawde checked her tone. She feared Nicholas would evict Perry if the King dismissed his plan. 'Perry already spends almost every waking hour working here for us.' She resisted adding that Nicholas did very little other than sit in his parlour daydreaming about a day when he might enjoy greater wealth. 'Can't you pay men from the village to tend the fire every night?'

Nicholas placed his palms on the table and gave Mawde a stony stare. 'As master of this house, I'm responsible for our income and I make the rules. Our last harvest was as dismal as everyone else's, and this year, Henry and I need to plant more fields. That will require significant expenditure; therefore, I need to raise the money while making savings elsewhere. I'm sure Perry understands and will be only too pleased to help.'

'I'm happy to sit by the fire every third night,' Perry said affably. 'I've mastered the art of dozing in short bursts.'

Mawde thought about the gold and silverware Nicholas had locked away in his parlour. Surely there was plenty there to cover the cost of seeds. She could not risk mentioning it to Nicholas because then he would know she had been snooping. She took a few sips of Portuguese wine and finished eating her dinner in silence.

# CHAPTER ELEVEN

Agnes opened the kitchen door and stepped inside from the courtyard. A sudden squall caught the door and slammed it shut behind her. 'Clare was telling me the village has a new blacksmith,' Agnes said, placing a small pile of laundered clothes on the bench tucked beneath the table.

'It's about time.' Mawde placed a steaming pie on a rack to cool. 'Let us hope he doesn't drink himself to death and end up in a ditch like the last one.' She looked towards the hearth. 'I think I'll pay the blacksmith a visit. We need an extra spit iron and a couple of pot hooks. Would you like to walk there with me?'

'I'd be glad to.' Agnes left the kitchen and returned with two heavy woollen capes. 'We'll need these. It's still blustery outside.'

Branches creaked in the stiff breeze and white caps ruffled the sea. Mawde pulled her cape tighter around her and leaned into the wind. By the time they reached the village square, Agnes was pale and wheezing.

'Stop a moment,' Mawde said, grasping her sister's elbow and turning so their backs faced the wind. 'Catch your breath.'

Waves crashed against the harbour wall and sprinkled them with sea spray. The sound of metal clanging against metal carried on the wind. Mawde watched Agnes purse her lips in a battle to control her breathing. At last, colour returned to her cheeks and she announced she was feeling better.

The moment they stepped inside the forge, the black-smith's tools fell silent. There was a loud sizzle and hiss of steam as he plunged a red-hot piece of iron into a cauldron of water. He put the iron rod to one side and wiped his hands on his apron. When he turned to greet them, Mawde felt as if she had been punched in the chest. An awkward silence followed.

'Mawde!' Agnes dug her elbow into Mawde's side. 'Say something,' she whispered.

Mawde shivered despite the hot flames rising from the fire. Dark shadows chased through her thoughts; a barrage of bitter memories collected in her childhood. 'Julian Viker,' she said, the words pricking at her lips. His insults echoed in her mind and cut her like a knife. She recalled the time he had caused her to fall and spill the food from her bowl, a time when there was too little to eat and her stomach had growled and hurt. She reached for the pocket hanging at her side and wrapped her fingers around the carving of Madonna and Child. Julian had accused her of stealing the carving, but her father had not believed his lies. She stroked the smooth contours of the Madonna's robes. Da would not want her cowering now.

'My apologies for intruding,' Mawde said, her voice wavering. 'It was a mistake to come here today.' She felt

Agnes's arm slip out from her own and sensed her sister's confusion.

The blacksmith took a step towards her. 'I didn't expect to find you in this village,' he said gently. 'I heard you left many years ago and assumed you would have settled in Devon.'

'Then I'm sorry to disappoint you.' Acrid soot had dried Mawde's mouth, and she found it hard to swallow. 'Come, Agnes, we're leaving.' Mawde turned towards the door.

'Wait!'

Mawde stopped and spun round. The blacksmith was striding towards her. 'You murdered my brother!' she cried, jabbing him in the chest.

The blacksmith caught her hand in his. 'I did no such thing.'

Mawde's skin flamed beneath his touch. She snatched her hand away. 'I don't believe you,' she said. 'I will find another blacksmith to make what I need. Agnes, follow me.'

'But—'

'Now!' Mawde's legs trembled as she walked towards the door. She glanced over her shoulder to check Agnes was following.

'I didn't kill your brother, Mawde,' the blacksmith called after them. 'I admit I did not treat you well, but I swear before God and on everything holy, I did not hurt baby John.'

Mawde paused with her hand on the door handle.

'I was a dreadful bully, though,' Julian added, 'and I beg for your forgiveness.'

'My forgiveness?' Mawde turned to look at him. 'Your spite and cruelty destroyed my childhood.'

The blacksmith hung his head. 'I know, and I'm sorry.'

He paused. 'But tell me, Mawde, who among us hasn't performed at least one deed we regret?'

Images tumbled through Mawde's mind, the contents of her nightmares: the last time she saw her father, hurrying to catch a boat because she had forgotten to pass on a message; the inferno of what had been her home and charred wood dust floating in the air; the smell of her grandmother's burning flesh while she pleaded for Mawde's help; Cromwell's flaccid belly as he rolled towards her in his bed.

Mawde opened the door and stepped outside. The low winter sunlight blanched her vision after the gloom of the forge. She lost her footing on a rut in the road and landed on her hands and knees. Her stumble sent a herring gull scurrying with a fierce flap of its wings and a shriek so shrill that Mawde had to cover her ears. Tears of regret soaked her cheeks, and she maintained a stubborn silence all the way home, ignoring her sister's questions.

When they reached home, Mawde fled to her bedchamber. She sat on the bed and buried her face in her hands. Her grandmother had favoured Julian and almost encouraged his bullying behaviour. If Julian had not served as her father's apprentice, Mawde's life would have followed a different path. Her grandmother might have been kinder towards her, and Mawde might have saved her from the fire.

*God has put Julian in this village as a reminder of my childhood sins.* Mawde wrung her hands together. *I know God wants me to atone, but what does He want me to do?*

She rocked back and forth and then fell to her knees to pray for God's guidance. The hours slipped by and daylight faded, but still Mawde could find no answers. Her temples throbbed, her neck ached and her stomach twinged with hunger.

'Hunger!' Mawde smiled and crossed herself, thanking God for giving her a sign. He wanted her to do more to ease the suffering in the village. It had to be more than gifts and alms, and Mawde vowed to find the answer, because then God would forgive every one of her sins and free her from her nightmares.

# CHAPTER TWELVE

DAFFODILS RIPPLED in the churchyard of St Just, their golden yellow trumpets at odds with the smell of damp soil rising from a freshly dug grave. Mawde's heart ached for Cousin Henry. He looked weary and gaunt; his normal masculinity had been stripped away by the devastating loss of his wife.

As they filed away from the graveside, Mawde saw Sir Hugh and Lady Trevanion waiting to offer their condolences to Henry. A breath caught in her throat. Sir Hugh was tugging the frill of his cuff, and it reminded her of the time she had watched him undress in the brothel at Greenwich.

'Sir Hugh, Lady Trevanion,' Mawde said, dipping her head in deference. 'It's kind of you to support my cousin today.'

Lady Trevanion gave a sad smile. 'How could we not? He's a charming fellow and always eager to help. Only last night, he was up all hours with three of our ewes which were struggling with lambing.' She looked towards Henry.

'May the Lord bless him while he grieves, and his three dear little children.'

'He's always been a selfless man,' Mawde said, wishing she thought the same about Nicholas. 'Sir Hugh, may I speak with you about a village matter? It should only take a moment.'

Lady Trevanion rested her hand on her husband's forearm. 'I will offer condolences on behalf of us both and leave you to hear Mistress Sherman's concerns.'

Sir Hugh drew himself to his full height and cast a shadow over Mawde. His stare was cold, his mouth tight. 'How might I assist you?'

Mawde's tongue felt large in her mouth as she parted her lips to speak. She hoped Sir Hugh could not hear the catch in her breath. 'I was wondering if you had reconsidered allowing the villagers to graze their animals on your pasture at the top of the hill beyond the Holy Well?'

Sir Hugh shook his head. 'I told you that land is private and my sheep graze there now.'

'Please, Sir Hugh. The common land is in a poor state after the heavy rains of winter. If you cannot offer the Chapel Hill pasture, at least offer something else. The villagers are desperate.'

A tall man approached with his wife and a boy. All three appeared tired and wan. The man and his son doffed their hats to Sir Hugh before continuing on their way.

'That was Goodman Tomas and his family,' Mawde said. 'He was one of the priory carpenters, but now the priory no longer exists, he cannot find paid work. Did you see how thin he looks, and his wife and child, too?'

Sir Henry stared after them as they walked down the hill towards the village. He rested his hands on his ample belly. 'Well, yes, I suppose they do look a little underfed.'

'A little! Goodman Tomas is a proud man,' Mawde

66

said. 'He's hard-working, uncomplaining, and not the type to ask for help. Every winter is hard on families, but the last was harder than most. God willing, this warm spring weather will restore the grazing land, but I dread to think what will happen when it's overgrazed again.' She waited for a group of mourners to pass. 'Please, Sir Hugh, I beg you. One small area of pasture, that's all I'm asking for.'

Sir Hugh snorted. 'No.'

Mawde felt herself shrink a little beneath his disdain. She angled her body so they could both see Lady Trevanion. 'Tell me, is your wife aware of your penchant for visiting the Greenwich stews?'

'My what?' Sir Hugh's face contorted. He reminded Mawde of how a child might look after being caught with their fingers in a honey pot.

'Virgins are your preference, are they not?' Mawde took a moment to steady the quivering of her legs. 'And I know you like to rod a woman while you're being watched.'

'Keep your voice down!' Sir Hugh's eyes darted towards a group of village gossips standing almost within earshot. A deep pink flush stained his cheeks and the heat of embarrassment radiated from him.

Mawde moved closer to Sir Hugh. 'Do you brag to your wife about your immoral behaviour? Or would such a revelation cause her to swoon?'

Sir Hugh's eyes sought his wife. His Adam's apple bobbed up and down. 'You saw me in Greenwich?'

'I did.'

He kept his gaze fixed on his wife. 'Why were you in the stews?' While Mawde sought the words for a credible answer, his face relaxed and he guffawed. 'Don't tell me you worked there?'

Mawde drew away from him. 'No, I did not. I worked as a confectioner for Cromwell, and he arranged for me to work in the kitchens at Greenwich Palace. My accommodation was close to that neighbourhood, and I saw you as I passed. My companion pointed you out to me. She knew all about your shocking demands. You know how word gets around.' Mawde hoped God would forgive her for twisting the truth and not deem it another sin to add to her tariff. She reassured herself she was picking her words to help poor residents of the village. She could only hope Sir Hugh did not recognise her from the time she had watched him fornicate with her dear friend, Nan. Thank God for Cromwell's man removing her from the brothel before she serviced a customer herself! 'Ah, Lady Trevanion approaches. Let us share what we have discussed and see how she reacts.'

The colour drained from Sir Hugh's florid face. Sweat beaded on his brow. 'Have the damn pasture! But promise me you'll make it known that I'm gifting it as common land.'

Mawde's tension ebbed away, and a ripple of exhilaration passed through her body. 'On behalf of the village, I give sincere thanks.'

'Is all well, my dear?' Lady Trevanion asked, stroking Sir Hugh's cheek with her gloved fingers. 'You seem out of sorts.'

'I'm fine.' Sir Hugh used a linen kerchief to blot his brow. 'I feel a little nauseous because of the delay to breaking our fast. It will pass when I have something to eat.'

'Your husband was sympathising with the plight of the villagers, Lady Trevanion,' Mawde said, revelling in Sir Hugh's discomfort. 'I was telling him about the poor state of the common grazing land after the heavy rain in the winter. It's worse now than it has ever been, especially now the priory has closed and more villagers need to use it. Sir

Hugh has donated an area of his pasture to rectify the problem at once.'

'May God bless you for your kindness, Hugh.' Lady Trevanion took both of Sir Hugh's hands in hers. 'You are an example to all gentlemen.'

Mawde wanted to laugh and cry as joy fizzed inside her. She had achieved a small victory for the people of her village and in full sight of God in His churchyard.

# CHAPTER THIRTEEN

OVER THE FOLLOWING WEEKS, Mawde noticed a slight thaw in the attitudes of the villagers. Conversations still paused whenever she approached, but most of the women politely smiled when returning her greeting. The spring sunshine also restored the vitality of the common grazing land. Vibrant green grass rippled in the breeze and butterflies basked on carpets of pink clover. Even Mawde's night-mares grew less frequent.

May arrived with a balmy day and a summons from Cromwell for Nicholas. The atmosphere in the house grew lighter without him. Mawde sang as she worked in her kitchen, pickling radishes to store in the larder and boiling rhubarb for pots of conserve. When Nicholas returned after a four-week absence, he, too, was in a buoyant mood.

'Come,' he said, taking Mawde's hand after two village boys had finished unloading his cart. He led Mawde to his parlour and pointed at a trunk in the middle of the floor. 'Open it!'

Mawde loosened the leather straps and raised the heavy lid. She widened her eyes at the bounty inside and slowly shook her head. She counted four bolts of good-quality linen and another of fine mist-grey wool. There was a length of lawn that would make several partlets and sleeves she could edge with lace. The bottom of the chest held eight pewter plates, eight pewter cups, four green glasses embellished with enamel flowers, and a dozen pewter spoons.

Mawde's heart fluttered as she embraced Nicholas and kissed him on the cheek. His skin smelled of a summer breeze mixed with lemon and spice – the aroma of a gentleman. 'Thank you, sweeting, for such wonderful gifts.'

'I'm glad you like them.' Nicholas's eyes shone as he pulled Mawde closer and dusted her lips with kisses. Her heartbeat quickened and she returned his affection. This was the Nicholas she had fallen in love with.

'Do I infer from this trunk that your visit went well, and our fortunes are now on the rise?'

'My dear wife, I believe they are.' Nicholas nuzzled Mawde's neck, causing her to squeal. He held her at arm's length and added, 'The King approved my proposal for St Anthony's fire without pressing for better terms. And he rewarded me well for my latest efforts regarding matters of royal business. But that is not all! When I met with Cromwell, the High Steward of Cornwall joined us and Thomas Treffry of Fowey, too. They confirmed a castle is to be built in St Mawes, and Treffry will be the Clerk of the Works.' Nicholas kissed Mawde on the forehead before adding, 'They appointed me as Treffry's deputy.'

Mawde felt a tightness in her chest. 'But you have no experience of building!'

Nicholas released her. 'I don't see why that matters.' His expression darkened. 'You think me incapable of over-seeing a few labourers?'

'No, of course not.' Mawde reached for his hand but he brushed her away.

'It's not as if I'm to build the castle myself. If I keep each man's mind on the task, the build should go according to plan.'

Mawde was not so sure. It was one thing to watch a builder or carpenter at work, but quite another to recognise if he was going about his business in the correct manner. She kept her doubts to herself.

Nicholas's mood shifted and a glimmer of a smile played on his lips. 'Our wheel of fortune is turning, Mawde. Soon I'll have the means to make investments and increase my wealth. I'll take my place at the right level of society, and all of Cornwall's gentry will want us as their guests.'

Nicholas lifted a goblet from the trunk and held it to the light streaming through the parlour window. The glass glistened like a giant emerald. Mawde imagined filling it with wine. She would play hostess as lady of her house, dressed in fine robes and expensive jewellery befitting of her higher social status. And she would have the means to give more generous alms to the poorest people in the village.

A seedling of doubt grew in Mawde's mind. 'Is it possible for us to move from yeoman to gentry?'

Nicholas put the goblet on his desk and reached out to stroke Mawde's cheek. 'Anything is possible if we strive hard enough. Did you know there are men at court who started life as peasants?' Voices carried from the hall. Nicholas stepped away from Mawde to close the parlour door. The embroidery of his doublet seemed to shimmer as he returned to her. 'Through calculated risks and shrewd decision-making, those men gained money and land. They often attend the royal court and spend time in the King's presence! He sees those men as the gentlemen they are today, untarnished by their humble backgrounds. If those men can better themselves, so too can I!'

A cloud passed in front of the sun and plunged the parlour into shadow.

'I can't see St Anthony's fire generating enough money,' Mawde said. 'Nor a wage for observing construction. Do you have something else in mind?'

Nicholas closed the lid of the trunk and turned to look at Mawde. 'I intend to offer credit.'

'To whom?'

'The men in the village.'

Mawde's stomach twisted. She lowered her voice to a whisper. 'Nicholas, you can't! They'll arrest you and charge you with usury.'

Nicholas tutted. 'Don't worry about things you don't understand, Mawde. There are ways to get around the outdated Canon laws. Even Cromwell is in the business of lending money.'

'Skirting laws won't stop it from being a sin,' Mawde said, taking care to mind her tone. 'On Judgement Day, the Lord might punish you and condemn you to eternity in purgatory.'

'I'm willing to take my chances.' Nicholas unfastened his doublet and loosened the laces of his shirt. 'I've had a long journey,' he said, sounding distant. 'I need to change my clothes.'

The clouds shifted and the sun's rays illuminated the leafy pattern woven into Nicholas's doublet. *Ivy*, Mawde thought. *A creeping plant that finds cracks in walls and damages weakened houses.* She shivered and hugged her arms to her chest. Desperate men would borrow money and struggle to repay it. Whatever moneylending scheme Nicholas had planned could only be destructive.

# CHAPTER FOURTEEN

A WALL of flames stole Mawde's breath as she reached towards Nicholas. Their fingertips almost touched, but Nicholas lost his footing on the wall and fell backwards into the fire pit. His mouth hung open in a perpetual scream while demons danced on glowing embers. Mawde woke, gasping for breath. Her shift was drenched with sweat. The nightmare had been the most vivid yet – Nicholas had died and gone to Hell, condemned to remain there for eternity. Mawde had begged for his soul to be spared, but a jury made up of her grandmother, Tamsin and Queen Anne Boleyn had sentenced her to join him.

Nicholas was fast asleep, snoring beside her. Too agitated to wait for the cock's crow, Mawde slipped out from beneath the bedcovers and knelt on the rush-matted floor to offer her morning prayers. Afterwards, she tiptoed to the window and waited for the sun to rise and cast its golden glow on the water. Corpus Christi Day was three weeks away. Mawde's mood darkened as she recalled a previous Corpus Christi Day spent with her cousin Tamsin. They had taken a ferry from St Mawes to Penryn and enjoyed the parade of pageant wagons, mystery plays, music and dancing. But her joy had evaporated because of Julian Viker, the indispensable village blacksmith. She recalled how she had stumbled when he bumped against her to sneak the wooden Madonna and Child into her pocket. He had tried so hard to earn Mawde a beating, but her father had taken her word over his. Mawde took the small carving from her pocket. Tears misted her eyes as she recalled vague memories of her father: his smell at the end of a long day's work, rough callouses on his hands, his gentle manner, his kind eyes and his unwavering love. The smooth wooden folds of the Madonna's robe felt warm against Mawde's palm. She imagined her father was holding her hand, reassuring her all would be well.

Nicholas stirred and rolled over in the bed, but soon resumed snoring. Mawde wondered what her father what have thought of the man she had wed. Most of the time Nicholas was pleasant and civil, but in recent months his dark moods were longer-lasting and more frequent. And it had not escaped Mawde's notice that he had developed a penchant for drinking large quantities of wine. Only last night he had consumed two full pitchers, making him unsteady and slurring his words. What a fool Mawde had been to believe a man would still love her after several years apart! How she regretted rushing into their marriage when they should have taken the time to reacquaint themselves first. She unfastened the ribbon that held the new pendant and placed it in her palm. A snowflake – brittle, ice-cold and transient. Mawde stowed it in a box which already contained the flower pendant Nicholas had given her nine years earlier, a gift she had cherished for several years as a token of his love. She closed the lid and turned the key before burying the box in a trunk of old kirtles.

Nicholas's secrets and ill moods were his price for bringing her home.

Mawde pulled her night shift over her head and used it to dry her eyes. She pulled on a clean shift and her favourite yellow kirtle, then pinned her hair into place. She pinched her cheeks to add warmth to her pallor, then turned to find Nicholas awake.

'Did you sleep well?' Mawde asked, forcing a smile.

'Well enough.' Nicholas grimaced. 'I have an unholy headache.'

'I'll make a tisane of chamomile and feverfew,' Mawde said. 'That should ease your pain.'

Nicholas stared at her through bloodshot eyes. 'It's my fault. I've developed a taste for red Bordeaux wine.'

Mawde moved to the washstand and soaked a cloth in the water. 'This might help.' She wrung out the cloth and folded it twice before laying it across Nicholas's brow. 'I was wondering if we could organise something to celebrate Corpus Christi Day,' she said, gently pressing the cloth against Nicholas's forehead. 'It will be a quieter affair than in previous years, but we could spread a little goodwill through the village. Few families can spare coins to take a boat to celebrate in Penryn, and who knows how long it will be before the King forbids such festivities altogether?'

Nicholas eased himself up to sitting and perched on the edge of the bed. He seemed to take an age to consider Mawde's request. At last, his lips slid from a grimace to a smile. 'My clever wife,' he said, peeling off the damp cloth and massaging his temples. 'That would help us win local favour. Tell me, what do you have in mind?'

Mawde took the cloth from Nicholas and passed him a laundered shirt. She returned to the window and stared towards the sea. Despite the early hour, the waterway was crowded with small merchant vessels, fishing boats and the ferry that sailed back and forth to Penryn.

'I believe the Trevanions are leaving for Truro today or tomorrow,' Mawde said. 'That means there will be no food or drink provided by the manor. Perhaps we could take it upon ourselves to provide sustenance and entertainment.'

Nicholas walked across the room and wrapped his arms around Mawde's waist. 'An excellent idea. It will prove to the villagers we're as worthy of respect as any lord and lady of a manor.'

He rested his chin on Mawde's shoulder. She baulked at the stench of his breath. She tried to step away, but Nicholas pinned her against the windowsill and fumbled with the layers of her skirts. With her forehead and palms pressed to the glass, Mawde watched a herring gull circle in the sky. She submitted to Nicholas's gropes and thrusts, wishing she, too, could fly.

# CHAPTER FIFTEEN

Mawde was eager to speak to the vicar about the feast of Corpus Christi and approached him after the Sunday service.

'Father, may I ask you something?'

The vicar was flushed, with sweat glistening on his face despite the shade of the chapel porch. 'Please, ask away.'

'I was thinking about Corpus Christi Day. It's only three weeks away and there's been no mention of a celebration.' She watched a young boy in ragged clothes dart behind a gravestone to hide from his mother. The boy was reasonably nourished, but his mother was too thin. 'I think the villagers would enjoy a parade of the Host through the village,' Mawde said. 'Many of us used to travel to Penryn for the celebration, but few people these days can afford the ferryman's fare.'

The vicar fanned himself with his missal. 'The same thought crossed my mind, Mistress Sherman, but with the King forbidding the marking of Saints' Days...'

'Please, Father! I'm sure the King wouldn't disapprove

of us celebrating Corpus Christi. He'll doubtless insist upon a celebration at the royal court.'

The vicar pursed his lips and let out a slow breath. 'I'm not sure about that, Mistress Sherman, and I don't want to risk arrest.' A bead of sweat trickled down the side of his face. 'I'll ask Sir Hugh's opinion when I see him next. He'll know if the King would permit such a celebration.' The vicar regarded Mawde with a doubtful expression. 'I would caution you against optimism. Sir Hugh has found it easier than most to abandon Catholic traditions.'

Anger simmered in Mawde's chest. Wasn't it enough for the King to close the priory? Must he quash the spirit of his people by cancelling every feast day, too? 'Sir Hugh won't object,' she said. 'He cannot. Not while he's away at one of his other manors.'

A resigned expression settled on the vicar's face. 'Sir Hugh and his wife are in St Mawes. I prayed with them earlier this morning. Sir Hugh injured his back after falling on the stairs, and dear Lady Trevanion is sick with an ague. Sir Hugh was in a black mood, as you can imagine.' A fly landed on the vicar's robe. He used his missal to swipe it away. 'I'll call at the manor again this afternoon and ask for his views about a parade. I agree it would be good for village morale – provided he consents.'

'I'll go,' Mawde said, certain the vicar was too mild-mannered to persuade an irascible Sir Hugh. 'I have another matter to discuss with him and will ask about Corpus Christi Day afterwards.' She hoped God would forgive the mistruth, but she wanted to bring joy to the village. 'If Sir Hugh's agreeable, the children can make banners for the parade, and perhaps the older boys can perform a mystery play.'

The vicar hugged his missal to his chest and smiled.

'Excellent ideas. I can teach them the lines they need to recite, and their mothers can make costumes.'

Mawde wasn't so sure about the women having material to spare for costumes, but she still had the cloth salvaged from the shipwreck. The saltwater had rendered it unsuitable for kirtles, but it was adequate for mystery play outfits.

'In that case, Father, I bid you a good day. I'll visit Sir Hugh this morning and send word to you when I have his approval.'

While the rest of Mawde's family set off for Henry's farm to join him and Aunt Mary for Sunday dinner, Mawde hurried home to collect three pots of Perry's honey. By the time she reached the manor, she was hot and thirsty. She followed the steward through the hall wishing she had taken a moment to tidy herself before lifting the heavy iron door-knocker.

'You!' Sir Hugh paced the length of his library with his hands clasped to his back. 'What do you want this time?'

Mawde caught the steward's smirk as he retreated from the room. She glanced down at her dishevelled skirt that was coated with a film of earthen dust. She waited for the door to close before turning to look at Sir Hugh. His piggy eyes stared back at her, challenging her to speak.

Mawde cleared her throat. 'I wanted to ask if you'll be in the village for this year's Corpus Christi.'

'Why do my social arrangements concern you?' Sir Hugh grimaced and groaned as he eased himself into his chair.

'My husband and I thought the villagers would enjoy a small feast and perhaps a little dancing. Nothing too extravagant, of course. We didn't know if you intended to host a feast this year and did not wish to offend you by arranging one ourselves.'

Sir Hugh struggled up from the chair and resumed pacing the room. He stopped in front of Mawde. 'You wish to celebrate Corpus Christi as a feast day?'

Mawde shrank under his intense glare. 'No!' She clenched her fingers around the handle of her basket and willed herself not to show weakness. 'Well, yes. But not to offend the King. We thought it might be an event King Henry himself will celebrate.' Sir Hugh's glare softened a little, suggesting that might be the case. 'Oh, I almost forgot!' Mawde reached into her basket and placed the pots of honey on Sir Hugh's desk.

'Are you trying to bribe me with paltry gifts?' He threw his head back to laugh but cried out with pain instead. Deep furrows appeared on his brow. Mawde almost pitied him.

'No, sir. I heard your wife is sick with an ague. The honey is from our own hives and it might help her chills.'

'What do you care about the health of my wife?' Sir Hugh staggered towards a wall and leant with his forehead and arms against it.

Mawde started doubting the thinking behind her visit. She spent a moment searching for words she hoped would sway his opinion. The sound of footsteps passing beyond the door gave her an idea. 'I hope Lady Trevanion hasn't fallen ill because she learned of your transgressions.'

Sir Hugh turned slowly towards her. His eyes narrowed and his nostrils flared. 'How would she know? I haven't told her.'

Mawde swallowed. 'Have you considered that someone else might know? Servants are privy to many secrets but don't always hold their silence. I heard many a rumour traded in the corridors when I worked at Greenwich Palace.'

Sir Hugh took a breath as if he would speak, but a

knock at the door stopped him from responding. His steward entered the library followed by the pungent aroma of overcooked fish. 'The apothecary has arrived, sir. Shall I escort him upstairs to your wife or would you like to see him first?'

'Take him to Lady Trevanion's bedchamber. I'll see him afterwards.'

The steward bowed and retreated from the library, closing the door behind him. Sir Hugh rounded on Mawde. 'Are you trying to blackmail me again?'

Mawde feigned surprise. 'Blackmail? Goodness, no, Sir Hugh! I'm only trying to make it clear that servants are prone to spill secrets.'

Wide bands of sunlight illuminated Sir Hugh's desk. Mawde drew her fingertip through a thick layer of dust.

Sir Hugh's feet scuffed across a square of thick carpet as he shuffled towards the window. 'Do what you like! Organise a feast! My wife and I will leave the village next week, provided we are well enough to travel.'

'Thank you, Sir Hugh.' Mawde suppressed a smile. 'Once again, the villagers will be grateful to you.' She walked towards the door and turned. 'I wish you and Lady Trevanion a quick recovery, and I hope Lady Trevanion enjoys the honey.

# CHAPTER SIXTEEN

When Corpus Christi Day arrived, the village atmosphere was the happiest Mawde had experienced since her return to St Mawes. Adults greeted each other with smiles, and children laughed and squealed while playing chase or hide-and-seek. Mawde bought pancakes for herself, Mamm and Agnes, the batter fried to a thin crisp and sweetened with Perry's honey. Musicians played in the town square, filling the air with lilting pipe notes and beats of tabor drums. Mawde felt a small flush of pride.

'Mamm! Mawde! There's something in the water.' Agnes was leaning over the sea wall pointing to the middle of the harbour.

'What is it?' Mawde shielded her eyes from the sun and watched something dark slide beneath the ripples. The creature broke through the surface of the water and its sleek body shimmered in the glare of the June sunlight. 'Oh Agnes, it's a dolphin! Let us hope it's a good omen.'

Men, women and children hurried towards the sea wall. The dolphin leapt out of the water, making children cry out with glee. The dolphin made a second leap and then swam back towards the sea. 'It must be almost time for the parade,' Mawde said, turning to face the street.

A few minutes later, four adolescent boys walked past them, each holding a pole that supported an opulent embroidered awning. The vicar walked beneath the awning, carrying the blessed sacrament. Polished silverware glistened in the sunlight, casting bright rays onto the sacred wafer.

Mawde linked arms with Mamm and Agnes, and they edged through the crowd towards the village square. They watched the boys position the awning on a small trestle table covered with an altar cloth. The boys then took their positions at each corner while the vicar placed the sacrament on the board. With a broad smile, he turned to face the crowd. Mawde clapped and cheered with everyone else – it was time for the wagon parade.

Cousin Henry's carts came first, with swags of greenery adorning the sides. Girls from the village sat on small benches, each one of them wearing a garland of wildflowers and coronets of elderflower, buttercups and daisies. Henry's eldest daughter sat on a raised stool. Mawde thought her as regal as any queen surrounded by ladies-in-waiting. Farmhands and labourers followed, sitting on straw bales and throwing straw dollies to little girls in the crowd. Fishermen came next, posing on a cart festooned with nets and old leather fenders. They held tankards of beer and heckled at the crowd.

The last cart carried the boys who would perform the mystery plays. They stood tall with their chests puffed out and shouted to their friends. Mawde's attention drifted away from the cart as she saw Nicholas slinking through the crowd. She would have lost sight of him if not for a large orange feather protruding from his cap.

'I have an errand to run,' Mawde said. 'I'll be back in time for the mystery plays.'

Mawde kept her eyes fixed on the feather. It stopped outside the alehouse and then disappeared inside. Mawde moved as close as she dared. It was rare for women to enter the alehouse, and she had no reason to be there. The building was scruffy, with a faded sign outside, and it reeked of neglect and dirt. A muffled conversation drifted through an open shutter. Mawde was certain she picked out Nicholas's voice, but no matter how hard she strained her ears, she could not make out his words. The conversation soon ended, and a squeak of old hinges caused Mawde's muscles to tense. Someone had opened the alehouse door and would soon emerge outside.

'You won't regret your decision. I'll return with the papers tomorrow.' The voice belonged to Nicholas.

Mawde's heartbeat hammered in her chest. She merged with a small crowd that was moving towards the village square, not daring to look back. She found Mamm and Agnes sitting under a sycamore tree, waiting for the mystery play to start.

'Is all well, my dear?' Mamm asked. 'You seem a little breathless.'

'All is well. I rushed to get back in time to watch the play.' Mawde scanned the surrounding men and women. 'I thought Aunt Mary and Beth would be here with Henry's younger children.'

'They probably took the children to the barn where the parade started. I'm sure they'll find us soon.'

A roar of applause stopped all conversation and the mystery plays began. The boys appeared nervous at first, but grew increasingly confident as they recited their lines. Mawde spied Nicholas at the back of the audience. He was talking to two young men and was looking handsome in a new jacquard doublet. Mawde was admiring the rich russet fabric and tailoring of the cloth when a breath became trapped in her throat. One of the men had grasped Nicholas's hand while the other man slapped his back. Nicholas stopped talking. Mawde froze. After a second that felt like a minute, Nicholas laughed and slapped one man on the back. As he strutted away, pulling his cuffs over his wrists, Mawde's heart skipped a few beats. The clasp of hands, a slapped back and the mention of papers for the alehouse landlord were all signs that Nicholas had started lending money.

Mawde forced herself to smile while handing out food from the long trestle table Perry had set up outside the village hall. Men, women and children thronged around her, eager to sample her fragrant meat pies, ginger comfits and sweet honey biscuits.

By mid-afternoon, all the food had been eaten and Mawde joined Agnes for an evening of dancing. She tried to shut out all thoughts of Nicholas while moving her feet to the music. When the circle stopped at the end of a tune, Mawde caught sight of Mamm. She was staring into the distance, her brow ridged with concern. Mawde broke away from the ring of dancers.

'Mamm?' she called, hurrying towards her mother. 'You look troubled.'

Tears welled in Mamm's eyes. 'I've searched the crowd, but I haven't found my sister, nor Beth and Henry's children. Something untoward has happened or Mary would be here!'

Mawde placed her hand on her mother's arm. 'Try not

to fret, Mamm. I'll walk up to the farm and find out what kept them away. I'll return as fast as I can.'

Mawde's feet ached as she climbed the steep hill with the evening sun on her back. She paused by the Holy Well and saw Beth coming down towards her. Her head was uncovered and her fiery hair glowed like the sunset. She had used a shawl to tie Henry's baby to her chest, and she was grasping the hand of his smallest daughter. Beth's face was ashen despite the warmth of the evening.

A chill passed through Mawde's body. 'Beth? Is Aunt Mary unwell?'

Beth's chin trembled. 'I'm so sorry, Mawde.' Laughter wafted up to them from the direction of the alehouse, followed by the pungent smell of burning pig on a spit. 'We were preparing to leave the farm to come down to the village when your aunt had a fearsome pain in her chest.' Beth's face puckered. 'There was nothing I could do.'

Mawde swayed a little. She staggered towards the side of the hill and sat on a low stone wall. Her head throbbed with the hum of cheerful chatter until a song thrush cut through the noise, its subdued lament blocking out the gaiety and echoing Mawde's distress. *This is my husband's fault.* God had made her pay for her sins by taking people she loved. Now He had punished her again for a sin that was not her fault. The guilt of Nicholas's ambition and greed weighed heavy on Mawde's heart.

# CHAPTER SEVENTEEN

THE SUN BEAT down on the St Just Church graveyard, casting a golden light on the lichen-dappled headstones. Mawde felt her mother buckle beside her and caught her arm to save her from collapsing into Aunt Mary's open grave. Da, baby John, Grandmother and Tamsin were all buried nearby. Mawde's heart lurched. A forgotten message and a dislike of her grandmother had played a part in three of their fates. They might still be alive now if not for choices Mawde had made.

'Will you walk to the creek with me?' Nicholas asked, intruding on her thoughts.

Mawde hesitated. Nicholas had been distant since Corpus Christi Day. She tried to read his expression and thought she saw warmth in his eyes.

'Go,' Mamm said, releasing her arm from Mawde's grip. 'Agnes will stay with me.'

Mawde followed Nicholas through the graveyard, past the church and down to the water's edge. Small ripples lapped against the beach, distorting the reflections of the church and trees. Empty mussel shells lay in clusters, interrupting a swathe of silver shingle with patches of dark blue. A regal white swan glided through the shallows leading a parade of four small cygnets.

'I've always loved this creek,' Mawde said, watching her reflection tremble on the water. 'But circumstances have usually been sad when I've visited this beach.'

A wood pigeon cooed from a tree behind them, then flew from its branch with a clatter of wingbeats. The outgoing tide whispered as it dragged waves over small stones, exposing patches of river silt and releasing an earthy odour.

Nicholas laid his summer cloak on a dry patch of shingle. He waited for Mawde to sit before settling beside her. 'I know I've been difficult of late, but you're a good wife, Mawde. I want you to know that.'

Mawde turned to look at him and thought she saw warmth in his eyes. 'I thought you had regrets about marrying me.'

A look of surprise flickered on his face. 'Lord, no!' He picked up a pebble and launched it towards the water. It landed with a small splash, sending out ripples in perfect circles. 'I've had a few matters on my mind. Complicated issues I'd rather not discuss.' He reached for her hand and kissed her fingers. 'Things will be better from now on, I promise.'

Mawde rested her head against his shoulder. 'Your moods have taken you to dark places. I thought I was the cause.'

Nicholas released her hand and hurled another pebble at the water. 'I think, sometimes, I've handled matters badly, or meddled in affairs that should never have arisen.' He looked into her eyes. 'I'm sorry if I hurt you with cruel words.'

Mawde smiled at him. She felt a fluttering deep inside

her and a quickening of her pulse. 'Thank you for saying that.'

Nicholas returned her smile. The blue of his eyes grew more intense as he lowered her onto her back. Mawde cupped his face in her hands and drew him closer towards her. She closed her eyes. Their lips touched. His kisses set her tingling. The sounds of the creek faded away and Mawde felt as if she was floating. She wanted the moment to last forever, but Nicholas drew away.

'Do you remember the first time I kissed you?' he asked.

'I do. We were in the lane at Powderham. It seems like a lifetime ago.' Mawde sat up and removed her bonnet to brush off sand and stones. 'We should go,' she said, replacing it over her linen coif. 'They'll be looking for us at the wake.'

Nicholas rose to his feet and brushed his breeches and hose with his palms. He gave Mawde a deep bow, then offered her his hands. 'My lady, may I have the honour of helping you to stand?'

Mawde laughed and grasped his wrists. After another lingering kiss, they hurried through the churchyard and along the lanes to Henry's farm, giggling like lovers who had shared intimacy for the first time.

When the farmhouse came into view, Nicholas came to a sudden stop and pulled Mawde into his arms. 'With all my heart, I love you,' he said. He kissed her passionately, and Mawde believed he meant it.

Later that evening, when it was time to prepare for bed, Mawde studied her face in the mirror. She looked younger than her six and twenty years. She tilted the mirror to study her eyes and caught Nicholas watching her reflection. Recalling the kisses from earlier that day, a flush of warmth rose deep inside her. Mawde stowed her mirror and rose from her stool to remove her kirtle, petticoat and shift. She turned to face Nicholas and loosened the ribbons that supported her half-leg hose. Naked, she stood at the side of the bed, and started to lift the sheet.

Nicholas snatched the sheet from her hand. 'Where's the snowflake pendant?'

Mawde touched her bare throat with her fingertips. 'I took it off.'

'Why?'

Mawde hesitated, desperate to find a credible excuse. 'I had work to do in the garden,' she blurted. 'I feared the ribbon might come undone and I'd lose the pendant in the soil. It slipped my mind to put it on again.'

'Do it now,' Nicholas said, his voice syrupy with longing.

Mawde stepped away from the bed to retrieve the pendant from its hiding place in her trunk of winter kirtles. As she secured the ribbon behind her neck, she sensed Nicholas coming up behind her. He cupped his hands around her breasts and nuzzled his face against her neck.

'That's better,' he said, sliding his hands towards her belly, and then moving them lower. The heat of his arousal burned against Mawde's skin. He turned her and guided her back towards the bed, then lay her down and kissed her lips, her chin, her throat, her breasts. He stretched out beside her and Mawde caressed his chest.

'Lower,' Nicholas murmured.

Mawde teased him by tracing a snake slowly across his abdomen, revelling in the catch of his breath and his look of expectation. Soon, they were clinging to each other and moving together as one.

When their energy was spent and their carnal appetites were sated, Mawde rolled onto her side and gazed at her husband. His body glowed in the candlelight as if covered in a veil of gold. She watched his eyes wander from her face to her chest, and he caressed the contours of her breasts, sending a delightful shiver through her.

'God willing, our union will have blessed us with an heir,' Nicholas said, sliding his fingertips between her thighs. 'But just to be sure,' he said, kissing her neck, 'we should do that again.'

After making love a second time, Nicholas blew out the candles. Mawde stared into the darkness. A gentle draught crept through the open window and parted the drapes. The feeble light of a crescent moon illuminated the bedcovers. Mawde listened to the swishing of waves breaking on the rocks and thought she heard the distant hoot of an owl calling to its mate.

Nicholas rolled onto his side and traced a circle on her belly. 'If everything goes according to plan, I will make a lot of money.' After a long pause, he added, 'We will have much to celebrate if my success coincides with you birthing an heir.'

Mawde turned her head to meet Nicholas's intense gaze. A shard of moonlight cut across his face, making his features sharp and severe. 'What kind of good fortune?'

Nicholas tapped her lightly on the nose. 'The elevation of our social status is already underway. Soon, I will own the village.'

Mawde's throat constricted. 'Own it? How?'

'How is not your concern, but when I acquire a good number of houses, we will do well from the rent.' Nicholas yawned. 'It won't be long before that damned cock crows. We should go to sleep.'

The shard of moonlight disappeared and plunged them into darkness, leaving Mawde to toss and turn, wondering what Nicholas was planning.

# CHAPTER EIGHTEEN

For the next three weeks, Mawde endured sleepless nights and long hot days of exhaustion. She apologised daily for her snappy moods, which worsened with the arrival of her courses. The only activity that brought her joy was baking bread and making sweetmeats.

A rumble of cartwheels and the heavy thud of hoof-beats announced a visitor's presence in the courtyard.

'Who can that be?' Mawde said, throwing a ball of dough onto the tabletop.

Agnes lifted a cauldron of pottage onto a hook over the fire before opening the kitchen door. 'It's the blacksmith,' she said. 'Mamm placed an order a week ago. Master Viker said he would deliver it.'

Mawde stepped into the courtyard and stared at the cartload of kitchen items: pots of varying sizes; knives; a skillet and hooks. 'We don't need all of this.'

'Yes, we do.' Agnes reached into the cart and lifted out a cooking pot. 'Mamm's are old and dented, and a couple have turned to rust. And there's no such thing as too many knives in a kitchen. You often say so yourself.'

The blacksmith offered Mawde an item covered with a small blanket. 'Your mamm said you might like one of these. Consider it a gift.'

Mawde stepped away from him. 'I'll not accept gifts from you.'

The blacksmith's face dropped. 'Please?' He removed the blanket to reveal a swinging pan. 'Your mamm said you wanted this to make comfits.'

Mawde had not used a swinging pan since the day she left Greenwich. If she chose to accept the gift, she would be able to make perfect comfits. That would please Nicholas when he started bringing guests. 'I'll take it,' she said with a frostiness in her voice. 'But I insist on paying for it.'

'I'd rather you didn't. I realise a gift won't undo any past unkindness,' the blacksmith said mildly, 'but I hope it goes some way towards making amends.'

Mawde looked sideways at him and felt a surprising quickening of her heartbeat. Julian Viker was a fine-looking man. He was taller than Nicholas, with well-defined cheekbones, broad shoulders and a muscular build. His smile was natural and warm.

'I will pay for it,' Mawde insisted, struggling to keep her voice calm. The blacksmith's eyes shone with a kindness far removed the cruel youth who had shared Mawde's childhood home.

'May I offer you a cup of cool, refreshing ale, Master Viker?' Agnes said, stepping between them.

'The blacksmith has no time to tarry with us, Agnes. He has a busy forge to run.' Mawde glared at him, challenging him to contradict her.

'This is the last of my deliveries, so I have no need to hurry. I accept your offer of ale. The forge is hard work on a hot day like this, and I have a raging thirst.' He tethered his horse to a gatepost and gestured for Agnes to help herself to the cart's contents. 'And, please, call me Julian. Your family has known me since I was a lad.'

Mawde seethed as Agnes beamed at him.

'Julian it is then.' Agnes made her way back to the kitchen with cooking pots piled in her arms. She returned to the courtyard with a flagon and cup and poured a drink for the blacksmith. Mawde caught an exchange of smiles and a bloom in Agnes's cheeks.

Mawde snatched the flagon from Agnes. 'Go and stir the pottage before it boils over.'

She waited for Agnes to enter the house before rounding on Julian. 'You took my brother from me! I'll not give you my sister too.'

'I've told you before, I did not kill your brother, and I swear that's the truth.' Julian narrowed his eyes. 'And anyway, it's you I wish to see, not your sister.' His expression softened again. 'That said, my prospects are good, and Agnes could do worse than me.'

'Still arrogant, I see.' Mawde forced herself to keep her eyes locked on his.

Julian shook his head. 'Confident, not arrogant.'

'And your accent has changed.'

'It has.' Julian looked away. 'I paid attention to the speech of educated folk and adapted my words to suit theirs. It's better for business – or at least it was in Truro.'

Agnes returned to the courtyard and smiled at Julian. 'Can I offer you something to eat? My sister has made a batch of lavender biscuits, and we have fresh onion bread.'

Mawde spoke before he had a chance to reply. 'Go to the farm, Agnes, and ask Henry for a cheese. Ours spoiled in the heat.'

'It was fine yesterday when we ate supper.'

Mawde glowered at Agnes. 'It is not fine today.'

'But—'

'Go!'

An uncomfortable silence settled in the courtyard after Agnes left for the farm. Mawde was first to speak. 'You said you didn't kill baby John, but I think you know what happened to him.'

Julian removed his hat and passed it from one hand to the other. 'I swear by Almighty God, I did not kill your brother.' He looked at Mawde with solemn eyes. 'It's not the easiest story to tell. May we sit in the shade?'

Mawde hesitated.

'Please? It's a burden I've carried all these years. You deserve to know the truth. A few minutes is all I ask.' Julian wiped the sweat from his brow. 'Please may we sit somewhere cooler than this?'

Mawde nodded and led the way indoors and to the main hall. The room was in darkness, the thick drapes pulled across the windows to block out the rays of the sun. Mawde pulled one drape aside to let in a band of light.

'Sit,' she said, pointing to the nearest bench. She moved to the other side of the table and settled opposite him. 'Now, tell me your story.'

Julian took a slow breath. 'It was a hot day like today, when baby John died.'

Mawde thought she saw Julian's eyes mist but steeled herself against feeling sympathy. It was her brother that died, not his!

'The air inside your father's workshop was almost suffocating, so your da sent me for ale.' Julian met Mawde's piercing gaze for a few moments and then lowered his eyes. 'Baby John was restless, mewling in his crib. Your grandmother was sleeping. I feared John might cry and wake her, so I gently stroked his face, just like I'd seen your mother do to soothe him when he was fretful. My shirt laces were loose – I'd untied them earlier to cool my chest. One lace dangled lower than the other and John grabbed it in his fist.' Julian gave a sad smile. 'He looked so pleased with himself. He released it and caught it again, holding tighter this time. It turned into a little game. I teased him with the lace and he tried to grasp it. I remember the way he looked at me with a big gummy smile.' Julian took a slow breath. 'That lace was old and frayed. A piece broke off in John's hand. He tried to put it into his mouth, but I took it from him and tickled his cheek with it instead. He liked that. I kept doing it, and after a while, he drifted off to sleep. He looked so peaceful.' Julian dabbed his eyes with the backs of his hands. 'I can't be sure what happened after that, but it's haunted me to this day. Your da called my name, asked what was taking so long, so I hurried to fetch the ale.' His voice cracked. 'I must have dropped the lace into the crib. John must have found it when he woke and pushed it into his mouth.'

Mawde pictured her brother lying dead in his crib, and recalled her mother's anguished pleas while her father tried to revive him. 'How could you!' she cried.

'But I didn't kill him!' Julian reached for Mawde's hands, but she snatched them away and crossed them on her lap.

'You let my grandmother blame me for it! Everyone wondered if I'd killed baby John out of some kind of petty jealousy.' Tears drenched Mawde's cheeks. She dried them on her sleeves.

A bird flew at the window, hitting it hard with its beak. Mawde hurried over and peered outside. A sparrow had landed in a flower bed and showed no sign of movement. After a few seconds, the bird ruffled its feathers and then flew away. Mawde watched it shrink into the distance, hoping it would survive.

Julian's voice brought her attention back to their conversation. 'I've served a penance every day since,' he said.

'How?' Mawde's tone was curt.

'I see your brother every night in my dreams, and whenever a baby cries. I will never marry because of what happened – I don't deserve children of my own. How could I watch my child grow after what happened to baby John? Instead, I put everything into my work, and I try to be respectable and kind.'

Mawde returned to the table and looked him in the eyes. 'Do you swear that's the truth?'

Julian crossed himself. 'I swear it on my life.' He cleared his throat. 'Now that you've heard my confession, there's something I want to ask you.'

'What?'

'There are rumours circulating in the village. Rumours about you.'

Mawde stiffened. 'What of them?'

'They say you had something to do with the fire that killed your grandmother and cousin. Is it true?'

Mawde tried to swallow but her throat was tight. 'I didn't start the fire,' she said in a croaking voice, 'if that's what you were asking.'

'And I didn't stuff the lace into your baby brother's mouth,' Julian said quietly. 'It seems we might both be spending the rest of our lives atoning for a moment's hesitation or an innocent mistake.'

Mawde could tell from the look in his eyes that Julian knew the pain and sorrow of guilt and regret. He reached across the table and she put her hand in his. Unable to find suitable words, Mawde gently squeezed his fingers to accept his offer of a truce.

# CHAPTER NINETEEN

July parched the land with searing sunshine, but August brought cooling showers which revived the crops on Nicholas's land and provided a bountiful harvest. Mawde and her family celebrated with a feast made merry by the news of Beth's betrothal to Henry.

Later that evening, Mawde searched for Nicholas and found him in his parlour poring over a ledger. He closed the ledger as Mawde approached and rose from his chair.

'It was a wonderful surprise to learn of Beth and Henry's betrothal,' Mawde said as Nicholas guided her out of his parlour and towards one of the hall windows. 'I believe they will suit each other well.'

'It was not a surprise to me,' Nicholas said, releasing the window catch. 'I suggested to Henry he should marry my sister soon after he became a widower.'

Mawde gasped. 'Nicholas!'

'You said yourself they are well-suited.'

Mawde stared at him, lost for words.

'You might think me cruel-hearted for the timing of my

suggestion, but the reality for Henry is that he needs a mother for his children – even more so since his mother passed. I offered an attractive dowry for him to take my sister.' He gave a resigned shake of his head. 'Now I believe I was too hasty to make a generous offer. He seems genuinely fond of my sister and probably would have settled for less.'

Mawde peered sideways at Nicholas. His face was pinched and his eyes narrowed as he stared into the distance. 'Would your parents have approved of the marriage?'

Nicholas pushed the window open as wide as it would go. 'Your cousin is a hard-working man and respected in the village, so yes, my parents would have approved of him as a husband for Beth.' Nicholas spent several moments scrutinising the ships in the estuary. He tutted and closed the window.

'Is something wrong?' Mawde asked.

Nicholas pinched his lips together while considering his answer. 'I invested in a merchant ship bound for Southern Spain. It was due back in Penryn more than a month ago.' He ran his hand across his forehead as if trying to soothe a pain. 'I was given an assertion it would be a successful venture and double my investment.' He swayed and steadied himself by grasping the windowsill. 'I fear the ship foundered in a storm or was seized by pirates.'

Mawde thought about the altar plate locked away in his parlour. Was that what he had used to fund his investment? 'Do we stand to lose much if the ship doesn't return?'

Nicholas turned his back towards the window. 'Most of what I had put aside to secure our future.' He met Mawde's worried gaze. 'Beth's dowry will clear out all that remains.' His face appeared to relax a little. 'I cannot recover that which is missing but there is something I can do to raise more money.' Nicholas strode towards his parlour and stopped by the door. 'I'll probably be up late tonight refining my plans. Don't wait up for me.' He disappeared into his room and firmly closed the door.

It was a perfect September day for celebrating a marriage. The air was warm, the sky was blue and the atmosphere was vibrant as Beth and Henry led the dancing in the village square.

Mawde felt envious watching the newlyweds together. Beth and Henry laughed and smiled with an obvious deep affection.

'May I have the pleasure of dancing with you?' Julian was by her side in his Sunday doublet and hose.

Mawde smiled. 'I thank you for your offer, but I must dance with my husband first.'

Nicholas waved her away. 'I'm not in the mood. I'd rather find refreshment.'

Mawde hesitated. 'Shall I go with you?'

'No need.' A vein flickered in Nicholas's temple. 'I heard someone complain that the bride ale's running low. I'll go to the alehouse and pay for more barrels. You stay here and dance with the blacksmith.'

Julian bowed and offered Mawde his hand. 'My lady, will you dance with me now that your husband has given his approval?'

Mawde waited for Nicholas to stride away before accepting Julian's hand and moving towards the dancers. She lost herself in the music as she marked out the steps but she soon grew breathless with a quickening of the pace.

When the music ended, she fell into Julian's arms, smiling and laughing. They moved to a grassy bank to recover from their exertions. Julian lay on his back with his eyes closed and his chest heaving. He was of a similar age to Nicholas but looked a few years younger. And he was handsome. Mawde was still observing him when he opened his eyes. A soothing warmth engulfed her when he held her gaze and smiled.

Julian pushed himself up on his elbows and surveyed the nearby crowd. 'Look, there's your sister,' Julian said, beckoning for Agnes to join them. He stood as Agnes drew nearer and offered her his arm. 'May I have the pleasure of dancing with you, Agnes?'

Agnes flushed a deep shade of scarlet as she linked her arm with his. Mawde pitied her sister's attraction to a man who harboured no desire for a wife. Mawde left them to enjoy the music while she searched for Nicholas. She scoured the square and the village streets, but without success. Next, she dared to enter the alehouse after hearing women's voices from beyond the door. A new sign hung outside bearing the name *The Dolphin*. The door had a fresh coat of wax. Straw and herbs covered the floor inside. The landlord's son said he'd been serving all afternoon but had not seen Nicholas there. Puzzled, Mawde returned to the village square. She filled a wooden beaker with ale and sipped it while watching the dancers. When the music ended, she stared at the barrels stacked against a wall. The ale had flowed freely from the barrel she had used, and two barrels next to it were yet to be tapped. Anger fizzed in the pit of her stomach. The ale turned bitter in her mouth. Nicholas had lied about the bride ale running low.

Feigning a headache, Mawde left the celebrations and walked home at a brisk pace. She entered via the kitchen and sat on a stool to slip off her shoes. The cold flagstones soothed her sore feet, which had blistered while she was dancing. She was about to pour herself a drink when she heard a man's voice in the hall. Mawde forced her feet back into her shoes and limped out of the kitchen. Two men were sitting at her table; one was the cordwainer, the other was a local builder.

'Gentlemen, forgive me,' Mawde said, checking her hair was tucked in her coif. 'I didn't know you were here. May I offer you refreshment?'

Both men stood and greeted her politely but declined her offer of a drink. The door to Nicholas's parlour opened and another man entered the hall. It was the landlord of the alehouse. When Nicholas emerged, his face contorted as if he was angered by Mawde's presence. Not wanting to cause a spectacle, she retreated to the kitchen. She pressed her ear to the solid wooden door, hoping to overhear their conversations. But the voices were far too low, and she heard only murmurs.

Mawde waited for the murmurs to stop before returning to the hall with a pitcher and cups. The cordwainer was alone at the table. 'In case you change your mind,' she said. She climbed the stairs to her bedchamber and dozed until Nicholas joined her.

'What business did those men have with you?' Mawde said, trying not to sound accusatory.

'Nothing untoward.'

Mawde found his word choice unsettling. 'What do you mean by nothing untoward?'

Nicholas yawned and climbed into the bed. 'Word is out that I have experience in financial matters and those men sought my help.' He kissed her on the cheek and then rolled on to his side, signalling their conversation was over and he wished to go to sleep.

Mawde stared at his dark silhouette. She was certain he

was practising usury and their evening visitors were in his debt. More were likely to follow. She slipped out of bed and dropped to her knees to pray for God's intervention. Nicholas was driven by greed and the villagers needed protection.

# CHAPTER TWENTY

An easterly wind whipped the surface of the sea into small jagged peaks. Leaves withered and fell from the trees, and the air was sharp with a chill.

Mawde watched Nicholas heft a travelling chest onto his cart. 'How long will you be gone?' she asked, pulling her shawl tight around her.

Nicholas checked the girth of his horse before mounting it and settling in the saddle. 'Several weeks. After I've overseen the closure of Buckland Abbey, I must deliver the seized goods to the King's receiver at the Tower.' He grinned down at her. 'I didn't think I'd be doing this again, but the opportunity was too good to turn down. I'll receive a handsome payout when the task is complete.'

Mawde wondered how much money and altar plate Nicholas intended to declare and how much he would keep for himself.

'May you be blessed with fair winds and untroubled waters, and may the Lord guide you home with safe passage.'

Nicholas gave a mock salute. 'And God willing, when I return, you'll have my heir in your belly.'

Mawde placed her hand across her lower abdomen. The gripe inside confirmed her monthly bleed was imminent. Nicholas flicked the reins and urged the horse to move forward. Hooves and cartwheels crunched across gravel until the horse and cart passed through the gate and onto the dried mud of the lane. Perry walked beside him to escort him to the harbour and would then return with the horse and empty cart. Mawde waited for them to shrink into the distance before joining Mamm and Agnes in the kitchen. The pungent scent of vinegar irritated the back of her throat. She left the door open to sweeten the air and swapped her shawl for her apron. She had a long day stretching ahead, filled with pickling autumn vegetables and salting a butchered pig.

Late in the afternoon, someone knocked on Mawde's front door. Wiping salt from her sore fingers she went to greet her visitor.

The landlord of *The Dolphin* doffed his knitted cap and then wrung it in his hands. 'Begging your pardon, mistress, but I was hoping to speak to your husband.' He shuffled uneasily from one foot to the other. Mawde detected the tang of sweat from underneath his jerkin. She suspected the sweat was from stress and worry rather than heavy toil.

Mawde stepped aside and beckoned for him to enter. 'My husband is away on business, but perhaps I can help?'

One of the landlord's eyelids twitched. 'I should wait until your husband's home,' he said, stumbling over his words.

'He left only this morning and will be away for several weeks.' Mawde gave the landlord a sympathetic smile. 'Now that you're here, I might as well try to help.'

The landlord averted his gaze. 'How much do you know about our... business arrangement?'

'Only that my husband was happy to oblige. Do you need more money?'

The landlord paled. 'He said I shouldn't discuss it with anyone but him.' He rubbed his face with his hand as if trying to erase his own presence. 'I'll work something out. Forgive me for intruding, Mistress Sherman. I'll bid you a good day.'

Mawde closed the door behind him and slammed the oak with her palm. If she had pressed a little harder, he might have let something slip. She returned to the kitchen to find Mamm and Agnes taking a break from the salting. Mawde took a sharp knife and chopped some cauliflower for pickling. The blade slipped and nicked the tip of her index finger. She sucked the wound to clean it of blood, still thinking about the landlord. He was clearly in a state of distress due to his arrangement with Nicholas. Somehow she had to find out why, and do something to help him.

After two days of salting and pickling, Mawde joined Perry in the vegetable garden. They passed an hour in companionable silence, pulling carrots and beetroots from the ground. When their task was complete, they settled on a dry patch of grass to quench their thirsts with a small flagon of ale. As Mawde pulled the stopper from the flagon, Agnes came running towards them.

'Come quickly,' she said, her chest heaving. 'It's Julian. He's injured in the lane.' Her face crinkled. 'It looks bad!'

Mawde felt a tremor creep up her legs. A sour taste filled her mouth. She dropped the flagon and ran towards the house, stumbling on clods of earth. She passed through the courtyard, kicking up small stones, and saw a horse and overturned cart at the bend in the lane. Julian was lying on the ground.

'Julian!'

The horse pulled against his harness and made a deep, throaty sound. It flared its nostrils and rolled its eyes, rearing and kicking its front legs. Julian gave an anguished cry and said his left leg was trapped. Mawde's heart started pounding. 'Perry!' she yelled. 'Hurry!'

'Already here.' Perry sprinted past her, giving the flustered horse a wide berth. He tried to lift the cart off Julian's leg, but the cart would not budge.

Mawde grabbed the loose reins. She tried to settle the horse with soothing words and by stroking its neck. Agnes arrived, pursing her lips and struggling to catch her breath. 'Take over from me, Agnes.' Mawde passed her the reins. 'Speak calmly to this poor creature while I free him from the harness.'

As soon as she had released the buckles, Mawde hurried towards the cart. Perry was working up a sweat unloading sacks and crates. 'I've only two more sacks to go,' he said. 'Then we'll try to lift it.'

Mawde knelt by Julian's head and cradled his face between her hands. She spoke softly to reassure him while the seconds it took for Perry to shift the sacks felt like several minutes.

'The pain's easing,' Julian said, his voice sounding distant. 'It hardly hurts at all now.' He gave Mawde a weak smile. 'Thank goodness I wore my sturdy boots.' Julian closed his eyes.

Mawde gently slapped his cheeks. 'Open your eyes, Julian! I need you to stay awake.'

'I'm here,' Agnes announced, kneeling next to Mawde.

'The horse has settled well enough. I tied the reins to a tree.'

'Good. Keep Julian awake,' Mawde said, shuffling towards the cart to help Perry.

'Count of three,' Perry said. 'One, two, three.'

Between them, they lifted it a couple of inches, but could not hold its weight.

'Shall I run and get help from the village?' Agnes offered.

'No time,' Perry said. 'I'll find something to wedge underneath.'

Mawde glanced at Julian. His eyes were closed and his fingers were clenched. 'We'll soon have you out from under there,' she said, hoping she spoke the truth.

Perry returned with an armful of split logs of varying thickness. They tried lifting the cart again and raised it a couple of inches. Perry used his foot to kick logs into the gap. They lifted again. Mawde's arm muscles burned, her fingers cramped, but at last they raised the cart high enough to drag Julian free. Perry used a sturdy branch to splint Julian's injured leg, then Mawde and Perry took one arm each to support Julian's weight between them. They made slow progress towards the house with Mawde weeping tears of relief and Julian shrieking with pain.

After settling Julian on a cushioned chair, Mawde knelt to remove his boots. His lower leg had doubled in size and the skin was taut and splitting. Mawde watched Perry appraise the injury. He had a grim expression on his face.

'I saw an injury similar to this at the priory years ago,' he said. 'The bone is undamaged but if we don't cut into the swelling, he will lose his leg.'

'Does he need a surgeon?'

'Ideally.' Perry studied Julian's wound again. 'I don't believe we have time to wait. I'm willing to do it.'

Mawde pressed her lips together. 'Very well,' she said at last.

Perry went to fetch a knife. Sweat beaded on Julian's brow. His whole body trembled and his face turned deathly pale.

'Agnes, help me lie him on the floor. He looks fit to faint.'

Mawde used cushions from the settle to make Julian comfortable and support his injured leg.

When Perry returned, he had her sharpest knife in his hand. Mawde sent Agnes upstairs to fetch a blanket, and she averted her eyes while Perry used the blade. Julian screamed. He grasped Mawde's hand and squeezed so hard that she feared her fingers would break.

'It's done,' Perry said at last.

Mawde stole a glance at Julian's leg. Blood poured from the wound.

'I think we should apply a salve to help heal his leg,' Mawde said to Perry.

Perry thought for a moment. 'For most wounds, the infirmerer favoured a mixture made with honey, egg whites and rosewater, but he always cleaned the wound first.'

'There's rosewater in the still room,' Mawde said. 'And honey and eggs in the kitchen. Do what you can to reproduce the infirmerer's recipe while I use vinegar and water to clean out the dirt.'

While Mawde and Perry worked on his leg, Julian drifted in and out of consciousness. Afterwards, Mawde sat by his side and stroked his calloused hand, willing him to recover. For all that had happened between them, she had grown fond of Julian. She asked Agnes to prepare a broth so he would have something easy to swallow while he fought the pain.

The sun sank low in the sky. The light in the room

dimmed. Mawde was trying to make herself comfortable when Julian reached for her arm.

'You don't have to sit with me,' he said. 'You've been kneeling there for hours.'

'How do you feel?' Mawde asked.

'Tired.' Julian grimaced. 'And my leg is throbbing, but not as bad as I feared. Perry knew what he was doing.'

'We're lucky to have him.' Mawde stroked the side of Julian's brow then snatched her hand away, chastising herself for touching him with such an intimate gesture. 'I'll find something in my still room to ease that pain for you.'

'I should return to the forge,' Julian said, trying to raise himself up on his elbows.

Mawde pressed on his shoulder. 'You're in no state to do that today, and I insist you stay here tonight.'

Julian collapsed back onto the cushions. 'I don't wish to be a burden. Perry can take me home and settle me in my bed.'

'No, Julian. Not tonight.' Mawde stroked his brow again. 'We'll review the situation in the morning.'

# CHAPTER TWENTY-ONE

Mawde stayed awake for most of the night. Every time Julian moved, he cried out with pain. She tried to calm him with a chamomile tisane interspersed with cups of strong beer. The following morning, fearing the worst, Mawde peeled away the dressing. The swelling had subsided a little, and the absence of a putrefying smell suggested it would heal, albeit with a scar. Mawde applied a fresh layer of honey and rosewater unguent before binding his leg with clean linen.

'Perry will help you in the forge for the next few days,' she said, securing the binding with dress pins. 'You must rest your leg on a stool to keep the shin and calf from swelling.'

'No.' Julian shook his head. 'Perry doesn't have the strength or skill to work metal. He can take me home, but he will not take over my work.'

'But your leg,' Mawde protested. 'The heat from the forge and standing all day will make it worse.'

Julian pushed himself up to sitting. 'Your concern

means everything to me, Mawde, but I'll not leave my work to another man. I'll be sensible and only do what is necessary. Few things are urgent when it comes to metalwork. I'll spend today getting my accounts in order and relight the fire tomorrow.'

'Accounts,' Mawde echoed. She wondered if Nicholas kept a ledger and a list of the men who had sought his help. 'Julian, did you know my husband has been advising men in the village regarding matters of money?'

Julian took a sudden interest in the fastenings of his doublet. 'I'm aware of a few men who have sought his counsel and expressed satisfaction afterwards, although none of them discussed the specifics.' He gave Mawde a sideways glance. 'It was as if they were under instruction not to.'

'I have the horse and cart ready,' Perry said, emerging from the kitchen. He helped Julian to stand and then handed him a stick. 'I carved this for you last night to keep some of your weight off your injured leg when you're standing and walking.'

When Mawde heard the cartwheels crunch across the gravel as it left the courtyard, she slipped into Nicholas's parlour. She sat on his chair and stared at the desk, which was littered with documents and letters. Most of the documents related to his farm, which he left Henry to manage for him. There were receipts for sickles and scythes and a note to acknowledge payment for a pair of oxen.

The only ledger Mawde could see was the one she used for her household accounts. A gull's shriek drew her gaze towards the window, but her view of the sea was obscured by a mist yet to burn off in the sun. She shivered. Winter would soon be upon them. She rose from the chair and went to the corner of the room where Nicholas kept her coffer of coins for food and household items. The coffer was on top of Nicholas's locked chest where he had stored his looted gold and silver. A new, larger coffer nestled beside it – and the key was in its lock.

Mawde's heartbeat quickened as she carried the coffer to the desk. She perched on the edge of the chair and dried her palms on her skirt. When she turned the key, the lock shifted with ease. Mawde lifted the lid and found documents inside. She lifted one out and traced her fingertip across the red wax seal. There were words embossed along the edge, and at the centre it bore an image: a phoenix rising from a fire.

'*De cinere ad lucem*,' Mawde read aloud. She had made excellent progress reading and writing under Perry's instruction and recalled that *lucem* was the Latin word for light. The word *cinere*, however, was unfamiliar, but from the image of the phoenix she assumed it had something to do with fire. 'From flames to the light?' she mumbled to herself. No, that made little sense. After all, flames were light. *Cinere* sounded like something had been burnt, like wood that had burned to ashes. Ashes! Mawde smiled. Perhaps that was it! 'From ashes to the light,' she said. 'That makes better sense.'

Her glee was short-lived when she considered the meaning. It seemed an arrogant way to announce the achievements of a man who had accrued modest wealth. She wondered about the contents of the letter but dared not break the seal. Nicholas erupted at the slightest provocation and there was no telling how he would react if he discovered she had been snooping. She replaced the folded parchment and riffled through the others. Each one bore an identical seal. Mawde locked the coffer and replaced it on the chest, then returned to the desk to search for the stamp. She pulled out one of the drawers. It held only quills and a small pot of ink. She opened the other drawer. There was a knife for sharpening quill tips and a partly used block of wax. Mawde slammed the drawer shut. She would have to delay reading the documents until she found the phoenix stamp and could reseal each letter afterwards.

# CHAPTER TWENTY-TWO

The winter months crept by, shrouded by thick sea mists. When Nicholas arrived home on a damp day in January, he smiled and jingled a heavy purse of coins. His reward, he said, for closing Buckland Abbey. By the end of the month, there were rumours that work would start on building the castle, but several more weeks passed before Treffry sent a team of workers to start breaking ground in the spring.

Cartloads of tools and stone salvaged from the priory trundled past Mawde's house. There were more labourers than she had been expecting, and Nicholas announced it was up to her to feed them. Unable to produce enough bread in her ovens, Mawde went into the village.

'Mistress Sherman!' The cordwainer's wife elbowed her way to the front of the baker's queue and stood facing Mawde. 'I'd like a word with you.'

'Good day to you,' Mawde said, smiling warmly.

'I wish that were so.'

The cordwainer's wife was younger than Mawde but

already had grey hair. Her face looked gaunt, her clothes smelled musty, and the leather of her shoes was breaking down. Mawde felt the curious gazes of other customers turn towards her. A cold sweat prickled on her skin.

'I hear your husband's involved with the castle build,' the cordwainer's wife continued. 'We've all seen the carts moving up and down the street, and a long line of workers. Outsiders they are, too! When's your husband going to honour his promise of work for our men?'

Mawde's chest tightened as the other women closed in.

'Yes, tell us,' another woman shouted. 'He said they'd earn decent money when the build began but was quick to turn my husband away when he turned up to work this morning.'

'Same happened to my oldest lad,' declared someone else. 'We can't believe anything her husband says.' She gave Mawde a shove that sent her stumbling against the counter. 'Tell us, then, when will our men get the jobs?'

Mawde felt like a hen surrounded by foxes. These women were never warm towards her, but most days they were civil.

'I… I'll ask him,' she stammered. 'I'm sure it will be soon. Now they've started digging the foundations, perhaps he'll need them when the build starts?'

The cordwainer's wife moved closer until she and Mawde were breathing the same air. 'It's all very well your husband making offers built on promises of rewards, but he should fulfil his end of the deal. There's no telling what might happen if he's not as good as his word.'

'What do you mean?' Mawde asked, taking a step backwards and trampling on another woman's toes. 'So sorry,' she said, hoping for a forgiving smile, but receiving another rough shove instead.

'He guaranteed our men'd have wages. That's why so many of them accepted his deals.'

Mawde felt the colour drain from her cheeks. 'What deals?'

The cordwainer's wife snorted. 'As if you don't know. Paid work for them all, he said, no matter what their skills. It's about time he proved himself.'

The bakery walls seem to wobble and close in towards Mawde. 'I'll ask him as soon as I get home,' she said.

'Aye, you do that. We're eager to learn what he says.'

Mawde edged her way towards the bakery door. She stepped outside and filled her lungs with rapid gulps of air, wondering how she could persuade Nicholas to employ local men.

Mawde sent Perry to the building site with a handcart laden with food for the workmen. Next, she filled a basket with a flagon of small beer, two earthenware cups, cold meat and a pot of pickled vegetables. She slipped the handle over her forearm and left the house to search for Nicholas.

She passed a large group of men erecting tents and tried to pick out familiar faces, but the village women had been right about all the men being outsiders.

She heard Nicholas before she saw him. He was having a heated exchange with a tall, burly stonemason. When their argument ended, Nicholas strode towards her, his face pinched and ruddy.

'That whoreson accused me of being unqualified for my task! I told him to watch his tongue if he wants to continue earning money here.'

'The Hockynge brothers are stonemasons,' Mawde said, hoping it might offer an opportunity to bring locals into the building site. 'They would be glad of the work.'

Nicholas grimaced. 'It's one thing to build a house or barn, but something else to build a castle. They're not much use to me here.'

'Are the principles not the same?' Mawde asked. 'Perry said the priory used them to repair the church walls and that they were fast workers who performed the task well.'

'The monk is a mason as well now, is he?' Nicholas leaned towards the basket and sniffed. 'What have you brought for me?'

'Bread, salt pork and pickled cauliflower. I also have a few cinnamon biscuits.' Mawde pointed towards a low pile of stones. 'Why don't we sit there to eat?'

Mawde poured them each some beer while Nicholas rummaged in the basket, helping himself to bread and meat. They ate in silence, watching ships entering and leaving the estuary.

'You must have about thirty men working on the foundations,' Mawde said when she had finished eating. She had counted fifteen men setting up the little tented village while others marked out areas for digging. 'I haven't seen a single man I recognise.'

'They're all Treffry's men,' Nicholas replied, cutting another slice of pork. 'He sent them over from Fowey. They've worked on fortifications for him, so he's using their experience here.'

'For the foundations?'

Nicholas took a large slug of ale. 'For the entire build.'

Mawde had a sinking feeling. 'So, what will you have the local men do? Will you use them for plastering and decorating the interior?'

Nicholas laughed. 'It's a fort, not a royal palace. It will need little interior decoration.'

'What about carpentry, then?'

'I doubt we'll use locals for anything.' Nicholas stood and brushed crumbs from his breeches. 'Why would we when we have the experience of Treffry's men?'

Conversations carried through the air. A few men sang while they worked.

'You made promises,' Mawde said, too softly for Nicholas to hear.

'Treffry's coming to visit the site tomorrow.' Nicolas said, removing his leather jerkin and slinging it over his shoulder. 'I'll invite him to lodge with us overnight. If you're still concerned about who does the work, you can raise the issue with him.'

Mawde found Treffry more affable than she had imagined. He praised her beef with red wine glaze and raved about her rabbit pie. He closed his eyes to savour the capon smothered with mustard sauce, then devoured two slices of a pork and onion pie. Mawde plied his glass with Burgundy wine while listening to him and Nicholas discuss the progress of the build.

'That was the most delicious dinner I've eaten in a long while,' Treffry said, dabbing his mouth with a linen napkin. 'I could do with you visiting my cook and refining his skills to your standards. That food was fit for the King!'

'Thank you, Master Treffry. I am fortunate to have cooked for nobility and worked at the confectionery at Greenwich Palace.'

Master Treffry looked taken aback. 'Your husband never mentioned that you worked in a kitchen.'

'It was a long time ago,' Nicholas replied.

Mawde almost corrected him but checked herself. 'I have one last treat for you, Master Treffry, if you will excuse me.'

'Of course. I'm eager to see what delights you'll bring next.'

Mawde seethed as she carried used plates and serving platters into the kitchen. Nicholas had not tried to advocate for the local workmen. She picked up her best pewter serving platter and carried it into the hall.

'Well, well, well.' Treffry stared at the platter with greedy eyes. 'You have outdone yourself.' He reached for a marchpane biscuit shaped like a miniature castle. 'If our castle looks as fine as this, we will have done our work well.'

'Speaking of work,' Mawde said, taking her place on the bench, 'I noticed that men have arrived from Fowey to build the castle walls. Had you considered using locals for the task instead?' Nicholas kicked her under the trestle, but she pressed on regardless. 'We have skilled workmen here in St Mawes: masons, carpenters and labourers. They were born into their trades and honed their skills at the priory until it had to close. Some of them worked on Lanihorne Castle and Glasney College, too.'

'I did not know that.' Treffry helped himself to another biscuit. 'These really are delicious. Sherman, you're a fortunate man to have your wife prepare delicious meals while I must suffer lesser offerings from a cantankerous cook.'

Nicholas dipped his head. 'Mawde insists on cooking every meal despite my pleas to employ a cook.'

Mawde stole a glance at Nicholas. He had pleaded no such thing. 'Lord knows the men of this village are desperate for employment,' she said, determined to turn the conversation back to the castle. 'Surely they'd be cheaper than men brought in from other villages or towns?'

'The daily wage would be the same irrespective of who does the work.' Small crumbs flew from Treffry's lips as he spoke. They landed like spits of rain on the clean white tablecloth. 'No, Mistress Sherman, I'll continue to use the men I know and trust.' He drained the wine from his glass and dabbed his mouth with his napkin. 'That was a fine dinner, Mistress Sherman, but now you must excuse us. Come, Nicholas, we should return to the build site and plan the next stage of the works.'

By the time Nicholas returned home that evening, it was time to retire to bed. Mawde was in a rage.

'Why didn't you advocate for our men?' she said, bristling at her own temper.

Nicholas shrugged. 'I knew what Treffry would say. It would have been a waste of words.'

'You should have tried! You should have said something to support me when I raised the possibility.'

Nicholas took her comb from her hand and steered her towards the bed. 'Enough of your little tantrum, Mawde. Do not raise your voice to me.'

'But you know how desperate they are in the village. They're barely getting by.'

Nicholas held her face in his hand. His nails dug into her cheeks. 'If you raise your voice to me again, I'll put you in a scold's bridle.'

Mawde shuddered and wondered if he would really do such a thing.

'I will advocate for your friends,' Nicholas said, releasing her. 'But not yet.'

'When?'

'After a few more have declared their need for my help.'

'For your business advice, I presume.' Mawde struggled

to soften her tone. Pressure was building at the back of her head.

Nicholas removed his shirt and untied the fastenings of his breeches. 'You keep your mind on matters that are your responsibility and stop trying to meddle with mine.' He pulled back the coverlet and climbed into bed. 'Hurry, Mawde. Undress now. I crave attention from my wife.'

# CHAPTER TWENTY-THREE

THE LAUNDRY DRIED QUICKLY in the warm spring air. Mawde folded clean smocks and shifts, enjoying the fresh smell of linens that Clare had rinsed in rose-infused water. She opened the clothes press where Nicholas kept his shirt and found a small, jewelled trinket box protruding from a pile of clothes. Mawde took the box to the window. Small gemstones sparkled in the light with little bursts of orange, yellow, pink and white. The box had a silver catch shaped like a padlock, but it needed no key. She ran her finger over the catch, wondering why Nicholas had buried it among his clothes. She shook the box. Something rattled inside. She released the catch and lifted the lid.

The box had a lining of blue velvet and contained a silver gilt fob. It had an imprint of a phoenix on its base and words around the edge. Mawde pressed the cool metal to her lips and thanked God for revealing it at last. She stowed the fob in her pocket and finished putting away the clothes, then shook out some kirtles Clare had brushed clean and hung them on her dress rail to air. With the cold winter behind her, she would not need her heavier kirtles for five or six months.

After dinner, Mawde settled at the trestle table and pretended to update her household accounts. She waited for Nicholas to return to the castle site and then seized her chance. Armed with a sharp knife and the seal fob, she entered Nicholas's parlour. The coffer containing sealed documents still had the key in the lock. Mawde felt a flutter of apprehension as she lifted the lid. More folded papers had been crammed together inside. She selected a sealed letter and placed it on Nicholas's desk. After peering into the hall to make sure she no one would disturb her, she slipped her blade beneath the wax seal and prised it away from the paper. The dried wax snapped on one side, leaving remnants clinging to the paper. Mawde unfolded the document and flattened it with her hand. An untidy scrawl almost filled the page, and the letters seemed to swirl. Mawde closed her eyes and reminded herself that Perry had taught her well. She opened her eyes and tried again, following the words with her fingertip and sounding them out letter by letter.

*On this thirtieth day of May in the year of Our Lord 1539, Humphrie Tomas, landlord of the Dolphin Alehouse, is bound by obligation in £15 to pay Nicholas Sherman £10 by Easter in the year of our Lord 1542 or forfeit his goods and lands.*

The landlord had written his initials 'H' and 'T', and Nicholas had signed with a flourish. Mawde read the document again to make sure she had understood it correctly. Her cheeks burned and her fingers tightened, crumpling the edge of the paper. 'So, this is how he intends to own the village. With usury disguised.' Mawde refolded the letter. She opened the drawer to take out the sealing wax and gasped in horror. There were quill pens, sheets of paper and two pots of ink. But no wax. She opened the other drawer to find only old letters and the knife for sharpening quills. She stared at the letter in her hand. By breaking the seal, she had rendered the deed invalid. Mawde ran her fingertip over the fragments of wax. She would have to try to reuse them. She pressed the tip of her knife between the wax and the paper but the seal remnant broke away with a shard of paper clinging to it. 'No!' Mawde tried to pick off the paper but the stubborn wax held on to it, leaving her no way of disguising the fact that the letter had been opened. An ache gripped her chest. She considered the other letters in the coffer and suspected they too were bonds for debts. She doubted Nicholas counted the deeds whenever he opened the coffer and therefore might not notice if only one was missing. She closed the lid of the coffer, turned the key and replaced the box on the larger chest exactly where she had found it. Her hand trembled as she stuffed the landlord's bond in her pocket. She would have to burn it.

Mawde replaced the sealing fob in Nicholas's trinket box and covered it with clean laundry. Two years had yet to pass before the landlord's debt was due for settlement. Surely Nicholas was unlikely to look for the bond before then? Breaking the seal was starting to feel like a small victory for Mawde, but when it was time for Nicholas to call in the debt, it would be a huge victory for the landlord of *The Dolphin*.

# CHAPTER TWENTY-FOUR

Mawde was in a cheerful mood as she walked into the village. The sky was clear, the air was warm, and vibrant yellow crocuses gave off a delicate scent of honey. A fishing boat sailed into St Mawes harbour. Mawde hoped the skipper might have a lobster or two she could cook for supper. Her mouth watered at the thought of the sweet meat glazed with a melting herb butter. The sound of a man's melodic voice drew her gaze towards *The Dolphin*. The landlord was fixing a window shutter and singing while he worked. Mawde smiled, imagining his joy when he discovered his bond of debt was missing.

'Look at 'er strutting about in 'er finery and smiling to 'erself.' The baker's wife stepped in front of Mawde and stood with her arms folded.

'It's such a beautiful day,' Mawde said.

The baker's wife squinted at Mawde. 'Sunshine will bring me joy when it learns to pay my rent.' She narrowed her eyes. 'You said you'd do something about getting our men work at the castle. That was months ago and still nothing's 'appened.'

'I know.' Mawde's smile faded. 'I tried to persuade my husband, and I spoke to Captain Treffry.' Her gaze drifted towards the bakery. 'Your husband wouldn't work on the build, would he?'

Mistress Michell snorted. 'Course not! But I 'ave two sons who would, and they 'ave families to feed.'

Something struck Mawde hard on her arm and exploded with a foul odour. A rotten egg. Another egg struck her shoulder. The baker's wife sniggered.

'Stop!' Mawde raised her hands to protect her face as a blackened carrot flew towards her.

Women thronged around her. Mawde turned to walk away, but there was no chance of escape. She clutched the handle of her basket, preparing to swing it if necessary.

'Outsiders are keeping our husbands out of work,' a woman shouted in Mawde's ear.

'What hope is there for our children?' yelled another. 'We can barely feed them, let alone buy them clothes.'

The women moved in closer. Mawde's knees trembled.

'None of that is my doing,' she said. 'I tried to persuade Captain Treffry, but he refused to change his mind.'

The baker's wife grabbed Mawde's arm and yanked Mawde towards her. 'Your 'usband made promises to our men. Said the castle would bring prosperity. We thought 'e meant for all of us, not just you and 'im. You see your 'usband fixes the situation soon, or we'll make no apologies for what our 'usbands are planning.'

'Wh... what are they planning?' Mawde tried to still the trembling of her chin. 'I have no more control over my husband than I do of Captain Treffry!'

'If you care about your 'usband or us, you'd better think of something.'

'Break it up!'

Mawde almost cried with relief at the sound of Julian's voice.

'Away with you! Now! Your troubles aren't of Mistress Sherman's making, and she has tried to help.' Julian barged his way through the crowd of women, his walking stick clacking on the sun-baked street. 'Go!'

The women muttered amongst themselves as they ambled away.

Mawde pressed a hand to her chest and let out a long breath. 'Thank you, Julian.'

'They're an intimidating bunch of women,' Julian said, leaning on his stick.

'They are.' Mawde gave Julian a sidelong glance. 'Do you recall that Whitsuntide when you and your friends harassed me and my cousin Tamsin?'

Julian dipped his head. 'I do, and believe me, I'm ashamed.' He looked up to meet Mawde's gaze. 'Come back to the forge with me. Despite your smile, you seem shaken.'

'I should go home.' Mawde pointed at the egg drying on her sleeve. 'This stinks.'

'Shall I walk you home?'

'A kind offer, but I'll be fine on my own.'

'Until next time, then.' Julian turned to walk away.

'Julian?'

He turned. 'Yes?'

'Is your business doing well?' Mawde felt the colour rise in her cheeks. She should have checked herself before asking such a personal question. 'It's just that since the priory closed—'

'You don't need to explain.' Julian smiled. 'My services are always in demand, and I'm supplying the ironwork needed for the new castle. And Lord knows how many cartwheels I've repaired from rims that have buckled under heavy loads. As for the villagers, they pay me in kind. I'm never short of foraged mushrooms and I'm sick of eating crabs. Mind you, if they keep plying me with ale, I'll be in danger of leaving the forge the same way as my predecessor.'

Mawde forced a smile. 'That's good.' She looked towards the small strip farms on the slopes near the Percuil River. 'There's not enough there to feed a village. It's a pity more villagers can't work for Sir Hugh. The King spared no thought for these people when he closed the priory. I wish there was something I could do.'

'Even though the women were cruel to you a few moments ago?'

'Especially because of that.'

Julian rubbed his injured shin. 'There is something I can do. I've more than enough work for one, so I'll take on an assistant, or perhaps an apprentice. That will ease the burden of at least one family.'

Mawde placed her hand on Julian's arm. 'You're a very different person to the youth I once knew.'

Julian covered her hand with his. Heat surged through Mawde's fingers.

'We can all change if we wish to, Mawde. You and I both know that.'

When Mawde arrived home, she went straight to her bedchamber and changed her sleeves for clean ones. As she finished tying them on, she heard Nicholas calling her name.

'I'm here,' Mawde called to him as she reached the bottom of the stairs.

'Come to my parlour.'

His tone conveyed a blend of frustration and annoyance. Mawde followed Nicholas with tentative steps, but as she entered the room her muscles relaxed. The coffer of debts was still in its place.

'I thought I'd share my plans with you,' Nicholas said, inviting her to sit at his desk.

'Business plans?' Mawde asked, surprised by his change of heart.

'No.' Nicholas rubbed his chin with the fingertips of his right hand. 'It won't be long before we outgrow this house, especially when we fill it with children. I've had plans drawn up for a sizeable extension.' He unfurled a large roll of parchment covered in sketches. 'If we take this wall down here,' he said, pointing to the downstairs parlour Beth had used as a bedchamber, 'we can make a larger parlour for family use during the cold months and build another small bedchamber beside it. Upstairs, you can have a large solar for entertaining ladies or indulging your pleasures when we have servants to do our bidding.'

Mawde tried to picture herself hosting ladies in a solar. It was something that came easily to women like Lady Trevanion, but not a role she had ever imagined fulfilling herself.

'Are you not pleased?' Nicholas snatched up the plans and furled the parchment. 'Is it not the type of house every wife desires?'

'Forgive me, Nicholas. I am pleased, but also a little distracted after an incident in the village.' She told Nicholas about her encounter with the women and the threats they had made.

'Pah!' said Nicholas, slapping his desk. 'I have nothing to fear. I have simply brokered deals and come to arrangements with the men. Women should not meddle in matters they do not understand.'

'Their husbands need employment, Nicholas, not ties to business deals.' Mawde recalled the wording of the bond the landlord had signed. No wonder the women were concerned if their husbands had similar debts. She softened her tone. 'May I ask the nature of the deals?'

Nicholas raised his hands in an exasperated gesture. 'I've lent money for starting businesses or making repairs to homes. If they repay me within the term agreed, the benefit is all theirs. If they don't repay within the time agreed, I will charge recompense for my inconvenience.'

'And if they can't pay?'

'They forfeit goods.'

Mawde fidgeted with the lace of her sleeve. 'What if they have no goods to forfeit?'

Nicholas shrugged. 'I will take their homes.'

'You can't! They must have somewhere to live!'

'I wouldn't evict anyone,' he said petulantly. 'It would be a simple matter of them assigning their properties or leases to me and then paying me rent.'

'But many of them lease their homes from Sir Hugh!'

Nicholas waved his hand dismissively. 'A mere paperwork issue. I'll recover any legal costs by increasing rents. Some villagers own their homes outright. They've passed through generations. For those people, the transaction will be straightforward.'

Mawde stared at Nicholas. The angle of his jaw seemed sharper; the set of his eyes looked more severe. The lines on his forehead marked a permanent frown and silver streaks peppered his hair. He was unrecognisable from the man she had fallen in love with.

'You've given loans men cannot repay without penalties or forfeits,' she said. 'Why would you do such a thing?'

Nicholas guffawed. 'God has made these villagers suffer so I'm doing what I can to help while ensuring I benefit myself. What's wrong with that? And if my actions condemn me to purgatory, well, at least it's warm in Hell.'

Mawde crossed herself. 'May God forgive your blasphemy!'

Nicholas glared at Mawde with malice in his eyes. 'We're told God's wisdom guides our actions, so He must be guiding mine.' Nicholas rose from his chair. 'God guides us to another task now. Follow me to our bedchamber.'

Mawde looked through the window. The sun was only halfway between its zenith and the horizon. 'Now?'

'Now.' Nicholas offered Mawde his hand. 'It's time God blessed us with a child.'

# CHAPTER TWENTY-FIVE

FOUR WEEKS LATER, the household had gathered for supper when a sharp cramp gripped Mawde's stomach. Until that moment, she had believed she was with child. She hunched forward, clutching her belly, and stifled a moan. Mamm stroked her forearm. Mawde closed her eyes, willing herself not to cry. She felt Nicholas's stare boring into her and looked up to meet his gaze. He raised his eyebrows. She shook her head. Nicholas thumped the table. Red wine slopped over the side of Mawde's goblet and stained the linen cloth.

Nicholas swept his plate to the floor. It landed with a loud clang and dented on one edge. His face was puce, his nostrils flaring. 'Despite my best efforts to get you with child, God still punishes us for your whoring.'

Perry gasped. Mamm coughed. Mawde tried to hold her head high and ignore the burning in her cheeks. 'I have lain only with one other man.' She crossed herself and added, 'As God is my witness, that's the truth.'

'God punishes us for something,' Nicholas hissed.

*Your sin of greed,* Mawde thought to herself. 'You knew

other women before you married me. Perhaps one of those women spoiled your seed and robbed you of fatherhood.'

Nicholas leaned across the corner of the trestle table and smacked her hard on the cheek. Mawde's eyes watered from the stinging pain. An uncomfortable silence followed. Mawde broke off a small piece of bread, but it turned to ash in her mouth. She held her napkin to her lips and discretely spat it out.

Perry broke the silence. 'I believe I can help.'

'How?'

'I have heard it said that red meat strengthens a man's seed, and also asparagus and carrots.' He looked at Mawde. 'Mistress, you might pray to St Agnes, blessed mother of the Holy Virgin and grandmother of Jesus.' He lowered his gaze before adding, 'It would also help if you both consumed dried pig's testicles sprinkled on your wine.'

'How in God's name are you qualified to give such advice?' Nicholas scuffed his chair across the flagstones and cast a shadow over the table.

Mawde shrank away from him, fearing he might strike her or Perry.

Perry appeared unperturbed. 'Forgive me, master, but I like to read. I choose texts that enable me to learn and help other people. A stonemason salvaged the infirmerer's book from the wreckage of the priory. We had talked about my interest in books, and he offered it to me as a gift. Shall I fetch it?'

'That won't be necessary,' Nicholas said.

Mawde reached out to touch the back of Nicholas's hand. 'I'm willing to try anything that might bless us with a child. Please say you will too.' She looked at Nicholas with imploring eyes, hoping a son might quell his ambitious appetite. 'Please, Nicholas. I want to bear your child and give you the heir you deserve. Shall we try Perry's recommendations?'

Nicholas withdrew his hand from hers. He looked as if he might refuse but gave a nod of assent.

Mawde gave Perry a grateful smile and finished her supper in silence.

Nicholas mellowed as summer arrived. Perry's suggestions seemed to have worked – Mawde's monthly bleed was overdue.

'Sweeting?' Nicholas was at the kitchen door. 'Can you spare a few moments to accompany me to the beach?'

Mawde watched Mamm cup her gnarled fingers around a pile of chopped onions and scooped them into a cooking pot.

'Mamm?'

Mamm nodded. 'Agnes can chop the rest for me when she comes back with the herbs.'

Mawde rinsed her hands and stepped outside to join Nicholas. They walked together in silence until they reached the beach. The sound of the waves slurping the shingle soothed Mawde's troubled soul. She had endured many nights of restless sleep, fretting about Nicholas's loans. And her nightmares were getting worse.

Three fishing boats lay at anchor. Nicholas pointed to the nearest one.

'She's a decent size,' he said. 'About twenty-five feet. Sturdy too. There's only one mast, but that's adequate for the work she does. What do you think of her?'

Mawde shielded her eyes from the sun and stared at the boat. She could make out bench seats running along the sides of the deck and a small fo'c'sle at the bow. 'It's like many of the fishing boats here. What's your interest in that one?'

'She's called *Mistress of Carrick*.' Nicholas cocked his head one way and then the other, as if sizing up a horse.

Mawde remained silent, her attention distracted by a movement in the water. 'Is that a seal?' she said, straining for another glimpse.

Nicholas spoke as if he hadn't heard her. 'If everything goes according to plan, and I have projected my income correctly, I will buy a piece of land upriver beyond the castle. Duchy land abuts my farmland and extends all the way to St Just. An acquaintance told me the King offered it to Sir Hugh but he chose to decline it. Rumour has it he's short of money.' Nicholas brushed imaginary creases from his jacket and drew himself to full height. 'I intend to ask the King to sell that land to me. I would pay Henry to farm some of it and use the rest for hunting. There's a perfect spot on the edge of a woodland overlooking the River Fal. A perfect location for a house.'

'What about your plans for the house we already have?' Mawde loved the view from her home, looking across to St Anthony's Head and to the open sea beyond. The view from the land beyond the castle faced more to the west and across a busy stretch of river.

Nicholas grasped her hands and squeezed her fingers. 'I have a vision of a grander home built with smart red brick. It will have fireplaces in every room and bedchambers for guests.' His eyes sparkled. 'We'll have a grand hall fit to entertain the King, and a separate building with a kitchen, buttery, servants' quarters and whatever else you think we need. We'll enjoy a life as decadent as any lord and lady.' Nicholas pulled her towards him and kissed her on the lips. 'We'll fill the house with children too and be the envy of the county.'

'The envy of the county?' Mawde struggled to swallow. 'A house of such grandeur will need a fortune to build it, and a substantial income to pay servants.'

Nicholas was undeterred. 'I've thought it through, Mawde. The castle build is going well. I'm hounding the workmen to quicken their pace so they finish ahead of schedule. That will save money from the King's purse and should earn a handsome reward for me. Then I'll persuade the King to sell his fields and woodland.'

Mawde recalled hungry childhood days when she and Julian had trapped rabbits in that woodland. Poaching. Another sin added to her tariff.

'My mother was of noble status,' Nicholas added, 'so I know he'll think me worthy.'

'Does the King know your mother married a black-smith? He might not think too well of that.'

Nicholas's face contorted. 'I don't see why not. The King is known for his romantic gestures. He'd understand why a woman would marry for love.' Nicholas closed his eyes and tilted his face towards the sun. 'I can see it now. You and me standing in our rose garden watching ships sail the Carrick Roads.' He opened his eyes and smiled at Mawde. 'You will be my Mistress of Carrick. That's why I had to have the boat.'

'You bought the boat?'

'Well, not bought exactly. I took it in lieu of a debt.'

'You did what?' Mawde sat on the shingle as the beach seemed to spin around her.

Nicholas knelt in front of her. 'Don't fret, sweeting, I gave the fellow two pounds to soften the pain of losing the boat and said he can fish for me.' Nicholas grinned. 'I even told him if he earns enough money, he can buy back the boat.'

Mawde stared at the *Mistress of Carrick*. She was in

excellent condition. 'That two pounds you gave the fellow, did you add it to his debt?'

Nicholas rolled his eyes and said nothing.

'Can a fisherman earn enough money to repay you and buy back his boat?'

Nicholas scooped a handful of shingle and separated out a few small shells. 'I doubt it. But if he works hard and catches enough fish, he'll earn enough to feed his family and put some money aside.' He brushed the shells from his hand. 'The boat won't generate a large income for me, and it will take time to recover the debt, but I have other men interested in similar agreements. In the long term, it should be lucrative.'

Mawde's thoughts drifted to the sealed bonds in Nicholas's coffer. 'How many villagers are in your debt?'

'Last time I counted, at least a score.'

Mawde pressed her fist to her lips. *A score!* She might have saved the landlord, but she could not save them all. She clambered to her feet. 'How could you!'

Nicholas shrugged and stared up at her. 'They're all short of money, Mawde. Should I let them starve instead?'

Mawde slowly shook her head and turned to walk away from him. By the time she reached home, she was certain Nicholas was continuing the King's work and ruining her village.

# CHAPTER TWENTY-SIX

THE KITCHEN GREW UNBEARABLY hot with the arrival of June. The courtyard air tasted of dust. The chickens were lethargic and sullen. A sweaty messenger arrived at the door and passed a letter to Mawde. Mawde gave the young man a farthing for his trouble and took the letter to Nicholas in his parlour.

Nicholas broke the letter's seal and quickly read the contents. He turned to Mawde grim-faced. 'It's from one of my contacts in London. Cromwell is dead.'

Mawde felt as if her breath had been knocked out of her. 'Does he say how?'

'Executed.'

'Why?'

'For failing to find the King a suitable queen.'

'But he did!' Mawde thought back to Queen Anne's arrest, an event that regularly haunted her thoughts. The crowded riverbank, the royal barge, the dignity shown by the terrified woman while the oarsmen rowed her towards the Tower. Cromwell had been the architect of Queen Anne's downfall, but Mawde had fuelled him with her lies.

She gathered herself together and held her head high. 'Cromwell made it possible for the King to marry his beloved Queen Jane.'

'True, but then gave him Anne of Cleves.' Nicholas placed the letter on the kitchen table and smoothed out the creases. 'It says here that Cromwell was also guilty of other things: corruption, protecting heretics, and plotting to take the King's daughter, Princess Mary, as his wife.'

'He would never have done such things!'

Nicholas snorted. 'And you would know.'

Mawde lowered her head and stared at her lap. Cromwell had given her a role in a royal kitchen. If not for him, she would never have had the privilege of making confections for the King. If not for Cromwell, she would have given up on her dream of returning to Roseland. Guilt wrapped itself around her and made her heart ache. She had lain with Cromwell and whispered scandalous gossip for money. Had her foolish behaviour contributed to his fate?

Nicholas refolded the letter and tucked it inside his jerkin. 'I must get back to the building site. I'm in the middle of appraising the workmen and finding more ways to improve their efficiency.'

Mawde waited for the door to close behind him before dropping to her knees to pray. She asked for forgiveness for every wrong she had committed and for Nicholas's sin of greed. After saying 'Amen', she started to weep and clasped her hands to her belly. Despite remedies, remorse and praying several times a day, Mawde was bleeding again.

Mawde left the windows and drapes open when she went to bed that night to cool the stifling air. Nicholas arrived home long after dark and staggered into the room.

'Sorry to wake you,' he slurred, flopping onto the mattress and rolling towards Mawde.

His breath was heavy with the smell of wine and his skin stank of sweat. Mawde tensed as he grappled with her night chemise and started pulling it up. She held her breath, summoning the courage to tell him her courses had arrived, but Nicholas suddenly released his grip and rolled onto his back.

'You and blasted Cromwell,' he said. 'How am I supposed to rise for you when I can't stop thinking about you rutting with that man?'

Mawde stared at the ceiling and shed a few tears of regret. Hours passed before she drifted off to sleep, but the cockerel's crow came early and woke her long before dawn.

Nicholas stirred beside her. 'Damn me, that's the third morning in a row. I'll ring its scrawny neck if it does it for a fourth.'

'It's too warm to sleep, anyway.' Mawde pushed the thin coverlet away and fanned herself with her hand.

Nicholas turned onto his side. 'Something's troubling you.'

Mawde closed her eyes for a few seconds. 'I'm afraid I'm not with child.' The revelation hung between them like a thundercloud. 'And I fear for the people of the village. The streams are running dry again and crops are already wilting.'

Nicholas harrumphed. 'You should think about your own future before worrying about everyone else's.'

'What do you mean?' Mawde tried to suppress her rising sense of panic.

The creeping dull light of dawn slipped through a

chink in the curtains and cast a grey light on Nicholas's furrowed brow. 'Henry came to see me yesterday afternoon. Our wheat's turning brittle in the fields and won't yield much of a harvest. We still have to feed the castle workforce so it will be a tough winter for everyone, and that includes us.'

'What about the men who owe you money? If the prices of bread and ale rise, they won't be able to repay you.'

Nicholas's lips twitched. 'If that should be the case, I'll own their homes by spring. A poor harvest might be just what we need.'

Mawde felt as if the wind had been kicked out of her. 'Dear God, how can you say such a thing?'

Nicholas turned his mean eyes towards her. 'It's not for us to question God's decision to allow crops to spoil. He has His reasons for letting men, women and children starve, but, by His grace, I'm able to come to their aid. My loans help them in a crisis and benefit us in the longer term. It's up to us to take every opportunity to balance our misfortunes.'

'Cromwell did that,' Mawde said. 'It didn't end well for him.'

Nicholas jabbed her shoulder. 'You should reflect on your own greed before casting judgement on others.'

Mawde looked him in the eyes. 'I do. I reflect on my mistakes during every waking hour. Every poor decision I made haunts me in my dreams. But I was blessed the day you found me and gave me a home of my own. I believe we should share our good fortune with our neighbours who are struggling to buy food and clothes.'

'We do,' Nicholas said pointedly. 'Every day you send Perry to the village with a basketful of leftovers. Did you think I wouldn't notice how you cook too much for every meal? It's my money paying for the food you like to give away. And who pays for the monk you took in?'

Mawde lowered her voice. 'He's not a monk.'

'Not anymore.'

*Because you took that from him.* 'Perry earns his keep by working in the garden and tending St Anthony's fire.'

Nicholas curled his lip as if finding the mention of Perry distasteful. 'Enough whining! We all live with at least one regret.'

'And I suppose I'm yours,' Mawde said, challenging him to agree.

Nicholas gave an exasperated sigh. 'Don't be ridiculous.'

Mawde sat up in the bed and massaged her temples to ease a building headache. She might not be Nicholas's regret, but he was fast becoming one of hers.

# CHAPTER TWENTY-SEVEN

Heavy showers soaked the ground and Mawde's garden recovered. She spent the summer stocking her larder until the shelves buckled under the weight of jams, pickles and salted meats.

One dreary afternoon in September, Nicholas received an urgent summons to Fowey. He arrived home two days later, his expression as dark as the rain clouds rolling across the sky. Mawde took his damp riding cloak and spread it across the settle in front of the fire to dry. The unpleasant aroma of wet wool leached into the air. Nicholas settled on his favourite cushioned chair and clamped his fingers around the armrests. He tipped his head back and closed his eyes and let out an exasperated sigh.

'You must be hungry,' Mawde said. 'Shall I bring you a plate of pork and bread? I have a sweet apple and gooseberry jam that tastes wonderful with the meat.'

Nicholas snapped his head up and gave Mawde a hostile glare. 'I have no appetite and I wish to be left alone.'

A chill of apprehension rippled through Mawde's skin.

Nicholas pressed his fingers to his forehead. For a fleeting moment, Mawde thought she saw a flicker of vulnerability, but whatever weakness Nicholas might have displayed, he soon replaced it with hostility. 'Treffry has set me aside.' Nicholas glared at the flames dancing and leaping in the grate. 'Whoreson!'

The room seemed to sway. Mawde sat down on the other chair. 'Why would he do that?'

A vein twitched in Nicholas's temple. 'The limpet blamed the King! Said the King complained the build is taking too long. It's a stone fort, for Christ's sake, not a farmyard wall!'

Mawde recoiled and crossed herself. She glanced around the hall to check no one else was within earshot.

The colour had drained from Nicholas's cheeks. His hands and lips were shaking. 'An army of builders might raise the walls faster, but not a handful of Treffry's men!'

*You should have used the local men.* Mawde kept the thought to herself.

Spittle bubbled at the corners of Nicholas's mouth. He leaned forward and grasped the chair's armrests so tightly Mawde feared his knuckle bones would break through his skin. 'Treffry wined and dined me. He praised my work in front of other guests. He said that, thanks to me, his men were working faster than they'd ever done before.' Nicholas pounded one of the armrests with his fist. 'He even said I've done so well that the build is under budget. We celebrated that very fact with three bottles of Gascon wine. I retired to bed believing all was well, but he as good as stabbed me this morning. We hadn't been celebrating my hard work but my success at saving Treffry's money!'

Mawde frowned. 'I don't understand. It's the King's castle.'

A log shifted in the fire. The wood crackled and sent up a fountain of sparks.

'Aye, it is, but King Henry told Treffry to oversee the build himself. Apparently, he was apoplectic when he discovered Treffry deputised that role to me and had added my wage to his bill. The King has trust issues, as we well know, and has commanded Treffry to take up residence on the build site until the whole thing is complete. He also insisted Treffry finish the build at his own expense.' The anger in Nicholas withered. He sighed and leaned back in the chair. 'I don't know who to be mad at most, the King or Treffry. I know Treffry has no choice but to abide by the King's rules, but he had no need to fire me.'

Mawde sympathised with Nicholas's plight, but a small part of her rejoiced in the fact that he was sharing the fate of many villagers.

A prolonged silence fell between them. Mawde dared to break it. 'Will we be short of money?'

'I don't think so. It's a setback, but Treffry settled my accrued earnings in full, so we've no immediate need to worry.' He met Mawde's gaze. 'Our harvest was good this year and I'll soon have income from other sources. By early spring, it will be time to start recovering debts. I'll do well from those who can't pay in full by the deadlines we agreed.'

'Please don't!' Mawde's voice cracked.

Nicholas bristled. 'I can and I will. Every man who borrowed from me understood the terms of their bond and signed his initials or made a mark with his thumb without coercion from me.'

'Where will they go if you take their homes?'

'I've no intention of making anyone homeless. Like I said before, I'll rent the houses back to them. I'll pay up to a sovereign for each house and any fees due to Sir Hugh. It won't take long to get my money back and start turning a tidy profit.' He smirked at Mawde. 'It looks like your wish will come true. Treffry's under pressure to get the building finished so he will have to employ some locals. When the job's finished, Treffry can scuttle back to Fowey and leave us all in peace.' Nicholas shifted his gaze back to the fire. 'I'm not able to build a new house and buy land from the Duchy, but when I have more money coming in, I'll add extra rooms to this house. The castle will need staff when, at last, it is complete, and they can pay to lodge with us.'

'Surely they will live within the castle walls?' Mawde feared that greed was getting the better of Nicholas and clouding his judgement. His money would soon run out if he started building and buying every house.

Nicholas's smile faded. 'You're right. They will.' He pushed himself up from the chair and paced back and forth, tapping his forehead and mumbling under his breath. He stopped in front of Mawde. 'King Henry enjoys a royal progress, and he's been here before. He'll want to visit again and review Treffry's work.' Nicholas laughed. 'The village won't recognise itself when that happens. The King will come with a large retinue. They'll all need somewhere to stay.' He resumed pacing but with faster steps. 'I expect the King will stay with the Trevanions, but gentry might stay here with us. If we can impress the men and women who flutter around the King's inner circle, the King might give me his royal favour.' Nicholas dropped to his knees and grasped Mawde's hands. 'Imagine what that would do for us, my love.'

Mawde wanted to remove her hands, but his fingers gripped her tightly. She tried to picture a scenario where royalty and nobility and their families and servants would purchase goods made within the village: shoes from the cordwainer, homespun yarns, ale and delicious pastries.

The fishing fleet might grow again. The tavern would over-flow with revellers celebrating their good fortune. Other taverns might open too, and maybe even an inn. St Mawes would feature on every map, with bold letters marking it out as clearly as Truro and Penryn. It was a vision Mawde wanted to believe would come true under the right circum-stances. But something about Nicholas and his lust for wealth added to her fears for the village.

# CHAPTER TWENTY-EIGHT

WINTER SET IN, damp and cold, then rain gave way to freezing mists and occasional snow flurries. The local men had still not received any offers of work from Treffry. On the third Sunday in January, the mood inside the ice-cold chapel was more sombre than usual. Everyone prayed for the health of the King, who was suffering from ulcers on his legs. Mawde prayed longer than everyone else, fearing the implications for St Mawes. The lean, jovial, athletic man Mawde had glimpsed at Greenwich Palace had enjoyed a hearty appetite for entertainment, sport and sweetmeats. Chronic pain and festering sores would have rendered King Henry sedentary, stripping away his good humour and making him cantankerous instead. He would have no desire to leave a comfortable palace to visit a small Cornish village so many miles away.

Mawde stepped outside the chapel and scanned the yard for Nicholas. She saw him standing by a wall and talking to a builder. Something hard struck Mawde's back and knocked the wind out of her. She turned in time for a second missile to hit her hard on her chest. She bent double, gasping for air, and saw a large ball of ice on the ground. The ball had split open to reveal a clod of stinking dung.

Mawde straightened up and turned to see a woman stamping on a frozen puddle. She bent over and scooped up a handful of broken ice.

'Nicholas!'

Mawde's warning came too late. The ice struck the back of Nicholas's knee. He buckled and turned to face the woman but lost his footing and slipped. He landed heavily on a patch of frozen mud, striking it with his bottom and then his back. A small crowd had gathered but no one helped him up. Mawde stepped towards him, feeling unsteady on the ice. Her pattens slipped but she kept her balance and helped Nicholas to his feet.

'Swindlers, the pair of ye!' A man spat at Nicholas's face.

'Thieves, more like.' His wife glared at Mawde. 'You should never have come back to St Mawes, and certainly not with him!'

'Pigs!' another woman yelled, her identity hidden by the swelling crowd. Mawde heard the rector beg them to disperse, but his pleas were swallowed by a barrage of insults.

People laughed and jeered as Mawde and Nicholas left the chapel grounds. Mamm, Agnes and Perry followed a few paces behind.

'That's right,' a man shouted. 'Use the innocent members of your family to shield you! You're cowards as well as thieves!'

Nicholas quickened his stride. 'I find their disrespect offensive after all I've done for this village.'

Mawde struggled to keep pace with him and kept slipping on patches of ice. 'They fear for their futures,

Nicholas.' She reached for his arm, hoping it would help steady her as well as slow his pace. 'They fear losing everything they own, so it's understandable they blame you.'

'They knew well enough what they were getting into when they came to borrow my money.' Nicholas released her hand from his arm. 'I should call in every one of their debts now – and sue the swines for slander.'

*It's not slander when they speak the truth,* Mawde thought. 'Can you do that? Call the debts in early?'

Nicholas glared at her. 'I can do whatever I like.'

When they reached home, Nicholas made straight for his parlour and slammed the door behind him. Mawde went up to their bedchamber to change into clean, comfortable clothes. She pulled on her favourite coif, wondering how to sweeten Nicholas's mood. To call in debts would be disastrous and would add fuel to the volatile mood in the village.

Later that morning, Mawde knocked on Nicholas's door and opened it without waiting for an answer. 'You did not break your fast after chapel, so I baked your favourite biscuits.'

The biscuits had not yet cooled, and they released a rich honey fragrance that made Mawde's mouth water. She hoped it was doing the same for Nicholas. She held the platter out towards him and he selected the largest biscuit. He took a bite and closed his eyes, munching and sighing with pleasure.

'Nicholas, please don't call the debts in early,' Mawde said as he took another bite. 'We need to get the villagers on our side, not upset them further.'

Nicholas chewed and swallowed. 'I will not tolerate their insults,' he said, brushing crumbs from his doublet. 'And anyway, we need the money. I'll start with Goodman

Wylde tomorrow, seeing as his wife was the instigator behind this morning's outburst.'

'Sweeting, they're desperate people who can't bear to see their children hungry or dressed in ragged clothes. There must be another way you can help them.'

'Like what?'

'I don't know. Goodman Wylde was a carpenter at the priory. Can you help him set up his own business? My father used to make children's toys, cups, trenchers and bowls when his carpentry work ran dry. Goodman Wylde could do the same if he had his own tools.'

Nicholas sneered. 'You don't know what you're talking about. That's investing, not lending, and there'd be no guarantee of getting my money back. Who in this village can afford to buy toys?'

Mawde moved across the room and rested her hand on one of Nicholas's locked chests. 'Might there be something in here that might help turn everyone's fortunes around?'

Nicholas's Adam's apple bobbed in his throat. 'That chest holds nothing but old business papers and a few worthless trinkets.'

Mawde suspected otherwise. 'What about the *Mistress of Carrick*? You could employ another fisherman or two so they can catch larger hauls of fish.'

'Don't be ridiculous. An extra fisherman won't make the boat any larger. It's already doing its best.'

Mawde was persistent. 'St Anthony's fire! You could increase the fee for keeping it alight.'

Nicholas's taut face muscles relaxed. 'That's a useful suggestion. We earn a paltry fee, but I can't increase it without the King's consent. There is one way to increase my share of it. Perry can go on alternate nights instead of one in every three.'

Mawde buried her face in her hands and chastised

herself for the suggestion. 'Perry already does too much. You cannot have him out there so often and expect him to continue working here. And he helps on the farm most days. The poor man will collapse.'

Nicholas stood and grasped Mawde by her shoulders.

'You're hurting me!' she said, trying to prise off his fingers.

'Hold your tongue, Mawde, or I *will* put you in a scold's bridal and parade you through the village.' He pushed her hard as he released her and she fell backwards against one of the wooden chests.

A sharp pain shot through Mawde's lower back. 'Forgive me, husband. I spoke out of turn.'

'I've told you before to leave business matters to me. Do not mention them again.' Nicholas helped her stand. He softened the tone of his voice. 'Those delicious biscuits have done little to satisfy my hunger. I'd like an early dinner.'

Nicholas spent the afternoon at the butts for Sunday archery practice. Night had fallen by the time he arrived home. He dropped a bulging leather purse onto the table and stared at it, shaking his head.

'I cannot fathom how he did it, but the carpenter settled early.'

'In full?'

'In full.'

Mawde's heart fluttered. The fact the carpenter had settled early meant he owed no interest. 'You must be relieved to have recovered such a large purse of money,' Mawde said.

Nicholas kept his gaze fixed on the purse. 'The loan

served no benefit to me. I might as well have not bothered.' He looked at Mawde. 'How did he do it? When I saw him at the butts, I threatened to call in his debt because of what happened this morning. He fell to his knees and begged me not to but approached me this evening with that purse. He has no regular work to generate such a sum, and the villagers pay him in kind. Wilting carrots and dried apples did not fill that bag with coins. So where did he get the money?'

Mawde left Nicholas to his musings and lost herself in her own thoughts while kneading dough for the next day's bread. His greed had earned them disrespect and hatred throughout the village. She pummelled the dough as an uncomfortable truth settled in her mind. She had fallen out of love with Nicholas. Mawde perched on a stool and wiped flour from her cheeks. While her husband had tried to ruin a poor community, she had failed to rescue it with charity and kindness. She needed to find something that would help in the longer term, rather than the temporary easing of hunger. It would have to be something that righted Nicholas's wrongs and ended her guilt-fuelled nightmares.

# CHAPTER TWENTY-NINE

MAWDE LINGERED near the entrance to the forge, the heat of the interior a welcome respite from the blustering wind outside. 'Do you have spit racks?' she said, attracting the attention of an unfamiliar young man.

The man lowered his tools and walked towards her. 'A couple, but they're heavy.' He tilted his head to look past her. 'Did you come by horse and cart?'

Mawde shook her head. 'I didn't think.'

'Not to worry. I'll deliver the racks this afternoon if you tell me where you live.'

'No need. I'll send a boy with a handcart.'

Mawde spun round towards the source of the voice. When she saw Julian's face her heartbeat was as fast as a bird's. His eyes seemed to sparkle with joy at seeing her, and she felt a comforting rush of warmth.

Julian's stick clacked across the compacted earth floor of the forge. He lifted a sack with his free hand and held it out to the young man. 'Take these locks and bolts to the manor. Tell Sir Hugh's steward I'll be along later to fit them.'

'Can't you take them when you go to fit them?'

'Not if I'm carrying a bag of tools in one hand and my stick in the other.'

The young man begrudgingly agreed and left with the bag.

'An apprentice?' Mawde asked, watching the young man stroll along the street.

'Journeyman,' Julian replied, 'but I've no intention of keeping him. He has an attitude I cannot take to.'

Mawde smiled. 'You had one of those yourself, if I recall.'

Julian looked away. 'Yes, I suppose I did.' He gestured for her to sit on a stool. 'Tell me, what brings you here? I doubt it was for spit racks seeing as you walked here.'

'You're right. I don't need spit racks.' Mawde looked around the forge. Tools sat neatly arranged on shelves or hanging from a line of hooks. It reminded her of her father's tidy workshop. 'I intended to take the boat to Penryn, but somehow I ended up here.' Mawde lowered her gaze to the earthen floor, where dropped tools had left small divots. She felt the colour rise in her cheeks.

Julian dragged another stool next to hers. He took a moment to settle himself and then reached for her hand. 'We go back a long way, Mawde. I cannot undo the suffering I caused but I can be a friend to you now.'

Julian released her hand. Mawde stared at her palm. The skin was still warm from where he had touched it.

'Mawde, you saved my leg, and possibly my life. That puts me in your debt. You have an aura of sadness about you, and I would like to help.'

Mawde looked towards the open door in time to see a woman walk past dragging a protesting little boy behind her. Her cloak looked too thin to protect her from the wind. 'The village wasn't affluent when I left, but it wasn't as poor as this. I feel for the families struggling to get by and keep a roof over their heads.'

Julian made a murmur of understanding. 'Don't feel guilty, Mawde. You have lived their life. And I've seen how generous you are with alms.'

'But it's not enough, Julian. The harvest was reasonable last year, but that isn't always so. Too often, the villagers' strip farms fail, and the animals lack flesh on their bones. I wish there was something I could do.'

'Trust in the Lord, Mawde. He will show you what to do.'

'He hasn't yet.'

'He will. And while you wait, if you need a friend, I'll always be here for you.'

'Master Viker?' A father and son entered the forge carrying a buckled wheel between them.

Julian grasped his stick and pushed himself up from his stool.

'Can you do something about this?' the father asked.

Julian limped towards them and made a quick appraisal. 'I can improve it, but it won't be perfect.'

Mawde raised her eyebrows. To her, the wheel looked beyond saving and yet Julian was willing to try.

The man ran his hand over the buckled rim. 'I'll appreciate anything you can do to keep it turning. Can't afford a new one.'

'Of course.' Julian used his stick to point to the cart outside. 'What about that? Is it badly damaged too? I've spare wood in my storeroom if it's of any help to you.'

'Aye, that would be grand,' the man replied. He doffed his hat to Mawde and smiled. 'Begging your pardon, mistress. I didn't see you there.'

'No apology necessary.' Mawde rose from her stool and

tried to keep her composure. 'It's time I left Master Viker to his work now that he knows what I need.'

Mawde smiled at Julian as she left the forge and bid the man and his son a good day. 'Spit racks!' she said, hurrying towards home, bubbling with joy for the first time in several months.

# CHAPTER THIRTY

For the rest of the winter, Mawde avoided forays into the village except for Sunday services at the chapel. She could not bear the scowls of the men and women, nor the way they muttered behind their hands. She felt like an outcast in her own village, and all because she had married an arrogant, greedy man. Mawde was also avoiding Julian. Her initial happiness after her visit to the forge had been displaced by shame. She had no business spending time alone with the blacksmith while she was a married woman.

Easter arrived in a blaze of sunshine. Bright yellow daffodils coloured the hedgerows, interspersed with delicate primroses. Mawde had hoped the villagers would drop their hostility in the spirit of Lenten confession, but when she and Nicholas filed out of the church at St Just, people turned their backs towards them.

Nicholas clenched his jaw muscles and tension creased his brow. 'I'll see you at home,' he said before walking away with fast strides and leaving Mawde staring after him.

Mamm hooked her arm through Mawde's. 'Come, my dear, ignore them all. They'll come to their senses soon.'

Mawde wished she could believe her. 'If only they knew how I've tried to persuade Nicholas against giving loans.'

'I know. Be patient, my dear. They'll realise in good time.' Mamm squeezed Mawde's arm. 'Look over there, by the church porch. The miller's son has sought Agnes's company again. He talks to her after every service. I believe he might be fond of her.'

Mawde smiled. 'Don't mention it to Nicholas or he'll have them married by the end of the day. I'd hate for Agnes to rush into something she'd later come to regret.'

Mamm gave a sympathetic sigh. 'Oh, my darling, have faith. Happiness will find you in the end.'

'Mistress Wyn. Mistress Sherman.' Julian doffed his hat and gave a little bow. 'I see Master Sherman has already departed. Perhaps I may escort you on the walk back to St Mawes?'

'Julian, that's kind of you,' Mamm said, slipping her arm from Mawde's. 'But Agnes and I are going to break our fast at my nephew's farm.'

'Mamm?' Mawde looked at her mother with enquiring eyes. 'We have food prepared at home.'

'Nicholas and Perry will be there to eat it, and I'm sure Julian would be glad to join the three of you.'

Mawde looked at Julian, willing him to accept. She found his company uplifting and they would have Perry as a chaperone.

Julian held Mawde's gaze. 'I regret I cannot accept your kind offer. Perhaps another time?'

Mawde was first to look away. 'Of course,' she said, disappointed.

'But I'd like to walk back to the village with you, if you can tolerate my slower pace.'

'That's settled then,' Mamm said, smiling at Julian. To

Mawde she added, 'My dear, I'll be home by mid-afternoon.'

Mawde, Perry and Julian set off on the long walk back to St Mawes. They followed a well-worn coastal path skirting the edge of Duchy woodland and then Nicholas's farmland. Perry strode on ahead, claiming he was weary after a long night tending St Anthony's fire and his body craved a nap.

'They'll not forgive you for fraternising with the moneylender's wife,' Mawde said to Julian, as scowls accompanied loud whispers from a trio of women who passed them. 'They'll turn their backs on you too if they think you're a friend to my family.'

'I don't fear gossips,' Julian said. 'I'm the only black-smith for several miles around. They need to nurture my goodwill. Few other blacksmiths would make pots and pans in return for a jug or two of ale or the promise of a shoulder of lamb.'

One woman glanced back towards Mawde and said something to make her friends laugh. Mawde's eyes mist-ed. 'I was so eager to return to St Mawes,' she said, recalling the intensity of her yearning. 'But it no longer feels like home. I might as well be a stranger here. The women stop their children accepting coins or biscuits from me for fear my husband will find out and demand recompense.' Mawde looked at Julian. 'Sometimes I wonder if I would be living a happier life if I had not returned.'

'Don't say that! I'm grateful for your presence here. If I could persuade those gossips to treat you kindly, I swear to you, I would.'

Julian's uneven gait made soft thuds on the earthen track. His shoe scuffed a small pile of stones, and he almost lost his footing.

'Where's your stick?' Mawde asked, grasping his arm to stop him from stumbling and releasing it just as quickly.

Julian smiled. 'I make do without it as often as I can. The scarring is unsightly, but my muscle strength has improved.'

He moved closer to her, and his arm brushed against her sleeve. Mawde kept her face angled away so he would not see her smile. 'Does your leg give you much pain?' she asked.

'Not like it used to.'

They continued the walk in a companionable silence. Soft clouds dotted the sky and butterflies danced over hawthorn flowers. Sweet-smelling gorse sweetened the air and hummed with hidden insects.

As Mawde's house came into view, she broke the silence. 'Julian, did you mean it when you said you would help me?'

'I did.'

Mawde swallowed. 'Will you call a public meeting? I've thought of something that might help sway opinions about me.' She felt Julian's gaze shift towards her and gave him a shy smile. 'I cannot bear the hostility any longer. There's something I must do.'

Julian returned her smile. 'I have a large barn behind the forge. Shall we hold the gathering there?'

'That sounds perfect.'

'When would you like this meeting to take place?'

Mawde thought for a moment. 'Today,' she said. 'After archery practice.'

Julian raised his eyebrows. 'So soon?'

'Yes,' Mawde said, looking into his eyes. 'I don't want to lose my nerve.'

# CHAPTER THIRTY-ONE

THE BARN WAS SMALLER than Mawde had expected, and it reeked of damp and neglect. The furthest wall showed signs of rot and looked as if it might collapse if someone pushed against it. Mawde stood in a corner and stared at a stage built from empty crates. Her hands shook as she imagined herself standing on it, speaking to a crowd. She grasped the sides of her skirt and tried to steady her nerves.

'Let's go home,' Mawde blurted to Mamm as she went to leave the barn.

Julian met her by the door. 'Where are you going in such a hurry?'

'There's little point in staying.' Mawde gestured to the almost empty barn. 'Archery practice finished ages ago. No one wants to hear what I have to say.'

'You're wrong,' he said, raising his fingers to his lips. 'Listen.'

Mawde sighed and closed her eyes. She heard distant voices approaching. She opened her eyes to see Beth and

Cousin Henry enter the barn and another man and woman close behind them. Others followed. Soon, the barn was full.

A woman nudged her husband and pointed at Mawde. 'What's she doing here?' she said, loud enough for everyone to hear her. 'I thought this meeting was for village folk.'

Mawde shrank towards the side of the barn. She heard more insults muttered about her and realised that they did not know it was she who had called the meeting. The barn smelled of stale breath and sweat. Mawde's lips tingled and her skin prickled as panic welled inside her.

'Your attention please!' Julian's voice cut through the chatter and everyone fell silent. 'Thank you for attending this meeting.' He extended his arm towards Mawde. 'Mistress Sherman has something to say.'

'Mistress Sherman!' the baker's wife shouted. 'I wouldn't 'ave bothered coming if I'd known this was 'er doing!'

More objections passed through the crowd. Several people turned away and surged towards the door.

'Stop!' boomed Cousin Henry. Mawde turned towards the sound of his voice. He had closed the barn door and blocked it with his muscular frame. 'Show a little courtesy and hear what she has to say.' He nodded at Mawde, encouraging her to join Julian on the stage.

'This should be interesting,' the cordwainer said, his tone laden with sarcasm.

People sniggered, some jeered. Conversations collided across the barn. Mawde took tentative steps towards Julian.

'Thank you all for coming.' Her words disappeared into the hubbub of agitated protests. She took a deep breath, then tried to project her voice. 'May I have your attention, please?'

Most people still ignored her.

'Stupid wench!' yelled a woman from the back of the barn.

Mawde's cheeks flamed. 'I can't do this,' she said, turning to leave the stage. Julian grasped her hand to stop her.

'Quiet!' he bellowed. 'You're here now, so listen to what Mistress Sherman has to say.'

'Why should we?' screeched the baker's wife. Others echoed her words.

'If you listen, you'll find out.' Julian released Mawde's hand and stepped away from her.

The noise died down and all eyes turned towards Mawde. 'Thank you all for coming.' Her voice wavered, and she found it hard to breathe. 'I ask only for a few minutes of your time.'

'That's all you'll get, too,' said one of the men nearest her. 'I've an appointment at the tavern and me beer's getting warm.' The quip received a hearty round of applause.

'That's enough!' Julian shouted, restoring order to the crowd. 'Listen to Mistress Sherman's words. I believe you will be glad of them.' Julian turned to Mawde and lowered his voice to a whisper. 'Don't think of them as men and women. Imagine you're talking to your chickens.'

Mawde's legs shook beneath her skirts. She picked out the baker's wife and imagined her covered in feathers. The image made her want to smile, and her trembling eased a little.

'I know how hard it can be to put food on the table. Winters here are always tough – I remember them well from my childhood. Like you, I scavenged the beach or trapped an occasional rabbit. I know how much hunger hurts and I wouldn't wish it on any of you.' Murmurs of assent boosted Mawde's confidence. 'The priory closing was a devastating blow. That put many of you out of work, and we lost our hospital and support for the poor.'

'Tell us something we don't know,' a scrawny young man commented. His eyes looked sunken and dark. His clothes were tatty and faded.

Mawde pressed on. 'It's difficult to envisage a day when life will get easier. But I believe it will. This village is unrecognisable from the days of my childhood when the market used to fill the street and bring visitors from miles around. Fishermen landed their catches here and merchant ships anchored in the bay. These things happen at Penryn now, instead of here. All we have left are a few basic trades with no one able to pay for them. It's time to take matters into our own hands and restore the village to what it once was.'

Someone shouted, 'I think she's right.' Mawde sensed a shift in the atmosphere as more people agreed.

The cordwainer elbowed his way towards her and stood with his hands on his hips. 'It's all very well saying we should restore the village, but how do you propose we do that?'

*Think of them as chickens.* Mawde scanned the crowd. 'Where are the fishermen among you? Please, raise your hands.'

No one responded. 'There must be at least one fisherman here,' she said, with a hint of desperation in her voice. She found the man who skippered the *Mistress of Carrick* and challenged him with her eyes. At first, he avoided her gaze, but his wife elbowed him hard in the side.

'Give her a chance,' she hissed, making him raise his hand. Another hand went up nearby, and then another two.

Mawde took a steadying breath. 'I understand why you offload your hauls at Penryn. That's where you make your money. Too many people here cannot afford to buy your fish. I therefore ask you to put aside two or three fish from every haul to give to the families who struggle the most.'

Her suggestion was met with expressions of disbelief. Mawde looked at the skipper of the *Mistress of Carrick*. 'Please?' she mouthed. He was still in debt to Nicholas for the use of the boat. Mawde hoped that would persuade him to take her side and then other fishermen might follow. He held her gaze, shaking his head. Bile rose into Mawde's throat. *Chickens.* 'Well?'

The fisherman shrugged. 'Two or three fish. Aye, I can do that.'

Smiling, Mawde sought the other skippers.

One of them raised a hand. 'Every single fish I catch has a price upon its fins. My boat is small and so is my catch. I can't give anything away.'

'I'm in a similar situation,' said another fisherman. 'To give a fish away for nothing is as good as taking food from the mouths of my children. I'm sorry, Mistress Sherman, but I can't do as you ask.'

Rumblings of discontent rippled through the barn.

'Quiet!' Julian bellowed. 'Mistress Sherman hasn't finished.'

'You cannot afford to give fish away for nothing,' Mawde said, adopting a more assertive tone. 'But would you accept payment in kind?'

'Like what?'

'I propose trading favours.' Mawde intertwined her fingers to try and quell her trembling. 'It's a common occurrence in other villages and towns and it used to happen here. I say the time has come to trade this way again, not only exchanging goods but working for each other too. We should keep a ledger of items given or services provided, and tick them off and note the date as soon as they're repaid. That way, the system is fair, whether the trades are paid for in coin or in kind.'

The skipper of the *Mistress of Carrick* approached the dais. 'What type of favour would repay me for fish?'

Mawde was quick to think of an answer. 'I often see you on the beach mending your nets. That takes valuable time you might want to spend at sea. Your repayment could be to have help with those repairs, leaving you more time to fish.'

'Aye, 'tis true enough. More time at sea means more money. We could also do with some work on our house.' He looked at his wife and then at Mawde. 'I'm willing to give it a try.'

'Thank you!' Mawde smiled. 'I believe there will come a time when circumstances change. Perhaps one day you'll own a boat again and work on it with your son.'

A look of understanding passed between them. 'Aye, Mistress Sherman, perhaps I will.' He turned to face others in the crowd. 'I will do as she suggests. Who else will do the same?'

'Wait!' The cordwainer shouted. 'If we're not careful, the favours we trade will convert into bonds of debt. Who will maintain this ledger you speak of, ensuring that isn't the case?' He gave Mawde a challenging stare. 'It should be someone we all trust.'

Mawde hesitated. She had planned to keep the ledger herself.

Julian joined Mawde on the stage. 'If no one has any objections, I will maintain the ledger.'

Mawde raised her eyebrows.

He responded with a smile.

A slow clap came from the back of the room. Mawde's stomach flipped. It was Nicholas. He was swaying from side to side like a man who had indulged in too much wine.

'I commend the blacksmith for indulging my wife's daft notions.' He hiccoughed. 'But *I* will not accept favours in return for advice or help.' He waved his arm like a drowning man grasping for a rope. 'My wife has wasted enough of your time. Join me at the alehouse and I'll buy you all a drink.'

Nicholas staggered out of the barn. Mawde expected an exodus of villagers, but no one moved to follow him.

Julian touched Mawde's arm. 'Keep heart,' he murmured. 'They're warming to you.' He raised his voice. 'I will take part in the scheme. I'll welcome repairs to my clothes or offers to launder my linens in return for small pieces of ironwork such as horseshoes, nails or hinges.'

The cordwainer raised his hand. 'I'll make new soles for a carpenter's shoes in return for a sign for my business.'

Henry raised his hand. 'I'll give the blacksmith butter and cheese in return for new shearing scissors.'

Other offers passed back and forth. Mawde shook her head with wonder.

A woman who had been a washerwoman at the priory entreated Mawde with desperate eyes. 'My child gets pains in his gut. Will you take needlework services for a tincture?'

'I will, and I'll also give you honey.'

The woman beamed at Mawde's reply. She turned to her neighbour and suggested sharing food and cooking meals together.

'Look at them.' Julian said. His hand brushed against Mawde's arm and made her heartbeat quicken. 'They're all eager to help each other now, and that's because of you.'

Tears of joy spilled onto Mawde's cheeks. She moved closer to Julian and reached for his hand. 'It's thanks to you too, Julian.' She gave him a warm smile. 'You gave me the courage.'

# CHAPTER THIRTY-TWO

AFTER THE SUCCESS of the village meeting, Mawde slept better than she had in years. She still woke once or twice a night, but her nightmares were abating. Women no longer talked behind their hands when they saw Mawde in the village, and children ran up to her with smiles on their faces, eager to devour her biscuits. Their clothes were still ragged but sported neat patches instead of holes and rips. They also had more flesh on their bones despite enduring another dry summer and the rising cost of wheat.

Mawde stood by the sea wall and watched a man drag a boat out of the water. He helped his wife climb out onto the beach and then lifted out two small children, a sheep and two disgruntled goats. Mawde smiled. He must have bought his animals from someone in another village.

'Mistress Sherman?' It was Julian, calling to her from the forge. 'Your order is ready.'

She made her way towards him and greeted him with a smile. 'I didn't place an order.'

Julian grinned and lowered his voice. 'I know that but no one else does. Come inside.'

'Is your journeyman still here?' Mawde said, looking around the forge. It was stifling inside.

'No,' Julian stood with his back to the fire to shield Mawde from the heat. 'A blacksmith's life wasn't for him, and he joined a ship bound for Spain last week. I'm not sorry he left. I have something for you.' Julian lifted a small package wrapped in a piece of cloth. He pressed it against Mawde's palm and closed her fingers around it. His hand lingered for several seconds before he drew it away.

Mawde opened the cloth wrapping to find an elegant brooch inside. 'Goodness, Julian, it's exquisite.' She traced the edges with her fingertip. The brooch was in the shape of a diamond with a small blue stone nestled in each corner. The edges were cast in the shape of a twisted rope and enclosed a Celtic knot in the centre. Mawde folded the cloth around the brooch and held it out to Julian. 'It's beautiful, but I can't accept it.'

'Why not? It's a small token of friendship.'

Mawde shook her head. 'My husband will not think so.'

'Persuade him.'

A lock of hair had escaped from Mawde's coif. Julian tucked it behind her ear. His fingertip lingered against her cheek. Mawde moved it away.

'Please don't,' she said, unable to make sense of the thoughts swirling in her mind.

'Have you told your husband of the history between us?'

'I've mentioned it.'

'Then tell him the brooch is a long overdue token of apology. He's welcome to confirm so with me.' Julian shifted his gaze towards the door. 'The weather will turn soon. I had hoped the brooch would secure your cloak and keep out the autumn chill.'

Mawde tightened her fingers around the gift. 'In that case, it will.'

'The favour ledger is working well.' Julian turned to retrieve a ledger from a shelf. 'Look at this.' Mawde cast her eyes over the page of entries: leather gloves traded for window shutters, a bowl of shellfish for a bowl of dried peas, a pitcher of ale in exchange for a pollock, and a shirt repair for new dress pins. Almost every entry had been ticked as repaid.

'There was a queue outside the butcher's this morning,' Mawde said, running her finger down the list. 'None of these entries are for meat.'

'And I've seen women step off the Penryn boat and struggle with the weight of their baskets.' Julian closed the ledger and returned it to the shelf. 'Good fortune has befallen the people of this village. Fewer favours have been traded in the last couple of weeks.'

'How so?'

'Alas, I cannot reveal the source. For the sake of our friendship, I will divulge that the answer lies close to home.'

'What do you mean? Is someone giving out money?'

Julian put his finger to his lips. 'I told you, I cannot say.'

When Mawde arrived home, she found the miller in her kitchen sipping a cup of ale. Her cheerful mood dissipated as he stood to greet her.

'Miller Pill, is all well?'

Mawde caught a concerned glance from Mamm. 'He's here to see your husband.'

'If it's about your bill, I can settle that now,' Mawde

said, reaching for the pocket at her waist. 'Tell me how much I owe you.'

'That's not why I'm here.' The miller fanned his face with his hat. Mawde thought she saw a tremor in his hands. 'Your husband settled your account last week. It's another matter I wish to discuss, and I'd prefer to do so today.'

'Nicholas doesn't know he's here,' Mamm said. 'He's in his parlour with the door closed. I didn't like to interrupt him.' Mamm's expression told Mawde Nicholas was in one of his moods.

'I'll let my husband know you're here. Follow me into the hall.' She asked the miller to wait by the table and tapped on Nicholas's door.

'Yes?' said a brusque voice from inside the parlour.

Mawde opened the door and peered inside. Nicholas looked dishevelled. 'Miller Pill is here to see you.'

Nicholas ran his hands through his hair. 'I wasn't expecting him until later this month.'

The miller cleared his throat.

'Will you see him now?'

Nicholas gave a curt nod and rose from his chair. Mawde beckoned for the miller to enter.

Mawde lingered in the doorway and watched Nicolas open a ledger. He ran his fingertip down a column of numbers and stopped a few entries from the bottom. 'Miller Pill, you are three weeks early.' He flicked his wrist to dismiss Mawde. 'Close the door behind you,' he said curtly.

Mawde made sure the door clicked as it closed and walked away with heavy footsteps. She slipped off her shoes, crept back to the door and pressed her ear against the wood. The creak of a hinge told her Nicholas was opening a chest. She assumed it was the coffer he used to store the bonds for debts.

'Here we are, Miller.' The thick oak door muffled the words, but Mawde heard them well enough. 'This is the deed you signed last year, and this is your entry in the ledger.' Nicolas's tone grew fainter. 'I agreed to a loan of £5 and you are in obligation to pay me £8 by the fourth Friday of September.'

Mawde pressed her hand to her mouth. An extortionate rate of interest!

Nicholas's voice grew louder again. 'Your time is almost up. If you're here to borrow more, I'm afraid you're out of luck. So, what is to be? Repayment of the debt, or will you forfeit goods and land?'

Mawde held her breath. At least Nicholas could not take the mill, because that belonged to Sir Hugh.

'What's that?' There was an unmistakable hint of disappointment in Nicholas's voice.

Mawde heard the clink of coins followed by the miller's voice. '£5 as full repayment of my debt.'

Mawde gave a little gasp of joy. How she wished she could see the expression on Nicholas's face.

'What do you mean, full repayment?'

'The purse contains £5. You're welcome to count it.'

Mawde heard the knocks and clinks of coins dropping onto the desk.

'It's all there,' the miller said. 'I trust there's no requirement for me to pay the penalty seeing as I have repaid in full before the due date?'

'That is correct.' There was a brief pause before Nicholas added, 'Here's your deed with the seal broken to confirm you owe me nothing.'

Mawde wanted to open the door and congratulate the miller. A scraping of chair legs had her rushing towards the sideboard. By the time Nicholas opened the door to his parlour, Mawde had one of their best goblets in her hand and was buffing it with a soft napkin.

'Good day, Mistress Sherman.' The miller gave her a broad smile and replaced his hat on his head.

'Good day, Miller Pill.'

Nicholas escorted the miller to the front door. He returned with his teeth clenched and cheek muscles twitching.

'How did the miller raise the money?' he said. 'I can't imagine he's doing well, not with wheat as expensive as it is.' He looked at Mawde's stockinged feet. 'Why aren't you wearing your shoes?'

Mawde stared down at her feet. Fragments of lavender that had been strewn on the floor were clinging to the wool. 'Oh... my um... I had to...'

'Doesn't matter.' Nicholas shook his head in disgust. 'I'm going to the alehouse.'

# CHAPTER THIRTY-THREE

THE LEAVES on the trees glowed red and golden and whispered in the sea-scented breeze. Mawde's apple trees hung heavy with fruit, thanks to Perry's careful watering throughout the summer months. Mawde loaded her basket with freshly picked Costards and walked back to the house. When she arrived home, she met a builder in the court-yard. He doffed his hat and wished her a good day before striding into the lane.

Nicholas was standing in the kitchen doorway, biting his bottom lip.

'What did the builder want?' Mawde said, resting her basket on the kitchen table.

'He came to settle his debt.' Nicholas ran his fingers through his hair. 'He's the third man to repay me this week. I don't know how they're doing it.'

Mawde hoped more men would visit with similar inten-tions. 'That's a good thing, isn't it?'

'From your point of view, perhaps. At least you needn't lose sleep over fears of me practising usury. I'm pleased to get my money back, but I've received no reward for lending it in the first place.' He grimaced and pressed his hand over his stomach.

'Nicholas? Are you sickening for something?'

His face was pale, and a sheen of sweat shimmered on his brow.

'I have a dreadful burning pain. Will you prepare a remedy?'

Mawde placed the back of her hand against his forehead. 'You don't have a fever, but a chamomile tisane will cool the fire in your stomach. I'll make a calming posset of lavender and honey, too. Lie down and rest a while. I'll bring them to the bedchamber.'

Mawde made the chamomile tisane and carried it upstairs to Nicholas along with a plate of bread. 'We're out of honey,' she said. 'Perry's harvesting today, so I'll go to the skeps and collect enough to make your soothing posset.'

Nicholas sipped the steaming tisane and ate a few mouthfuls of bread. 'That's helping already,' he said. He handed the cup and bread to Mawde and lay back on the bed.

Perry had built a large enclosure with rows of shelves separated by wooden walls to protect his numerous skeps. Mawde heard the droning hum of bees before she reached the enclosure. She watched Perry walk along a row and pause towards the end. He was wearing his hat with protective mesh, but his hands and forearms were exposed. He reached towards the domed lid of a skep.

'Perry, be careful!' Mawde shouted.

He turned and raised his hand before easing off the lid. When he reached inside, Mawde held her breath, fearing the bees would sting him. His hand did not linger long, and he carefully secured the lid.

'I'd never seen a skep with a lid until you made these,' Mawde said after Perry joined her.

Perry blew on his hand where a bee tottered on thin legs. The bee took off and drifted away back towards the skeps. 'I can't take any credit for the design,' he said. 'The beekeeper who taught me at the priory disliked destroying skeps to collect wax and honey. By making a lid he could secure well, he saved many hives. I'd hate my little angels to come to any harm, so I've continued with his methods. I can't always save the colonies at honey harvest time, but I try.'

Mawde reached for his hands and scoured them for signs of bee stings.

'I've not felt any stings on my skin today, so I doubt you'll find welts or blemishes.'

'Why don't they sting you?'

Perry gazed towards the skeps. 'It's all about respect.' Perry smiled. 'Tell me, mistress, what can I do for you? You didn't come to learn about beekeeping.'

'No, that's more my sister's domain. Nicholas has taken to bed with a burning in his stomach. I need a small pot of honey to make a posset.'

'I'll fetch one for you.' Perry started walking away but stopped and paused for a moment. He turned back towards Mawde. 'Mistress, I might know the cause of your husband's suffering. There's something you should see.'

He walked along a row of skeps and stopped before he reached the end.

Mawde hesitated. 'I have nothing to protect me from the bees.'

'You don't need it. Keep to the middle of the path and tread lightly.'

Perry waited for Mawde to join him by a skep before prising off the lid. He stepped back for her to peer inside.

Mawde craned her neck to peer over the edge. 'Oh my!' She had expected honeycombs and bees but saw a small pile of pouches instead. Some were made of cloth; others were made of leather. Perry withdrew one and pulled open the drawstring. He offered it to Mawde. She tipped the contents onto her palm – pennies, groats and angels.

'What is this?' she said. 'Why is there money in the skep?'

Perry lowered his head but stayed silent.

'It's you, isn't it?' Mawde put her finger under his chin to make him look at her. 'You're giving this money to the villagers so they can settle their debts with Nicholas.'

Perry raised both of his hands. 'Guilty.'

Mawde returned the coins to the pouch and returned it to the skep. 'How did you come by this money?'

Perry's bald patch shimmered in the evening sunlight as if crowned by a halo. 'I was guided by God,' he said. 'I believed He wanted me to put money aside from charitable donations given to the priory. Somehow, I knew the people of this village would need it.'

'You couldn't have known what my husband would do.'

Perry crossed his hands over his chest. 'The villagers would have suffered with or without his meddling.'

'But he made it worse for them!'

'Perhaps. That's not for me to judge.'

Mawde thought of the treasures she had discovered in Nicholas's parlour. 'Why were the purses not taken with the altar plate when the King sent his men to close the priory?'

Amusement played on Perry's lips. 'Do you remember the story I told you about the day your husband upset the bees?'

'I do.'

'Well, after that, he didn't dare antagonise them again, and he left the skeps in peace. I left the money hidden there after the priory closed. It took me a long while to find the courage to recover every purse, but I brought them here two at a time when returning from St Anthony's fire. I pass the old priory skeps on my way to the boat that brings me back to the village.'

'A lot of villagers are in debt to Nicholas,' Mawde said. 'What happens when the money runs out?'

'People will help one another. You've already reminded them how to do that by encouraging trade in favours. The community spirit had all but disappeared until you intervened.'

A robin landed on a skep. It ruffled its wings then cocked its head as if interested in their conversation.

'I fear community spirit means nothing to Nicholas,' Mawde said. 'You're a kind man, Perry. You could have used this money to rent a house and live comfortably on your own. You had no need to arrive at my door and offer yourself as a servant.'

A sparrowhawk circled above them. The robin chirruped and flew away.

'Using that money for my own benefit was never in the Lord's plan,' Perry said. 'Our beloved God brought you back to this village, and his reasons for that are now clear. He sent me to be your trusted servant, and it's my great honour to serve you.'

'Thank you, Perry.' A sob caught in Mawde's throat. 'I hope I learn to serve the village as loyally as you serve me.'

Mawde watched a cloud creep across the sun and turn the sea from blue to grey. She had believed kindness and charity paved the road to atonement, but now she knew that wasn't enough. The sparrowhawk dived into a clump of long grass and emerged with a mouse in its beak. 'It's a sign,' Mawde said, more to herself than Perry. She reached into her pocket and pulled out the amulet of the Madonna and Child. 'Difficult times are coming again.' She curled her fingers around the warm wood and wished her da was by her side to offer his fatherly wisdom.

# CHAPTER THIRTY-FOUR

Winter arrived with torrential rain, and storms battered buildings. Mawde's vegetable garden was almost destroyed, and her carrots and parsnips turned mouldy. Strip farms and gardens did not yield well for the people in the village. Food was scarce and the villagers stopped sharing. The favour trades dwindled as winter set in and the ledger fell into disuse.

On a bitter day in February, Nicholas called Mawde to his parlour to give her a purse of money to buy food and settle bills. A hearty fire warmed the room. Condensation trickled down the window.

'It's lighter than usual,' Nicholas said, handing her a small leather pouch. 'You've been giving too much away. It's time the villagers fended for themselves.'

Mawde closed her fingers around the purse. She did not need to look inside to know he had cut her housekeeping money by half. 'Nicholas, this will not last a fortnight.'

'It's up to you to see that it does.' Nicholas had an ugly twist to his mouth. His expression was hard and cold.

Mawde thought of the simple food she had eaten as a child when her father had been short of work or the harvest yield was paltry. Thin pottage, watery gruels and shellfish scavenged from the beach. The purse in her hand might be lighter than usual but it would feed them well enough.

A gust of wind rattled the window. Flames flickered in the grate. Mawde thought about the villagers who would be shivering with cold. 'The favour exchange was working so well,' she said. 'Desperate times are here again, so why do the villagers reject it? They know how they benefitted during the summer by sharing skills and resources.'

Nicholas turned to face his desk and reached for a pile of letters. 'Perhaps you meddled too much in something you don't understand. Concentrate on matters closer to home, like the entries in your own household ledger. They looked untidy when I reviewed them this morning.' He gave her a scolding stare. 'There were smudges in every column.'

Mawde felt a tide of anger rise inside her. 'Sometimes I forget to let the ink dry before turning the pages. I'll try to remember from now on. But Nicholas, there are bigger problems I'd rather address, like the plight of people in our village.'

Nicholas clenched his fingers. 'You can't help yourself, can you? Who do you think you are to them – some kind of guardian angel?'

'If only,' Mawde replied, refusing to cower beneath him. 'I'm trying my best to help them.'

Nicholas lifted the top letter from the pile. Mawde wished it was a summons that would take him away from home for at least a week or two. But with Cromwell dead and Treffry running the castle build, Nicholas had no reason to leave the village.

'There is some good news,' Nicholas said, cutting into her daydreaming. He folded the letter and placed it on the desk. 'From what I can tell, the castle is almost finished. That means we will have our royal visit.'

'But we all know the King still suffers with his legs. We pray for him every Sunday. If he's in as much pain as the rector says, King Henry will not travel.'

Nicholas moved his chair until he was facing Mawde. 'Our King is stronger than you give him credit for. He rides in comfort in grand carriages and in royal suites aboard ships. This castle was important to him. He'll want to see what Treffry has achieved. It's time this village prepared itself to welcome the King.' Nicholas drummed his fingers on the desktop. 'His entourage will need food and drink. They'll have money to spend on fripperies. They won't want to see a village in a state of decay, so it's time your villagers smartened their clothes and attended to repairs on their houses.' He smiled. 'Of course, for that, they'll need to invest money, and that's where I can help. They'll be able to pay me back when the royal entourage starts spending.' He turned away from Mawde and opened a drawer to find a clean sheet of paper. 'Leave me,' he said. 'I need to think this through and plan something that benefits everyone.'

'Please say you won't charge them interest or penalties?'

Nicholas gave Mawde a withering look. 'Sweeting, I have told you time and again to leave matters of business to me.'

Mawde left the parlour with mixed feelings. Most houses needed repairs and fresh coats of paint, and few people had goods to sell that would appeal to a king or gentry. But a village in a good state of repair might attract visitors who would buy local crafts and produce. The seed of a plan formed in her mind. She needed to speak to Perry.

Mawde pulled on an outdoor cloak that Clare had waterproofed with oil. The cloak was stiff and stank of fish but would shield her from the wind. She pulled the hood over her coif and set off for the skeps. Her boots slipped on slick mud. Twice, she almost fell. She found Perry beside a skep with his ear pressed to the wicker.

'Is all well?' Mawde asked softly, concerned for the welfare of the bees.

Perry straightened up and moved to the next skep to listen again. 'There's a faint buzzing inside, so I believe the bees are surviving.' He pointed to thick grey clouds darkening the sky. 'You should go indoors. There's another downpour coming.'

Mawde reached out and grasped Perry's hand. 'A quick word, first, if you don't mind.'

Perry raised an eyebrow.

'How much money do you have left in the skeps?'

'Thirteen pounds and seven shillings.'

'Not as much as I had hoped.'

Perry looked downcast. 'I couldn't refuse any request from families needing food and firewood.'

'That, I do understand.' Mawde relayed Nicholas's expectation of an impending royal visit. 'Do you think he's right and the King will come to St Mawes?'

Perry cocked his head to one side. 'He visited the priory several years ago, after he married Anne Boleyn. It's an area I believe he loves very much, and it's important for his coastal defences. Yes, I can see why he might want to pay a visit.'

'I hoped you might say that.' Mawde's optimism was on the rise. 'Perry, I have an idea. Tell me what you think.' She moved towards the end of the row and rested her hand on the money skep. 'What if we used the coins in here to prepare for the King's visit? We could buy lengths of linen and wool for the women to make shifts, caps and stockings. I'll also ask Julian if we can use his old barn to set up as a brewhouse. After all, it will take a large supply of ale and beer to quench the thirst of a royal entourage. And you could teach them how to make mead with our supply of honey.'

'Those are good ideas, mistress, but what about the people in debt?'

'They'll earn money from selling their brews and the garments they make. That will help their husbands repay whatever they owe to Nicholas.'

Perry pressed his ear to a skep. 'The landlord of *The Dolphin* won't like the women selling ale and beer.' He listened to another skep. 'But the women might do well from selling shifts and stockings if they use good-quality cloth.'

The sky darkened. Thick raindrops struck Mawde's cape.

'Not the brewhouse, then. But please, Perry, will you help me?'

Perry lifted the hood on his cape and covered his head. 'I will give you the coins you need.' He smiled. 'I will also teach a few village boys how to make ornamental wood carvings and pot-stoppers from stones. If we add more stalls to the village market, our visitors might spend well.'

The wind strengthened and raindrops struck the ground. Mawde shivered with cold.

'Thank you, Perry. I know my ideas aren't perfect yet, but together we'll give them more thought. Not in front of my husband, though. He must not learn about the coins.' She tugged Perry's sleeve. 'This rain looks set to last the day. It's time we both went indoors.'

Over the course of the following weeks, a steady stream of men arrived at Mawde's door. They sat at her table while they waited for Nicholas to discuss potential loans. Some men wanted to repair their houses while others desired bigger boats. They would fill their hulls with fish, they said, and earn a good living from their hauls. Their optimism was infectious and the mood of the village lifted.

By the time spring arrived, the village seemed to glow. The men had whitewashed the walls of their houses and applied fresh thatch to the roofs. After the spring sunshine dried the roads and tracks, the men filled potholes and ruts with stones. They trampled back and forth, pummelling the surface with heavy mallets until the surface was smooth and more suitable for supporting the King in a carriage. The women tidied inside their houses and made rush mats for their floors. Many made covers for extra mattresses, hoping for lodgers in their homes.

Mawde and Clare scrubbed every room and polished every window. Nicholas bought Italian glassware to impress any nobles or gentry who might call. He was certain that because their house was the largest after the manor and was nearest the castle, they might have the honour of entertaining King Henry himself.

Mawde bought lengths of linen, lightweight wool and lawn and distributed the bolts of cloth between the village women. She sketched designs for subtleties and listed sweetmeats she would make. She knew from her time in the Greenwich Palace kitchens that the King adored puddings, confectionery and cakes. She was as excited about a royal visit as everyone else in the village. All they needed now was a date.

# CHAPTER THIRTY-FIVE

LATE ONE APRIL AFTERNOON, the alehouse landlord knocked at Mawde's door.

'Forgive my intrusion,' he said, twisting his hat in his hands. 'I'd like to speak with Master Sherman.'

Mawde saw desperation in the set of his quivering jaw. 'Come inside.' She gestured for him to proceed into the hall. 'You're welcome to sit and wait for my husband. I'll tell him you're here.'

A tear rolled onto the landlord's cheek.

Mawde rested her hand on his upper arm. 'Remember, you can turn to the parish for help if you're in desperate need.'

'I know.' The landlord lowered his gaze and sniffed. 'I promised my wife she would never go hungry nor lack a roof over her head. I have failed on both counts.'

Mawde wanted to ease his anguish. She leaned towards him and whispered, 'Whatever you fear at this moment, please do not lose faith. I promise that all will be well.'

Nicholas's study door opened and Mawde snatched her hand away. 'Remember what I said.'

The landlord took a deep breath and walked towards Nicholas.

Mawde lingered in the hall, listening to the muffled voices coming from Nicholas's parlour. There was a lull in conversation and movement inside the room. A creak of hinges. A rustling of papers. The slamming of a heavy lid. Nicholas shouted obscenities and ordered the landlord to leave. The parlour door opened and the landlord emerged with an expression of amusement mixed with disbelief.

'Mawde! Come here!'

'I'll see myself out,' the landlord said kindly. 'Good day to you, Mistress Sherman.'

Mawde stepped into the parlour and gasped at the mess Nicholas had created. He had pulled the chests away from the wall, and coffers sat open on his chair. Sealed documents were scattered across the floor and letters were strewn over his desk.

Nicholas was rummaging in a trunk.

Mawde cleared her throat. 'Husband?'

Nicholas slammed the lid of the trunk and spun round to face her. His cheeks were pale and his eyes had narrowed into angry-looking slits. His top lip twitched.

Mawde stepped towards him, feigning concern while trying to stifle her fear. 'What has happened?'

'It's gone.' Nicholas paced back and forth across the room. 'How did I lose it?'

'Lose what?'

'The loan bond.' Nicholas smacked the side of his head. 'Where can it be?' He stopped and stared at his desk. 'I recorded the debt in my ledger but cannot find the sealed bond.' He looked sideways at her. 'You haven't seen it, have you?'

Mawde felt a pressure on her chest. She struggled to take a breath. 'Me? No. Let me help you search.' She stepped forward and opened the drawer to his desk, trying to steady her shaking hand. 'What does the bond look like? Does it have a name on the paper?'

Nicholas grabbed Mawde's arm and pulled her away from his desk. 'I've already looked in there.' He covered his face with his hands. 'It was a large sum of money, Mawde. Too much to lose. Now I'll never get it back.'

'How much was it?' Mawde said, thinking Nicholas would expect her to ask.

'Ten pounds.'

'Ten pounds! That's more than a year's wage for most men! Why would you lend a man so much money?'

'I wanted the alehouse!' Nicholas snapped as he resumed his pacing.

'Are other bonds missing too?'

'I don't believe so.' Nicholas stared at the chaos of paperwork littering his parlour. 'I'll take my time to check through all of this while I tidy it away. If it's just the one bond missing, I can live with that.' He chewed his top lip. 'It would have been lucrative for us – a property and a good business.'

'It must have been God's will to free the landlord from debt.'

Nicholas cursed under his breath. 'You and your damned preoccupation with charity.' He waved her away. 'Leave me. I want to be alone.'

'As you wish.' Mawde closed the door softly behind her and sighed with relief.

Mawde was painting a batch of eggs to give as Easter Sunday gifts when Agnes and Mamm arrived home from visiting Cousin Henry.

'Beth's with child!' Agnes said, breathless with excitement.

'Goodness.' Mawde lowered the brush she had been using. She wanted to share Agnes's glee, but the revelation left her feeling empty. She rested her palm over her belly and tried to imagine what it might be like to feel a baby stir inside. 'When is the baby due?' she asked, forcing herself to look happy.

'Mid-August, I'll wager,' Mamm said. 'She's already beginning to show.'

Mawde stared at the half-painted egg. 'They've been married for two years,' she said. 'I have been married for five.'

Mamm used a gnarled finger to tilt Mawde's face towards her. 'The Lord, in His wisdom, does not believe it's your time. Your day will come, Mawde. I'm certain of it.'

Mawde's bottom lip quivered. 'What if I'm barren?'

'Or your husband lacking seed?' Agnes said, knocking against her while reaching for a painted egg.

'Agnes!' Mamm said. 'How dare you suggest such a thing.'

Agnes turned petulant. 'It happens.'

It was a thought that had crossed Mawde's mind on more than one occasion. 'Tell her about Julian,' Agnes said, smiling again.

Mawde's heart lifted at the sound of Julian's name.

Mamm sat across the table from Mawde and rubbed her swollen knuckles. 'Poor Julian. He made four cannons hoping Treffry would buy them along with other armaments for the castle. Treffry knew Julian was making them but told him yesterday they wouldn't be required. Apparently, the King has ordered Dutch cannons, which have a longer firing range.'

'No wonder Julian was angry,' Mawde said. 'Perhaps a

few families with manors will buy them. If the King believes the Carrick Roads need protecting from invasion, so too will the gentry with land extending to the river.'

Agnes raised her eyebrows. 'That's what Julian said. Funny how you and Julian should have the same idea.'

'Here, Agnes, give that to me.' Mamm swapped the painted egg for one that had not been decorated. 'Help Mawde finish these while I prepare supper.'

Mawde stayed up late that night to paint a collection of eggs for Beth. Nicholas wandered into the kitchen and picked up an egg that was still wet. His lips curled into a sneer as he rubbed his thumb over the shell. It was one of a set of six Mawde had decorated with images of the Madonna and Child.

'So, my sister is with child,' Nicholas said, perching on the end of the bench.

Mawde nodded. 'I pray God blesses Beth and Henry with a healthy child.'

'As do I.' Nicholas turned the egg in his hand. 'Beautiful brush work. Shame about the smudges.' He replaced the egg on the table and picked up another. Mawde watched to see if the image spoiled in his hand but the paint had already dried.

Nicholas closed his fingers around the egg. 'If Beth has a son, I could make him my heir. As she's my half-sister, her child will have family blood.'

Mawde feared her heart might stop. She could think of nothing to say.

'Of course, I would rather sire my own heir than rely on another man's child.' He leaned towards her. 'If you can't give me what I want, what's the point of you being my wife?' Nicholas stood up and then smacked the egg onto the table. The shell cracked and egg white oozed out. 'Clean that up and put your brushes away. It's time to settle for the night.'

Mawde watched Nicholas leave the kitchen and listened to his heavy footsteps climb the stairs. Tears streamed down her cheeks and her whole body shook. She needed Beth's child to be a girl. Mawde needed time to conceive a son.

# CHAPTER THIRTY-SIX

THE FOLLOWING months dragged for Mawde. When nightmares didn't keep her awake, it was fear of Beth birthing a son. But the Good Lord listened and gave Beth a healthy girl.

As fast as Mawde's spirits lifted, the village atmosphere took a sharp downward turn. The castle build had finished, and a small garrison of armed men moved in at the start of June. Three local men were hired and trained to operate the Dutch cannons, but there was still no sign of employment for other local men.

One pleasant August morning, Mawde joined the baker's queue. Mamm had a fancy for honey bread and the baker's was better than her own. Hot air wafted through the bakery carrying the aromas of fish pies, freshly baked bread and small tarts filled with cheese. Cheat, barley and maslin loaves lined three display shelves. Another shelf held small biscuits speckled with pieces of dried fruits.

When Mawde reached the front of the queue, the baker's wife shook her head and glared. 'I thought we were supposed to 'ave 'ad a visit from the King!' she said. 'Seems unlikely 'e'll come now, seeing as summer's almost done.'

Other women echoed her words.

Mawde still harboured the same doubts but thought it best to keep them to herself. 'My husband still maintains the King will come to St Mawes.'

'Trouble is, though, we can't trust a word your 'usband says.' Her tone turned less hostile. 'What can I get you today?'

'I'll take two loaves of honey bread, please, and a couple of those cheese tarts.' Mawde paid and turned to leave but the cordwainer's wife barred her way.

'Do you realise there's not one family in this village that hasn't borrowed money from your husband? He sold us a dream of making money when the King comes this way. But you and your husband are the only ones who'll do well by calling in our debts.' She put her hands on Mawde's shoulders and fixed her with a steely gaze. 'There's a small part of me that wants to believe you're different to your husband, but I'm in the minority with that particular thought. So, let me give you a word of advice: prove you're one of us. Tell me you're not the same as him and you'll stop him destroying us all.'

Other women pressed closer and radiated desperation while waiting for her answer.

Mawde took a steadying breath and looked at each woman. 'I only want the best for you all. I'll see what I can do.'

The cordwainer's wife stepped aside. 'That's all we're asking.'

Mawde stepped through the door, seething and hurting inside. If only they knew how hard she had tried to combat Nicholas's greed! As she walked towards her house, the castle came into view, gleaming white in the bright sunlight and beckoning to Mawde. She quickened her steps. It was time to pay Captain Treffry a visit.

Treffry's office was stark and cold, with a north-facing window. Cobwebs clung to the whitewashed walls and dirt patches stained the wooden floor.

'A flagon of Burgundy wine and a honey loaf from the bakery,' Mawde said, placing the items on a rickety table. 'And a pot of Perry's honey.'

Treffry picked up the jar of honey and traced the bee-shaped stopper with his fingertip. 'To what do I owe the pleasure?' He gestured for Mawde to sit across from him on a chair that had a split in the seat.

'I'll not keep you long.' She moved towards a small window that looked into another room. It was in the shape of a four-leafed clover and carved out of smooth, cool stone. She wondered if the stone had come from the priory. 'The villagers are eager to welcome the King. I wondered if you had any idea when he will come to the village?'

Treffry clapped his hands and laughed. 'Why would the King visit this godforsaken place? There's nothing here but shabby houses and peasants reeking of fish.'

Mawde's mouth opened but her words lodged in her throat.

'My dear, you look like a puzzled pollock trapped in a fisherman's net.'

Mawde closed her mouth and forced herself to meet Treffry's gaze. 'I was of the impression that King Henry would visit when this castle was complete. The villagers used almost every coin they possessed to smarten up their village, ready to welcome King Henry. Are you telling me he's definitely not coming?'

Treffry studied Mawde for a long moment. 'You thought he would come to St Mawes?' He snorted. 'My dear, you were mistaken. The King is no longer inclined to travel. I can't recall the last time he left London. But one thing I know for certain is that he was never coming here.'

'Never?' Mawde felt her leg muscles weaken and gripped the back of the chair. 'But my husband was adamant he would come to the village.'

'I fear you must have misheard.' Treffry rose from his chair. 'Now, if you will excuse me, I must attend to matters of business.'

Mawde left the castle with tears in her eyes. She flung open the door to her kitchen and slammed it behind her.

'Did you know?' she demanded, barging into Nicholas's parlour.

Nicholas dipped his quill in an inkpot and wrote on a piece of paper. The sharpened tip made a scratching sound that caused Mawde to shudder. Nicholas blew gently across the damp words before looking towards her. 'Know what?'

'Did you know there would never be a royal visit?'

Nicholas smirked and folded his hands on his lap. 'Of course I knew.'

Mawde pressed her fist to her mouth. 'How could you?'

Anger flashed across Nicholas's face. 'Take your childish weeping away and leave me to my business.'

Mawde stayed where she was, her body juddering with suppressed sobs. 'All those people who borrowed money while believing your every word. You convinced them they would all make money while you intended to make them your serfs.'

'I wouldn't put it quite like that, but they had to believe something good might happen if they were to sign up to my loans.'

Mawde looked at the icy glint in his eyes. Anger and disappointment ripped at her heart. 'I don't know who you are!'

Mawde turned and fled from the house. She gathered her skirts into her hands and ran to the village square. Upset and breathless, she slowed to a gentle walk, ignoring the stares of curious children as she dried her tear-soaked cheeks. After taking a few moments to compose herself, Mawde walked into the forge.

'Mawde?' As Julian engulfed her in his arms, Mawde became distraught. She pressed her cheek against his shirt and soaked the linen with tears. The warmth and tenderness of Julian's embrace calmed her, and it was with reluctance that she freed herself from his arms.

Julian invited her to sit on a stool and waited for her to settle. He knelt beside her and held her hand, stroking the skin on the backs of her fingers. When Mawde felt able to talk, she relayed her conversations from the bakery and with Treffry and Nicholas.

'I cannot bear to look upon my husband, Julian. He has turned into a monster!'

Julian squeezed her hand. 'Even the worst storms pass,' he said. 'So too will this one.' He released her hand. 'I have ale and oatcakes back at my lodgings. Wait here while I fetch them.'

After Julian left the forge, Mawde stared at the low flames flickering in the fire. Suddenly, one flame climbed higher than the others. 'That's what I need to do,' she murmured. 'I need to rise above this.'

Julian soon returned and passed her a cup of ale. 'You look brighter,' he said, opening a folded cloth and offering her an oatcake.

Mawde shook her head. Her mouth was too dry to chew. 'I need to speak to everyone again,' she said. 'I know there will be consequences, but it's time they knew the truth. No more lies. No more false promises.'

'That sounds reasonable. I'll support you in any way I can.'

'Thank you, Julian.' Mawde took a few sips of ale. 'This isn't the kind of revelation that should spread by word of mouth. It would be better to call another public meeting. Will you do that for me?'

Julian nodded. 'When would you like to hold this meeting?'

'Is this evening too soon?'

Julian laughed. 'I should have guessed. I'll send a boy to spread the word there'll be a meeting in the barn at dusk.'

'Thank you.' Mawde hesitated. 'Julian?'

'Yes?'

The kindness in Julian's eyes caused Mawde to catch a breath. 'May I stay here until the meeting?'

She caught a slight twitch of Julian's eyebrows. He grinned and said, 'If you eat one of those awful oatcakes.'

The mood in the barn turned hostile as soon as Mawde announced there would be no royal visit. Women cried. Men blasphemed. Everyone heckled Mawde.

Mawde raised both of her hands and yelled above the cacophony. 'I beg your silence. Please!'

At last, the noise level dropped low enough for Mawde to make herself heard.

'I know this comes as a terrible disappointment. Believe me, I wish I had better news.' Her legs shook beneath her skirts. She steadied her nerves with a few deep breaths. 'I promise every one of you, I will do whatever I can to help.'

'Can you settle the debts we've run up with your husband?' the cordwainer shouted.

'Can you pay our tithes and our rent or buy our children clothes?' a man yelled from the middle of the crowd.

More people shouted. The temperature rose in the barn. Mawde looked from one to the other as they thronged towards her and called out their woes. Her gaze reached the back of the barn, where Nicholas was leaning against the wall. He was wearing a wide-brimmed hat and stood with his head bowed. Mawde thought he must have slipped in after the meeting started, hoping no one would notice.

Mawde read the simmering anger on the faces in the crowd. 'There's something else you should know,' she said. Her legs started to tremble.

'I think we've heard enough!' The baker scowled at Mawde and turned to press his way through the crowd. Others followed his example.

Mawde saw Nicholas lift his head to scan the barn. She imagined he was calculating how much money he was owed. When his gaze met hers, his lips curled into a sneer, but Mawde held her resolve. She refused to let him win.

'You'll all want to hear this before you leave,' Mawde shouted.

The throng stopped moving and seemed to turn as one. Mawde was met with a sea of despondent faces.

'This had better be good,' the cordwainer said.

'I promise you it is.' Mawde swallowed. 'Today, I learned that King Henry had no intention of visiting our village. You all borrowed money to prepare for an event that was never part of any plan.' She pointed towards Nicholas. 'And worse still, my husband knew all along.'

Murmurs of shock and disgust rippled through the crowd. Soon there was shouting, and the people turned away from Mawde. They thronged towards the back of the barn like a swarm of angry bees. Mawde watched Nicholas shrink away and cover his face with his arms.

As the noise level reached a crescendo, Julian reached for Mawde's hand. 'I need to get you out of here. I want you to go home.'

Mawde cast a sideways glance at him as he pulled her through the crowd. His lips were pinched together and his eyes had hardened with concern. He released the latch and opened the door just wide enough for Mawde to pass through. 'This is turning nasty,' he said, and ushered her out of the barn.

# CHAPTER THIRTY-SEVEN

MAWDE PACED THE HALL, biting her fingernails. The muffled crunch of footsteps on gravel brought her pacing to a halt. She heard the creak of a door opening, then scuffling in the kitchen. Her heart raced. Her shift clung to her skin.

A man's voice called to her. It was laced with a sense of urgency. 'Mistress? Mistress, are you there?' It took a moment for Mawde to register the voice belonged to Perry.

'I'm coming.' She scurried across the hall and entered the kitchen.

Perry and a fisherman carried a slumped man between them, the fisherman supporting him under the arms while Perry held his legs. The man's chest rose and fell with quick but shallow movements. His clothes hung in tatters, exposing red and purple bruises. Blood ran in a scarlet ribbon across the back of his hand. It pattered on a flagstone like early drops of rain.

'Dear God!' Mawde cried, grasping the doorframe.

'Mistress, clear the table,' Perry said, grimacing and

gasping for breath. 'Hurry! I can't hold his weight much longer.'

Mawde fought to gather her senses. 'Can you get him to the hall table? That one is longer.'

Perry grimaced. 'We can try.'

Nicholas gave a muted moan as they carried him through the kitchen. He had a swelling over his left eye, the skin so puffy that his eyelid was closed. His nose was misshapen and deviating to one side, and his top lip had a wide split covered with congealed blood.

'God forgive me,' Mawde said, crossing herself. 'This is my fault.'

Perry and the fisherman eased Nicholas onto the trestle table. Mawde ripped Nicholas's torn shirt sleeve to expose the rest of his arm. She stepped back, her palms pressed to her mouth. Nicholas had a large gaping wound in his forearm and a protruding broken bone.

'A bandage will not save his arm,' Mawde said, fighting a wave of nausea. 'Nicholas needs a surgeon.'

'I'll sail to Penryn,' the fisherman offered. 'There's a favourable wind tonight.'

Mawde's eyes darted towards him. 'You would do that for my husband?'

The fisherman shook his head. 'For your husband, no. But for you, mistress, I will.'

Mawde covered her mouth with her hand. 'Do you mean that?'

'Aye, I do.' The fisherman looked solemn and sincere. 'Any man in this village would do the same for you. We know your husband's greed is not of your making. Our wives have been unkind to you. They shouldn't have been, and we're all sorry.' Nicholas moved his injured arm and groaned. More blood gushed into the wound. 'No one likes to see a woman widowed, so I'll sail to Penryn for you.'

The fisherman gave Nicholas a pitiful stare. 'This is where his greed has got him.' To Mawde, he added, 'This is not your fault.'

Mawde spent a long night watching over Nicholas. Her fingers became stained with the colour of his blood from pressing cloths against his arm wound.

The surgeon arrived as dawn was breaking. He made a quick appraisal of Nicholas's injuries, then dismissed Mawde from the room. She sat in the kitchen with her hands over her ears, trying to block out Nicholas's screams. When he fell silent, she opened the door and peered into the hall. Nicholas was unconscious on a mattress on the floor. Perry was kneeling beside him and wrapping linen strips around his forearm. The surgeon wiped the blade of his knife on his stained leather apron. He looked up as Mawde approached and beckoned for her to join him.

'I've done what I can for your husband. I wish I could do more. When he comes round, the pain will be excruciating, so give him some henbane mixed with poppy syrup.'

Mawde watched the rise and fall of Nicholas's chest. The bruising around his eye had turned purple, and his split lip had doubled in size. 'Where will I find poppy syrup?' she said, after the surgeon left.

'If only we still had the priory infirmary.' Perry shook his head. 'The Penryn apothecary might have some. If not, Truro's our only chance. I'll leave now and return as fast as I can.'

'Thank you, Perry.' Blood soaked into the dressing that bound the stump of Nicholas's arm. Mawde grimaced. 'I'll make a tisane with dried poppy petals when he wakes. It won't help much, but it's better than nothing, and I'll give him a cup of strong beer.'

Overcome with fatigue, Mawde lay across the settle and drifted off to sleep. She woke to the sound of Nicholas sobbing and begging for God's forgiveness. She knelt by his side and held his hand while offering words of comfort.

By nightfall, Perry was still not home, and Nicholas was shrieking with agony. Poppy tea and the landlord's strongest beer had failed to give him relief. When Perry arrived in the early hours of the next morning, Nicholas was in the grip of a fever. He rolled his head from side to side and mumbled with delirium. Mawde trickled a spoonful of poppy juice between Nicholas's lips. His mumblings gradually eased as the poppy juice sent him to sleep.

Over the course of the following days, Nicholas drifted in and out of consciousness. When he was awake, he cried with pain and was too distressed to speak. On the third day after the surgeon's visit, his bandage was wet with brown and yellow stains. Perry unwrapped the strips of cloth, and Mawde's stomach heaved. Bile rose into her throat, and she hurried outside to be sick. When she returned, Perry was lighting a fire to burn the putrid dressings. Mawde steeled herself to look at Nicholas's arm. The stump was red and glistening with pus. It smelled like spoiled meat.

Mawde gently bathed the wound and smeared the angry flesh with honey. She wrapped the stump with a fresh linen bandage and supported it with a cushion. For hours, she sat by his side, watching for signs of recovery, but his lucid moments grew less frequent and fever burned on his skin. Mawde kept vigil day and night, rarely leaving his side. She dared to believe that when he recovered he would change his ways and they could be happy again. After five long days and nights, Nicholas finally mumbled her name.

'I'm here,' she said, reaching for his good hand and pressing it to her lips.

'Send for the rector.'

'No!' Mawde clasped his hand tighter, feeling the heat of his fever.

'Please, Mawde.' A sheen of sweat coated Nicholas's brow. He turned his head to look at her and lowered his voice to a whisper. 'I've done dreadful things, Mawde. I've even killed a man.'

Mawde gasped and dropped his hand. 'Who?'

Nicholas closed his eyes. 'The shipwreck. I stabbed him in the back.' His breaths came fast and shallow. 'Promise you'll pray for my soul?'

Mawde nodded. 'I will.'

Nicholas tried to take a deeper breath. 'The rector, Mawde. Hurry! I need absolution for my sins.'

Mawde asked Perry to find the rector while she tried to comfort Nicholas. His breathing slowed; his complexion paled. The stench of decay was cloying. Mawde searched her husband's face for the promise of a future together. But his skin was grey, his eyes were sunken, and his chin was an untidy patchwork of stubble. Gone was the man who took pride in his appearance, the handsome youth who had captured her heart. Nicholas was a man with a fading shadow and a fire that had burned to ash.

Mawde took his hand back in hers. His lips twitched. His eyelids fluttered. Then his face muscles slackened. Mawde watched him take his final breath and begged God to forgive him.

# CHAPTER THIRTY-EIGHT

Trees were shedding brown and yellow leaves which rained onto Nicholas's coffin. Men and women turned their backs as the cart trundled past them. Mawde hung her head with shame. Emotions knotted inside her – sadness at the passing of the man she once loved, and anger at what he had done to her village.

'Head up,' Mamm whispered sharply. 'Your veil will hide any tears you are shedding.'

There were no tears in Mawde's eyes. She had spent them many moons ago when the love dropped out of her marriage. She lifted her gaze and followed the cart all the way to St Just. The rector had assumed she wanted to lay Nicholas to rest near her departed family members. Mawde chose not to disagree as a last act of kindness to her husband.

The chill of the flagstones on the church floor caused an ache deep inside Mawde's knees, but the ache in her joints was no comparison to the emptiness in her heart. She was a childless widow.

As soon as the prayers were over, Mawde glanced

around the church. The sun streamed through the stained-glass windows and coloured the flagstones of the aisle. New pews sat in orderly rows and shone with layers of wax. Captain Treffry caught Mawde's gaze and solemnly dipped his head. Cousin Henry was comforting Beth, and Mamm was holding their baby. Agnes was fidgeting with a loose button on her sleeve. Perry was studying his missal. Mawde heard the rector clear his throat and turned her attention back to the pulpit.

After the service was over and Nicholas was placed in the ground, Mawde, Mamm, Agnes and Perry rode home on Henry's cart. When they arrived at St Mawes, Mawde could not believe her eyes; villagers lined the street, and men removed their hats.

'Come to the house,' Mawde called to them, as they offered their condolences. She hadn't felt confident about village support but had prepared food and drink in any case. Men and women from the village followed the cart and gathered in Mawde's courtyard. Perry and Agnes filled cups with ale while Mawde thanked each person for their support. Not one person uttered a bad word about Nicholas – no one dared speak ill of the dead.

Julian was the last villager to take his leave from the wake. After closing the door behind him, Mawde dropped to her knees and wept.

'What am I to do, Mamm?' Mawde said, wiping away her tears. 'I'm a barren woman and in my thirtieth year.'

Mamm gave a wry smile. 'It's a ripple, Mawde, not a storm. You've endured many setbacks and overcome each one. New opportunities will come your way, and, in the meantime, you have me, Agnes and Perry to support you in any way we can.'

Mawde stared at a small stain where tears had soaked

her skirt. 'You would have adored the Nicholas I fell in love with. He was a completely different man.'

'Of that, I'm certain, Mawde. I never took to my son-in-law, but I'm grateful he brought you home. Our dear Lord sets a path for us we do not always understand, but Nicholas is with Him now, and you must follow God's plan.'

'But what does He want me to do? I've striven every day of my married life to do what I think is right.'

Mamm put her arm around Mawde and kissed her on the cheek. 'I believe that one day you will do something remarkable, but what it will be, I cannot say. Now, help me stand and let's sit at the table. It's dusty on the floor.'

Agnes made a lavender posset. Mawde sipped the fragrant drink. Fatigue wrapped itself around her body and turned her muscles to lead. She made her excuses and went upstairs to prepare herself for bed.

For the first night in a very long time, she enjoyed a dreamless sleep.

# CHAPTER THIRTY-NINE

Mawde watched a ladybird explore the glass of one of the hall windows. It crawled from one corner to another, its red coat of armour glistening in the light. Mawde opened the window to set the ladybird free. She took a deep breath through her nose. The cool air was rich with earthy autumn scents and the fresh smell of the sea.

'Mawde?' Agnes joined her by the window. 'Captain Treffry's in the kitchen. He said he wishes to speak with you.' She lowered her voice. 'He doesn't look happy.'

Mawde furrowed her brow. 'I wonder why not. Offer him a goblet of wine, and sweetmeats if we have any.'

'My lady.' Agnes bobbed a curtsey, which caused Mawde to smile.

Mawde moved towards the settle, and stood facing the hearth. A low fire burned in the grate to stave off the evening chill. Mawde smoothed out the creases of her black skirt and pinched her cheeks to chase away her pallor.

'Captain Treffry,' she said, when Agnes ushered him towards her. She gestured towards the cushioned chair that

Nicholas had favoured. 'Please, make yourself comfortable.' She sat down on the settle.

Treffry made himself comfortable in the chair and loosened the fastenings of his jacket. 'My condolences for your husband's passing.'

'Thank you.' Mawde rested her hands on her lap and fixed him with her gaze. 'Something tells me there's another reason for your visit today.'

'I'm afraid so.' The severe tone of Treffry's voice set Mawde's pulse racing. He crossed one leg over the other and sat back in his chair. 'I'm here to collect your rent arrears.'

'Rent arrears?' A knot tightened in Mawde's stomach. 'I'm sorry, but I don't understand. Rent for what?'

Treffry's eyes roved across the room, taking in the grand hearth, the polished trestle table, the sideboard at the far end of the room. 'For the land allocated for your husband to farm,' he said, 'and the land upon which he built this fine house.'

A log shifted in the hearth and released a cloud of smoke. 'There must be some mistake,' Mawde said. 'My husband received this land as a gift for work he did for King Henry.'

'Is that what Nicholas told you?' Amusement played on Treffry's lips. 'The King gave your husband permission to build on this land, but he did not grant ownership.'

'He did! He appointed Nicholas as a yeoman farmer and gave him land bordering the river. All Nicholas had to do in return was supply your castle with food. And he did that. My cousin and I still do.' Mawde rose from the settle and threw a fresh log onto the fire. The dry wood caught, and a flame licked one end.

'My dear Mistress Sherman, are you so naïve? King

Henry rented the land to your husband for him to work as a tenant farmer.'

Mawde felt as if she was falling. She grasped the edge of the settle. 'There must be some mistake!'

Agnes arrived with a pitcher of wine and a dish of honeyed walnuts. She set them on a small table and retreated to the kitchen. Treffry helped himself to a walnut. He offered the plate to Mawde, but she shook her head to decline. Her mouth had turned as dry as ash and she was finding it hard to swallow.

Treffry crunched and swallowed the walnut, then took a large sip of wine. 'You know, Nicholas would have made a tidy profit if he'd done things right. But he wasn't interested in working the land and delegated to your cousin. Fortunately, your cousin is a hard-working man. He did so well with the land that your husband earned an income for doing nothing. I suppose you will now, too.'

Mawde stared at the silver buckles on Treffry's shoes. His words washed over her and made little sense. 'He told me this was our land,' she said, shaking her head. 'Why did he tell me that if it wasn't true?'

Treffry softened his voice. 'I'm sorry, Mistress Sherman, but your husband was not the man he pretended to be, and he was certainly no yeoman. Full of bravado, I'll give him that, but, alas, it was all an act. He had poor business acumen, drank too much and surrounded himself with women. Cromwell often praised him, and said he made a fine henchman. That's why he sent him to religious houses to ransack them for the King.' Treffry took another sip of wine. 'You strike me as a sensible woman. You must have had doubts about him?'

'Enough!' Mawde glared at Treffry. 'You're slandering my husband, may the Lord rest his soul.'

Treffry returned his goblet to the table. 'Forgive me, Mistress Sherman, I did not mean to offend.'

'And yet you did!' Mawde was unsure about what upset her most – the fact that Nicholas had left her with a debt, or that she'd misjudged him from the start.

'I presumed you knew about your husband's involvement with closing religious houses,' Treffry said. 'I suspect that was the reason the King wished to reward him. After all, the royal coffers filled quickly from acts of coercion and thuggery so it's really not surprising that he gave Nicholas favourable terms for land.'

Mawde felt the pressure build inside her chest as she accepted the cruel truth behind Treffry's words. No wonder Nicholas had altered from the time he left her at Powderham Manor to the day he found her at Greenwich. His arrogance and obsession with money were starting to make sense. He had been an ambitious young man who had failed to achieve his dreams.

'How much do I owe you?' she said, recalling the purpose of Treffry's visit.

'A full year's rent.'

'A full year! How is that possible? I've been a widow for only three weeks!'

'Many a time your husband requested deferment of payment, and kind soul that I am, I usually agreed. A few days before he passed, he told me he had a purse ready to pay his dues. I'll take it from you now, please, and leave you in peace.'

Mawde heard her cockerel crow and took it is as a warning not to buckle to Treffry's demand. 'Forgive my ignorance, Captain Treffry, but how much is the rent? You'll understand by now, it's not something my husband discussed.'

'For the farm, I will consider all dues paid while you

continue to supply the castle. But, for the use of the land upon which this house stands, the rent is twelve shillings per month. That's not an unreasonable amount.'

Mawde stared at the burning log. An icy chill passed through her. Had Nicholas set aside such a vast sum of money? Would more creditors come calling? She had not yet been through Nicholas's affairs, nor checked the contents of his coffers and chests. She would see to that right away after Treffry left. She tried to keep her composure, but her voice cracked when she spoke. 'I'm not well acquainted with matters of the law, Captain Treffry, but is it right for a widow to inherit her husband's debt?'

'I'm afraid so.' Treffry interlocked his fingers and pressed his palms out, making Mawde shudder as his knuckles cracked. 'Mistress Sherman, I do not wish to hound you over this matter, but Nicholas told me he had the funds to pay. Not only must you settle your husband's debt, but you must continue paying rent if you wish to stay here.' Treffry rose to his feet and tugged the sleeves of his doublet. 'I'm not an unreasonable man, and I can see I have upset you. I'll allow another deferment, but you must pay all rent outstanding when you pay your tithes at Lent.'

Mawde felt hollow as she escorted Treffry to the door. She paused before opening it. 'Captain Treffry, is it you I am indebted to, or the King?'

Treffry smiled. 'You're an astute woman, Mistress Sherman. It is, in fact, Duchy land upon which your house and farmland stands, but for as long as I'm Captain of St Mawes Castle, all benefits come to me.'

'I see.' Mawde stepped aside to allow Treffry to pass.

'Good day, Mistress Sherman.'

Mawde closed the door behind him and pressed her back against the wood. Even from beyond the grave, Nicholas was wreaking havoc. With a heavy heart, she walked across the hall and entered Nicholas's parlour. She opened a drawer and retrieved the keys to the coffers and large oak chests. Both coffers were full of deeds. Neither held purses of money. She raised the lid of one of the oak chests to find a tatty embroidered altar cloth speckled with wax stains. She lifted the cloth from the chest and found papers tied with ribbon. At the bottom, there was a small gold chalice encrusted with jewels and a large gold altar plate. Mawde moved to the other chest, hoping to find purses of money, but as soon as she peered inside, she cried out and dropped the lid. The second chest was empty.

# CHAPTER FORTY

Mawde sat at Nicholas's old desk with her face buried in her hands. No matter how often she stared at her ledger, the numbers did not improve. The autumn harvest had been bountiful, but Henry needed most of the profit to buy tools, carts and mules.

Winter arrived, cold and brutal, and Mawde had to buy extra firewood. By the time she had set money aside to pay tithes and Treffry's rent, there was too little left to buy clothes and food and to pay Clare and Jenet. She stared at the ledger Nicholas had used to record his loans to the villagers, each one backed by a bond secured with a wax seal.

'That's it!' Mawde said, jabbing an entry with her fingertip. 'Treffry will have a record.' She left the parlour and wrapped herself in her heavy oiled cloak. She tied on her pattens and stepped outside into a blustering gale. By the time she had covered the short distance to the castle, the rain had soaked her face and kirtle.

'I'm here to see Captain Treffry,' Mawde said to an officious young man at the guardhouse.

Several minutes later, Treffry's steward arrived and escorted Mawde to Treffry's office.

'Prove the land did not belong to my husband,' Mawde said as she entered the room.

Treffry looked taken aback at the tone of her voice. 'Mistress Sherman, how delightful to see you.'

Mawde dismissed his greeting with a huff. 'I would have known if Nicholas paid rent because I run the household ledger. I've studied the entries for the past five years and found no record of payments to you.'

Treffry dragged a chair towards the hearth and gestured for Mawde to sit. A burning log cracked and popped, scenting the room with woodsmoke.

'Mistress Sherman, we both know your husband was a man of secrets. The fact there's no record of payments to me does not mean they did not happen.'

He was right. Mawde felt a sob building in her throat. She tried to swallow it away. 'Please, Captain Treffry, show me the deed.'

'Very well.' He unlocked a drawer and searched through some papers, closed it and opened another. 'Here it is,' he said at last, removing a folded piece of parchment.

Mawde opened the folds. Her eyes were drawn to a flamboyant signature unmistakably written by Nicholas. She read the neat handwriting and found the meaning all too clear – Nicholas had never owned the land. Mawde refolded the parchment and passed it back to Treffry. 'May I see the ledger showing the payments he made?'

Treffry rang a small brass bell and an earnest young man appeared at the door. He had ink stains on his fingers. 'Fetch the ledger of lands and rents,' Treffry said.

The ledger confirmed Nicholas had fallen behind with payments twelve months before his death.

'Thank you, Captain Treffry.' Mawde's voice cracked

with sadness and disappointment. She understood the pain each villager had felt when they went into debt to Nicholas. 'You'll have your money by the end of February,' she said. 'That's before the date we agreed.'

'Very noble of you, Mistress Sherman. I look forward to our next encounter.'

Mawde rose to her feet. 'I wish I could say the same.'

The rain had stopped, and the wind had eased by the time Mawde left the castle. She picked her way across the rocks and onto the stony beach. She picked up a large grey pebble worn smooth by the power of the sea. Feeling as useless as the lump of stone, she hurled it into the water and watched the ripples spread and fade away. Never had she felt so vulnerable.

# CHAPTER FORTY-ONE

Mawde spent a sleepless night fretting about money. The following morning, she compiled a list of debtors and sent Perry to the village to ask each one of them to visit her at home.

The cordwainer was first to arrive. He entered the parlour with a worried expression and a tremor in his hands. Mawde found his ledger entry and read out the terms of his loan: £2 due for settlement by the end of the month.

'Mistress, I cannot raise the funds.' The cordwainer looked wretched. 'I spent the money on leather and tools expecting a full order book catering for locals and the King's entourage.' He looked at Mawde with shadowy eyes and deep lines on his brow. 'I beg you for an extension to the repayment date of my loan.'

'That's why I called you here,' Mawde said. 'I find myself in an awkward situation now my husband is dead. I need to recover the money he lent you, but in a manner that benefits us both.'

The cordwainer raised his eyebrows. 'How is that possible? I have a debt I cannot pay and must forfeit instead.'

'No, you will not. Your tools are of no use to me, and I do not want your house. That might have been my husband's ambition, but it certainly isn't mine.'

The cordwainer looked at Mawde with confusion in his eyes. 'So, what do you want?'

Mawde picked up a quill and stroked the feather with her fingertip while watching the barbs separate and slip neatly back into place. 'People in this village cannot afford to buy new shoes. Perhaps this is an opportunity to use your skills for other things? Instead of making new leather goods, why not work on leather repairs? Or make cheaper items such as aprons, belts or fastening straps for chests and trunks? If your trade still lacks demand, or you cannot compete with the cordwainers in Penryn, try your hand at a new skill that would be useful to the village.'

The cordwainer threw her a sideways glance. 'Such as?'

Mawde looked through the window towards St Anthony's Head. 'Sit with Perry when he guards the fire and learn the skills of woodcarving. Perry can teach you to make all manner of things such as bowls and trenchers and stoppers for jars. These are goods you can trade for favours or sell at the market.'

The cordwainer stroked his beard. 'I made a few leather repairs when we traded favours before. I'm willing to do so again.' He smiled at her. 'And I'll consider turning my hand to woodcarvings.' His face dropped. 'But what about my debt?'

'I would like to amend the terms of our arrangement,' Mawde said. 'I propose a weekly repayment and an extension to the term of your loan. Another twelve months should suffice. You may repay me sixpence per week, increasing to a shilling when your income improves.'

'And the additional cost for your inconvenience of the loan?'

Mawde shook her head. 'I do not seek to benefit from any villager's misfortune. I only wish to recover the money my husband gave out in the first place.' Mawde opened the desk drawer and drew out a clean sheet of paper. 'Do we have an agreement?'

The cordwainer smiled. 'Yes, Mistress Sherman, we do.'

Mawde wrote a deed to confirm their arrangement and asked him to sign at the bottom. She added her own signature and secured the document with a new wax seal – a simple monogram of the letter 'M'. Mawde crossed through the old entry in the ledger and entered the details of the revised loan on a new page. She handed the cordwainer the agreement bearing Nicholas's seal. 'I have no need for this,' she said.

The cordwainer broke the seal and ripped the letter in two. 'Thank you, Mistress Sherman. May God bless you for your kindness.'

By the end of the following week, Mawde had revised the terms of every debt. By the end of February, her coffer was full of farthings, pennies and halfpennies – enough to pay Clare and Jenet their wages and settle her debt to Treffry.

Mawde rearranged the parlour so that the desk faced the window. She wanted to take advantage of natural light for reading and writing in the ledger. She was huffing and puffing, pushing one of the chests when Perry appeared in the doorway.

'Let me do that for you,' he said. 'Where would you like it?'

Mawde pointed towards the wall where the desk had been located. Perry grasped a side handle and dragged the chest to its new position. 'That one too?'

Mawde nodded. 'I'd like them side by side.'

'You made that look easy,' Mawde said, when he had finished. She paused for a moment. 'I want to show you something.' She raised the lid of the chest containing the gold plate and chalice. When she lifted the altar cloth, Perry let out a gasp. 'Once upon a time, this trunk was full of gold,' she said, lifting out the altar plate. 'Now, this is all that remains. One altar plate and a small chalice.'

'May I?' Perry asked, reaching for the plate.

Mawde registered his look of surprise as he held it in his hand. 'Do you recognise it?'

Perry moved towards the window and studied the back of the plate. 'Every church had similar gold plates, but I know this came from Place Priory.'

'How can you tell?'

'Father Austin was a beekeeper at Place many years ago. When he became sub-prior of Place, he marked everything of value. See this here?' Perry pointed at a tiny marking scratched into the gold. It had four small vertical lines and a curved top. 'A tiny skep. His own special symbol.'

Mawde pulled the chalice from the chest and studied its underside. 'This has the same marking.'

Perry smiled. 'That's no surprise.'

'What do you mean?'

Perry started laughing. Tears streamed onto his cheeks. 'I'm sorry,' he said, 'I shouldn't laugh. Your husband, God rest his soul, was an extraordinarily greedy man, but Father Ambrose and I outsmarted him.'

'How?' Mawde asked, surprised by Perry's mirth.

Perry returned the plate to her. 'You'd better put that away,' he said, regaining his composure. 'All valuables from religious houses were supposed to go to the King, but your husband wasn't the only man to help himself to a share.' Perry's eyes danced with joy. 'Our dear departed Father Austin protected more treasure than my skep. There's plenty more where that came from, buried in his grave.'

Mawde's heart fluttered. 'Who else knows about it?'

'Only Father Ambrose and the carpenter who helped us to bury it.'

'Do you trust the carpenter to hold his silence?'

'I do. We rewarded him for his involvement.'

Mawde imagined refilling her chests with gold and silver items. She could use them one by one to help rebuild the village. Such great wealth would also ensure she would never want for anything, and neither would Mamm, Agnes or Perry.

'I should go,' Perry said. 'I promised your cousin I would help repair his barn.'

Mawde's pulse thundered in her ears. 'Perry, wait! The treasure you speak of, we should retrieve it. It won't be long before work begins on building a new house at Place. What if they dig up the grave to intern the prior somewhere else?'

Perry's brow puckered. 'It seemed like a good idea when we hid those valuable items but, in truth, they belong to the King. If you were found possessing that gold, you would face a severe punishment.' He met Mawde's gaze. 'You might even lose your life.'

'I realise that.' Mawde took a moment to calm her jangling nerves. 'Perry, that gold and silver could do so much good if we use it wisely.' She closed the lid of the chest. 'We could recreate our own version of the legend of Robin Hood, taking back what belonged to the priory and helping our poor neighbours.'

Mawde could see from the twitch of Perry's lips that she had almost persuaded him. 'Please, Perry? Isn't it God's will that we do what we can to help others?'

'Indeed.' Perry's expression turned serious. 'We cannot retrieve the hoard alone. It's bulky and heavy. But I know a man who might help us, a man we respect and trust.'

Mawde turned away from Perry to hide the glow in her cheeks. 'I know which man you speak of, Perry. I shall visit the village this afternoon and share our plan with the blacksmith.'

# CHAPTER FORTY-TWO

MAWDE HAD to wait a few weeks to put her plan into action. Beth injured her back in a fall and needed help with the children and the farmhouse. Mamm and Agnes needed little persuasion to stay at the farm for a few days, so when the perfect night arrived, Mawde and Perry were able to leave the house unheard and unseen.

The night sky was heavy with clouds split by slivers of moonlight. Mawde sat on the beach, huddled under her cape, waiting for Perry and Julian. Choppy little waves nibbled the beach. Branches creaked in trees. Shadows moved across the night sky, a few fast and darting, others slow and refined. Bats and owls, Mawde presumed, stalking their night-time feasts.

At last, the rhythmic sound of oars came from some-where on the water. A single-masted boat appeared through the gloom and bumped to a stop on the shore. Julian leapt out of the boat and limped towards Mawde.

'I don't want you to come,' he said. 'It's too dangerous. There's no telling what might happen when we reach the other side.'

'You're not leaving me behind!' Mawde rose and strode towards the bow of the boat, her boots crunching on the shingle. She grabbed the gunwale with both hands, but it was higher than she expected. She tried to pull herself up but lacked the strength in her arms.

'No, Mawde!' Julian tried to lead her away from the boat. 'We'll manage without you. I'd never forgive myself if you were caught.'

Mawde removed his hand from her arm. 'I'm going too,' she insisted. 'The task will be easier with three of us. While you and Perry open the grave, I will be your lookout.'

'I'd prefer it if you stayed behind,' Julian countered. 'Your skirts will encumber you.'

'What skirts?' Mawde opened her cloak. Beneath it, she was wearing a shorter cloak, a pair of Nicholas's old breeches and a sturdy pair of boots that rose to her knees. 'I believe I'm as well clad as you.'

Julian's eyes showed a mix of admiration and concern. 'I don't want you to get hurt,' he said quietly.

Mawde stepped closer to him. 'There are many wrongs I need to make right. This is my chance to do it. You and Perry have tools to carry, a lantern, and the prior's hoard. You cannot do it by yourselves, so I will play my part.'

'Very well.' Julian moved closer to Mawde and placed his hands on her waist. Her breath caught at the intimate contact. 'Forgive me,' he said, his breath brushing against her ear, 'but it's easier if I lift you. Bend your knees and push up to jump. I will do the rest.'

Mawde did as he asked. Her skin tingled beneath the pressure of his touch. Julian raised her high enough for her to step into the boat. She made her way towards the stern and settled on the bench. Julian pushed the boat off the beach and clambered into the bow. As the boat drifted away from the shore, Julian and Perry took an oar each and rowed towards the opposite coast. The boat rocked and slammed against the waves, sending up droplets of spray. Mawde tasted saltwater on her lips as she stared past the mast into the darkness. A small lamp burned at her feet, but she didn't dare lift it for fear they might be seen.

Mawde kept watch for boats resting at anchor and yelled to the rowers when they loomed into view. She gripped her seat with both hands and tried to ignore her nausea caused by the swell.

'Rocks to your left!' Mawde called out as they approached a small cove.

'Hard on your oar, Perry,' Julian shouted. 'Mawde, drop the anchor!'

Mawde hefted the heavy anchor over the side as the boat hit the beach with a thud.

Julian was first out and took the shovels and sacks from Perry. Once Perry was on the beach, Julian beckoned to Mawde. 'Bring the lamp and come all the way forward. I'll lift you down.'

Mawde sat on the gunwale and swung her legs over the side. Julian eased her on to the beach as if she were as light as a child. He lowered his head until their noses were almost touching. His breath caressed her lips. 'Are you sure you want to do this? You can wait here if you prefer.'

'No, Julian. I'm going with you.'

Julian took the lamp from Mawde and passed it to Perry. 'We'd better get this over with. The tide's coming in now but will turn in a couple of hours. If it ebbs beyond the boat, we'll be stranded and at risk of getting caught.'

They crept along the woodland paths like animals stalking prey. Wet leaves and slick mud made progress slow and slippery. Perry kept the lamp low, a thin arc of candle-light bobbing around in front of him. Julian followed, his limping gait scuffing the ground with alternate steps. Mawde was close behind him. Not one of them dared to speak. When they emerged from the woodland, the air was cold and damp. A fine drizzle hardened into heavier rain and soaked through the leather of Mawde's boots.

As they approached the old priory church, Perry stopped and pointed to a small stone cross that marked Father Austin's grave. The men stowed their tools under a bush and then continued forward. Mawde's breaths came fast and shallow as they stopped by the end of a wall. Perry placed the lamp on the ground and pressed his fingers to his lips. Mawde peered past him into what had once been the refectory. Old benches and trestles lay rotting in a pile, and the front wall was little more than a crumbling mound of rubble. Mawde caught her breath. A guard was asleep on a stool beneath a makeshift shelter. His back was leaning against a wall and his heels were resting on a bench. His boots lay discarded to one side and his jerkin was open, exposing his shirt despite the chill of the night. There was a flagon lying on the ground with liquid spilling from its neck and spreading towards a half-eaten pie. The guard made a loud snore which caused Mawde to laugh. Julian pressed his finger to her lips and urged with his eyes to be quiet. Three candles burned in recessed wall sconces, casting an eery light.

Julian grasped Mawde's hand and drew her deeper into the shadows. 'Watch him,' he said in a low whisper, his lips almost brushing her ear. 'Come to us if he wakes.'

Mawde crouched in her darkened corner and watched shadows play across the ruin. An occasional breeze caused the candle flames to flicker. One of them blew out. Mawde's thighs ached and she had cramp in her calf, but she dared not move for fear of waking the watchman. She scanned the ground for something to use should she need a weapon. Just out of reach, there was a length of wood that might once have been part of a trestle. The wood looked soft from rain and age but it was better than nothing. Slowly, she changed position and moved onto her knees. She reached for the end of the piece of wood and wrapped her fingers around it. Something tickled the back of her hand. She snatched it away and rubbed her knuckles on her cloak, hoping she had removed the creature. Gingerly, she reached forward again, grasped the wood and pulled. The far end caused something to fall and strike a flagstone with a thud. Mawde froze with her arm extended and counted slowly to ten. Satisfied the watchman was still asleep, she pulled the wood towards her hoping she wouldn't need to use it.

Time dragged. Mawde's jaw ached from stopping her teeth from chattering. The guard suddenly stirred on his stool as if he had heard a noise. He looked down at the flagon and cursed before fastening his jerkin. He rubbed his eyes and retrieved an axe from underneath his stool. Tension gripped the back of Mawde's neck – she had not spotted the weapon earlier. To her relief, the watchman belched and lay the axe across his lap. He settled his back against the wall and soon returned to sleep.

The rain eased. The clouds thinned. Fingers of moonlight touched the ruins. Bats fluttered across the sky like spectres in the night. Mawde's eyelids felt heavy and soon they were closed.

A clattering woke Mawde with a start. She immediately sought the watchman. His axe had fallen from his lap and landed on a flagstone. Mawde stayed as still as she could, resisting the urge to flee. The watchman retrieved his axe and staggered to his feet. He ambled to the far end of the wall and unfastened his breeches. At the sound of urine striking stone, Mawde eased herself out of her hiding place. She slipped through the breach in the wall and paused to take a deep breath. Three owl hoots came from the direction of the church. It was Julian's signal that he and Perry had completed their task.

By the time Mawde reached the graveside, Julian and Perry had replaced the earth and covered it with stones and leaf mulch. No passer-by would ever suspect the grave had been disturbed.

Mawde lifted a small sack. The contents rattled and clinked. She slung it over her shoulder and led the way back to the boat. Progress was slow going back through the woods because of the weight of the sacks, but they made it to the shore just in time to catch the outgoing tide.

Mawde shivered and trembled as they crossed the water. Her muscles ached and her teeth chattered as she considered the risks they had taken. She had put them all in danger by stealing the King's treasure, but she consoled herself with the knowledge that it would do so much good for the village.

'That's what Nicholas wanted me to be,' Mawde said, looking at the *Mistress of Carrick* as Julian lifted her onto the beach. 'He said that when he owned the village, we'd have a grand house overlooking the River Fal and I'd be his Mistress of Carrick.'

Julian considered the fishing boat, then turned to Mawde and smiled. 'I believe his wish will come true, but not in the way he imagined.'

# CHAPTER FORTY-THREE

For several days, Mawde hid plates, cups and candlesticks in her basket and smuggled them to Julian. He melted them into ingots and exchanged them for coins in Truro, St Austell and Bodmin. Eager to put the money to good use, Mawde visited Penryn market.

The marketplace was crowded despite thick frost on the ground. Musicians played on street corners and cooked meats scented the air. Mawde filled her basket with ribbons, threads and lengths of delicate lace. She bought jackets, jerkins, breeches and smocks with plenty of wear still left in the fabrics. She found a stall of leather boots and picked twelve pairs of different sizes, then she bought three dozen sewing needles and six bolts of cloth.

An icy breeze stung Mawde's cheeks on the ferry journey back to St Mawes. Her toes were numb and her fingers blue by the time she disembarked. She paid a boy from the village to offload her purchases from the boat and take them on an ox-drawn cart to her house.

Mamm stared with wide eyes as the boy piled linen, wool and canvas on the kitchen table. Then he stacked crates of clothes and boots on the flagstone floor. Mawde sent him home with a penny for his trouble and a cinnamon biscuit still warm from the oven.

'What in the Lord's name do you intend to do with all of this?' Mamm said. 'And how on earth did you pay for it?'

Mawde unfolded a length of wool cloth. 'This will do for shirts and hose.' She pointed to a length of canvas. 'And that's perfect for outdoor smocks. The clothes and boots are for anyone who needs them.' She ignored Mamm's question about payment.

Mamm furrowed her brow. 'You're giving it all away?'

'No, Mamm, not exactly. I've thought hard about the situation in the village. So far, we've reacted when things have gone wrong, but we've done nothing to plan ahead. Nicholas duped everyone into borrowing from him after promising a visit from the King, and now they've slipped back into pauperish ways and eking out an existence.' Mawde pulled a length of blue ribbon from her basket and wound it around her finger. 'The village market is nothing like it used to be. That's why we go to Penryn. Do you remember how visitors once thronged the streets, and you and I sold from baskets?'

Mamm had a faraway look in her eyes. 'Aye, I remember. Lavender bags and combs.'

'No merchants live here now, and the fishing fleet has shrunk.' Mawde sighed. 'I believe dressing like a pauper leads to thinking like a pauper, and I want that to change.' A cloud shifted in the sky and bright light flooded the kitchen. 'If the men, women and children were warmly dressed, well fed and positive of mind, they could restore the village to how it used to be.'

'And how would they do that?' Mamm shook her head. 'A change of clothes isn't the answer.'

Mawde dropped the ribbon back into her basket. 'I'm not entirely sure.' She placed her palm over her breast. 'It's God's will that I do this, Mamm. I feel it in here.'

'Very well.' Mamm scooped a pile of fabric into her arms. 'Help me clear this off the table. We have food to prepare and mustn't stain the cloth.'

Halfway through her supper of mutton stew, Mawde rested her spoon in her bowl. 'I noticed something missing from the market today.' She folded her napkin and placed it beside her bowl. 'Not a single stall had toys. Da used to make toys, didn't he, Mamm? Rattles for babies, little cups and balls.'

'He did.' A wistful look settled on Mamm's face. 'He also made spinning tops and little carved animals. He loved making things for children when he had the time.'

Mawde stared into her bowl. 'I don't recall the last time I saw children playing with toys. I see them playing knucklebones or playing at sword fights with sticks, but these days, none of the children play with proper toys.' An idea blossomed in Mawde's mind. 'Perry, do boys from the village still join you by St Anthony's fire?'

'They do. I teach them reading, writing and basic sums, and how to make stoppers from stone or wood.' He smiled. 'I can teach them how to whittle little toys. There's plenty of driftwood on the beaches. We can dry it and put it to use.'

'And when they're not with you, they can make toys at home, at first as gifts for village children and then for them to sell.' Mawde's words tumbled over each other. 'I'll rent a stall in Penryn where families can sell the toys. They might earn a small income that they can't earn here in St Mawes. Not yet anyway.'

'What about poppets for little girls?' Agnes said. 'I made one from straw for Beth's little girl and she plays with it all the time.'

Mawde clapped her hands. 'That's an excellent idea, Agnes. We can use Beth's old bedchamber as a workroom, and girls from the village can come to help you.'

Mawde saw the smile fade from her sister's lips. 'Agnes?'

Agnes looked down at her lap. 'I was going to ask you later, but I might as well ask now.' She sucked in her bottom lip. 'Will you allow me to move into the farmhouse?'

Mawde smiled with relief. 'You don't need my permission for that!'

'I know.' Agnes reached for Mawde's hand. 'You have Mamm to help you here, and Clare and Jenet. Beth has women in the dairy but no one in the house. She's already said she'll welcome me, but only if you agree.'

Mamm drummed the table with her fingertips. 'Might the arrangement offer more opportunities to see a certain miller's son?'

'Mamm!' Colour flooded Agnes's cheeks.

'Of course, you must stay at the farm,' Mawde said. 'I'll try to visit every week.'

'To collect the poppets we make?'

Mawde gave her sister a playful shove. 'Isn't that reason enough?'

'That's settled then.' Mamm stood and carried their empty bowls to the kitchen. 'Mawde?' she said, returning to the hall. 'May I have a piece of lace and a length of ribbon? My old neighbour is unwell, and I'd like to take her a gift when I visit her tomorrow.'

'Of course, Mamm. I'll walk you there in case it's icy again, like today.'

'I'll visit the forge too,' Mamm said. 'I'll invite Julian to join us for a hearty supper in return for walking me home.'

'He'll be busy, Mamm,' Mawde said. 'I'll walk you there and back.'

Mamm flicked her hand in dismissal. 'You won't want to wait around for me, and Julian won't mind. I'm sure he'll be glad of a decent meal.' She smiled. 'It's as clear as day you two have feelings for each other. You should spend more time with him.'

'Mamm! Whatever—'

'She's right,' Agnes said. 'I saw the looks that passed between you after Nicholas's funeral.'

'Agnes!' Mawde glared at her sister. 'How can you say that?'

Mamm raised her hand to silence Mawde. 'I might be old, but I'm not foolish. Neither is your sister. You and Julian are destined to be together so there's no point in fighting it.'

'That's ridiculous,' Mawde said, lacking conviction.

'I don't believe it's ridiculous,' Mamm said. 'But only time will tell.'

# CHAPTER FORTY-FOUR

IT SOON BECAME customary for Julian to visit on Sundays. He walked Mawde home after chapel and returned to her house after archery practice. One balmy Sunday in spring, he asked about the *Mistress of Carrick*. He hadn't seen her skipper in a while and asked if he still went fishing.

Mawde checked and double-checked the entries in her ledger. Fifteen weeks had elapsed since she had last received money from the skipper. She stared through the window at the cloudless sky. The bounty from the prior's grave had distracted her from the ledger and she had not noticed the omissions. She tried to recall the last time she had seen her boat's skipper at the village chapel or St Just Church. As far as she could remember, it was two Sundays before Christmas.

When Julian left for archery practice, Mawde set off for the beach. The tide was out and there were tiny fish darting through the glistening shallows. Crabs sidled by the water's edge following a line of seaweed. Several boats sat propped on the beach while fishermen carried out repairs. Mawde's mood darkened when she found the *Mistress of*

*Carrick*. The boat was listing to one side and her hull was thick with weed.

She called out to a fisherman. 'Do you know when this boat last sailed?'

The fisherman shrugged but said nothing.

Mawde gathered up her skirts and climbed the steep path up to the road. Flushed and sweaty, she hurried towards the village, where she found a group of fishermen huddled on the quay. They were discussing the previous day's bountiful catch, but her skipper wasn't among them. Clenching her fingers, she walked to his house and rapped hard on the door. After a brief pause, she knocked again, but no one came to answer. She moved towards the window and opened the flimsy shutter. The room inside was empty, with no sign of a recent fire. She kicked the door with the toe of her boot and smacked the door with both hands. Eventually, a neighbour appeared and told Mawde that no one was home.

'Where are they?' Mawde asked, feeling her temper rising.

'God only knows,' the woman said, wiping her hands on a threadbare apron. 'You must have heard about the men lured away by a stranger?'

'No. What stranger?'

'Like the Pied Piper of Hamelin, he was.' The woman shook her head. 'Lord knows, I pray every day to thank God my own husband wasn't tempted.'

Mawde cursed under her breath. 'For pity's sake, woman, what are you talking about?' The horrified expression on the woman's face brought Mawde to her senses. 'Forgive me, that was rude. I have an urgent matter of business to discuss with the skipper of my boat.'

'Well, I'm afraid you've missed your chance. Your man

was lured to a better life. He's gone to earn a decent wage building warships for the King.'

Mawde narrowed her eyes. 'Where? Penryn?'

'Goodness, no, my dear. Portsmouth, I believe, and they ain't been heard from since.' She stared at the empty house. 'No news. No money. So, his wife upped and left. Lord knows where she is now.'

Mawde apologised again for her rudeness and started walking home. With every step, her heart grew heavier. The King was gradually stripping the village of everything that mattered. He had taken the priory and their old religion, employment and now their men. Somehow, the thought eased her guilt about emptying the prior's grave. She had given out clothes, written off debts and donated to alms, but she had yet to find a way to break the cycle of poverty. A stall in Penryn was the right idea but would only help one or two families. She stopped to lean on the sea wall and regarded the ships in the estuary: merchant vessels, cargo ships, fishing boats and wherries. Mawde looked towards the village. Despite the men having borrowed from Nicholas, their homes needed decorating and repairing again. Buildings that had once formed merchant houses were now just clusters of rooms occupied by families whose hovels had fallen down. A few houses were in a reasonable state of repair, but the rest were patched and scruffy.

Mawde needed another haul of gold, larger than the prior's hoard, to improve the plight of the village. She turned back towards the water. There was only one place where she'd find such a sum, and that was aboard a ship.

# CHAPTER FORTY-FIVE

MAWDE STUDIED an image of Saint Maudez on the chapel wall. He was sitting on a stone step, while young men seated on the lower steps learned from his wisdom. The saint had a large book open on his lap and was pointing to a section of text. It reminded Mawde of the favour ledger and that she had not looked at it for many months.

Mawde left the chapel and made her way to the forge. Julian smiled when she sat down at his table but continued with his work. Mawde found several entries in the favour ledger. It was clear the villagers were trying to help one another, but the loans were as trivial as the repayments. A pail filled with winkles had been traded for a needle and a spool of thread. One of the women had washed a few clothes for carrots and a half-dozen eggs. Mawde could not decide whether the villagers disliked trading favours or if they had too little to give.

Julian heated a length of metal, then beat it with a hammer to shape the glowing iron into a shelf bracket. He plunged the bracket into a water trough, where it sizzled and gave off steam.

'You look troubled,' Julian said, adding the bracket to a pile of others.

Mawde shared the news about her boat and the absence of her skipper.

'I heard about that.' Julian limped across the forge and perched on a stool beside her. 'If I'd known your man was one of them, I would have said something.'

Mawde picked a small piece of ragged skin protruding beside her thumbnail. It smarted as it ripped away, leaving a tiny bead of blood on her skin. 'The King's done nothing but hurt this village. We should make him pay!'

'Careful, Mawde. You don't want anyone to hear you.'

Mawde gave a petulant shrug.

'I don't disagree with you, though.' Julian wrapped his hand around Mawde's. His skin felt rough, but warm.

Mawde gave him a sideways glance. 'I thought of something we could do.' She took her hand away from his and stared down at her lap. 'But you would think me foolish.'

'Try me.'

Mawde wrestled with her partial idea and gave Julian a sideways glance. 'We could seize a ship's cargo.'

A noise burst from Julian's throat as if he was stifling a laugh.

'You see!' Mawde angled herself away from him. 'I knew you'd react that way.'

Julian put his hand on Mawde's arm. 'How would we seize a cargo? The King's ships have armed guards who'd slit your throat if they caught you – that's assuming you succeeded in climbing aboard in the first place.'

Mawde shrank into herself. What had she been thinking? She covered Julian's hand with her own and turned her face towards him. 'My nightmares aren't as frequent now, but two or three nights of every week, I dream this village is burning. God has forgiven most of my sins, but I must still make amends for Nicholas. He didn't care for the people of St Mawes and caused them so much heartache. I've tried hard to help them all but I can't cure their poverty. The money we took from the prior's grave will only last so long and I don't know what else to do.' She looked at her hand where it touched Julian's. Her skin looked as pale as the moon while his was black with soot.

Julian drew his hand away. 'Forgive me, I'll mark your sleeve.'

'I'm not worried about that.'

Julian shook his head. 'You want to atone by robbing a ship, but that in itself is a sin.'

Mawde hung her head. 'I suppose it is.' They sat in silence for a minute or two, and Mawde recalled a conversation with Perry. 'Robin Hood,' she said, looking up. 'We'd be taking from the rich to give to the poor, just like Robin Hood in the legend.' Mawde's mood lifted. 'Isn't that what we've done already, you, me and Perry? Seizing the cargo from a ship wouldn't be any different, provided we used the haul for the greater good.'

Julian stood and paced the floor. 'I cannot see how we could rob a ship without getting caught.'

Mawde rose from her stool and closed the door to the forge. 'There is a way,' she said, walking towards him. She lowered her voice to a whisper. 'We could wreck it.'

'What?' The colour drained from Julian's face. 'Have you lost your senses?'

Mawde vigorously shook her head. 'No. We could lure it onto the rocks.'

Julian stared at her, his expression a mixture of shock and bewilderment. 'I don't know what to say.'

Mawde's thoughts were reeling. 'I know you think it's a

bad idea, but please, hear me out. There was a wreck back in '39 and there should have been survivors.'

'Should have been?'

Mawde sat on a stool and studied a thumbprint of soot on her sleeve. 'At least one man would have survived if not for the actions of my husband.'

Julian let out a noisy breath. 'I didn't know about that.' He closed and barred the door to the forge, plunging them into gloom.

'What I'm trying to say,' Mawde persisted, 'is that a wreck would not be the first on our coastline.'

'But you'd endanger the crew.'

Mawde waited for Julian to sit. She shuffled her stool towards him. 'I would not forgive myself if anyone was hurt, so I need a plan that does not cost lives. One ship would solve the problems of every person in the village.' As an afterthought, she added, 'Both of us included.'

A loud knock sounded at the door. 'Blacksmith? Are you there?''

Julian put his finger to his lips and spoke in a whisper. 'Let them think there's nobody here.'

An exchange of muffled voices followed, then the sound of retreating footsteps.

'They've gone,' Julian said.

Mawde took his hand and traced a callus on his palm. 'Will you help me?'

Julian folded his hand around her finger. 'I made a promise I would.' He leaned closer. 'There is something you could do.'

'What's that?'

'Let the fire go out.'

Mawde gasped. 'St Anthony's fire?' She lifted her head to look into his eyes. 'I see the port books when I collect the fire dues. I can look for a ship departing Penryn with a suitable cargo.' Mawde's breaths came quick and shallow. 'Many a captain sails in squally winds. If we were blessed with a thin mist, we could lure them aground with a fire further along the coast.'

Julian cupped the back of Mawde's head and pressed his forehead to hers. They bumped noses. Mawde giggled. Then Julian brushed his lips against hers.

'I'm sorry,' he said, pulling away.

Mawde covered her mouth with her fingers. 'Don't be,' she murmured.

'We could wreck a ship,' Julian said, 'but we couldn't take the cargo. Not unless the crew members perished, and we don't want blood on our hands.'

Mawde stared at the fire at the opposite end of the forge. The flames had burned low and the embers were glowing. A candle flickered in its sconce, making the forge look ethereal.

'I can't do it.' Mawde said. 'I cannot cause more deaths.'

She felt Julian's fingers rest against her cheek and turned her face towards him.

Julian's fingertips followed Mawde's jawline and stopped beneath her chin. 'We can wreck a ship, salvage the cargo and claim a handsome reward for everything we return. But instead of declaring every item we salvage, we could keep some back for your cause.'

Julian's eyes seemed to glow through the gloom. Mawde feared her heart might burst. 'You think it's possible? To do it without loss of life?'

'I do.' Julian's index finger moved up from her chin and along her bottom lip. His touch was as delicate as angel wings, and Mawde burned with longing. She kept her eyes fixed on his as he leaned closer towards her. She closed her eyes as their mouths met, first with a gentle touch of lips, then with a fervent passion. Mawde felt as if she'd been struck by lightning and her body was aflame. She let out a little moan of pleasure as heat coursed through her veins. Julian drew Mawde onto his lap and kissed her one more time. When he stopped, Mawde cupped his face in her palms and said, 'Please, Julian, do that again.'

Julian dusted the corners of her mouth with feather-light touches that triggered a deep and visceral yearning. He turned Mawde so her back was towards him and wrapped his arms around her waist. She could feel his manhood swell beneath her as he nuzzled the side of her neck. She arched her back and pressed against him, smiling at the catch in his breath.

'Ships don't just carry cargo like tin, cloth and spices.' Julian's voice was husky. 'Other items will wash up on the shore and those are the things we will keep.'

'What things?' Mawde asked, leaning against his chest.

'Gold and silver locked in coffers.' Julian chuckled. 'You'll have to refund your fee for the fire going out.'

Julian moved his hands to the lower region of Mawde's belly, making her muscles clench. Memories of Cromwell and Nicholas entered her mind, but she soon cast them aside. This was a deeper connection with a man, a sharing of minds as well as attraction. She turned and sat astride her blacksmith. He tightened his embrace. Mawde loosened the laces of his breeches but then heard her dead grandmother's voice.

*Sinful child! Rotten to the core. Selfish and cursed.*

Mawde's passion quickly dwindled, and she clambered to her feet.

'I'm sorry, Julian.' Mawde straightened her clothes. 'I should never have mentioned the idea of a wreck. We can't risk any lives.'

Julian retied his breeches. 'We'd have a rescue plan in

place.' He opened his arms, inviting Mawde back to him, but she stayed where she was. 'We would need a storm,' Julian said, shifting his attention to the ties of his shirt. 'There's an old cabin near St Anthony's fire where we could shelter until the rescue. Waiting for a storm to pass costs every captain money. It delays departure for his next venture, and the one after that. There's bound to be one captain foolish enough to risk departing in adverse weather. And I'm confident we could make the plan work without any risk to life.'

Mawde played out the scenario in her mind. If they were successful and no lives were lost, not only would they get their reward, but they would be proclaimed heroes. And the wreck or its cargo might even belong to the King.

'I'll think about it,' she said, preparing to leave.

'Mawde?'

She turned to see Julian looking intently at her.

'Yes?'

'Let me have one more kiss?'

She smiled and kissed him on the cheek.

# CHAPTER FORTY-SIX

THE FOLLOWING DAY, Perry stormed into the kitchen and slammed a basket of carrots onto the table. Small clods of wet soil fell from the leaves and created little muddy puddles on the freshly scrubbed oak.

'What's happened?' Mawde asked, moving the basket to the floor.

'I overheard Captain Treffry boasting to Sir Hugh that he reported two priories to Cromwell. He cited unseemly behaviour and idleness. One of them was Place!'

Mawde remained silent. She had never seen Perry look so wretched.

'How could he pass judgement? He never visited the priory. Even if he had, I doubt he could tell the difference between idleness and silent devotion to prayer.' Perry turned his miserable face towards Mawde. 'I longed to leave the religious life, but I never shirked responsibility and neither did the Brothers. It's fools like Treffry that helped destroy our religious houses and fuelled the King's eagerness to fill the royal coffers.'

*Oh, Treffry,* Mawde thought, *how could you?* Mawde

knew how gentry and nobles tried to manipulate the King and members of his inner circle. It hadn't turned out well for Cromwell, but it seemed to have worked for Treffry.

Perry gave a feeble smile. 'Forgive my moment of anger, mistress. I spoke out of turn.'

'Treffry will get his comeuppance, Perry, you'll see.'

Mawde considered Treffry a blight on her life. He had fired Nicholas, made him moody, and humiliated her over her rent. Now it was clear he had provoked the King's greed and hurt the people of her village. Mawde decided enough was enough. Treffry was the King's pawn, and she would make him pay.

Three days later, Mawde visited the port office. 'I'm here to collect the St Anthony fire dues,' she said, glancing at the port book on the clerk's desk.

The clerk pulled a small ledger from a shelf beside him. He opened it to the most recent entry and lay it on top of the port book.

'Sign please.' The clerk dipped a quill into a pot of ink and passed it to Mawde. She checked the entry and signed her name with an elegant flourish.

The clerk returned the ledger to the shelf before heaving himself from his chair. He waddled off to the adjacent office to fetch Mawde's fire dues purse.

Mawde peered at the port book. She struggled to read the upside-down entries, but her eyes picked out the name of Captain Thomas Treffry. The entry suggested one of his ships had arrived at Penryn that morning. There was nothing to suggest it had unloaded goods, so it must be there to collect cargo. The clerk returned and handed

Mawde a small purse of coins. She peered inside to check the amount and thanked him with a smile.

Mawde boarded the ferry bound for St Mawes. While she waited for it to cast off, she appraised the condition of the boats that had congregated in the harbour. There were two large three-masted ships and many smaller two-masted vessels. Most of the smaller ships were in a reasonable state, but several needed repairs. Mawde knew that years ago, the St Mawes boatyard was considered the best around. Now it managed simple repairs and struggled to build one boat per year. Perhaps one day she might build it up again – if she could acquire enough money.

A young boy released the ropes while his father hoisted the sails. The boy jumped aboard the boat as the wind carried it forward. As soon as they left the harbour, white caps crowned the waves.

'I don't much like the smell o' this wind.' The owner of the ferry heaved hard on a rope to adjust the angle of the sail. He sniffed deeply. 'Reeks of a storm.'

By the time the boat reached St Mawes, Mawde was feeling queasy. She stood on the quayside with her palms on the wall and drew deep draughts of air. When the ground stopped swaying beneath her, she walked to Julian's forge.

Her insides twisted and fluttered when Julian lay down his tools and wiped his hands on a cloth. She closed the door and walked towards his open arms. When Julian stooped to kiss her, Mawde tasted woodsmoke on his lips.

'This is a delightful surprise.' Julian held her at arm's length. 'What brings you here, Mistress Sherman?'

Mawde smiled at the formality of his tone, but reverted to a serious face when the door latch lifted with a loud click.

'That will be Simon, my apprentice.'

The door creaked as it opened and a youth step into the forge. His top lip curled with an arrogant air, and his hair was greasy and lank. He reminded Mawde of Julian when he was a youth. The apprentice strode towards the fire and banked it with wood.

'I came to seek your opinion about a sensitive matter.' Mawde hoped her tone conveyed she needed to speak with Julian alone.

Julian gave a slight dip of his head. He stuffed some pot hooks into a bag and handed it to his apprentice. 'Take these to the manor. The cook is expecting them.'

Mawde heard Simon tut and caught him rolling his eyes. Julian waited for the youth to leave, then closed the door behind him. 'Tell me, how can I help?'

Mawde relayed Perry's revelation about Captain Treffry. Her shoulders tightened as she tried to control her rage. 'Not content with his meddling with the priory, Treffry still hasn't employed more local men. And let's not forget how he treated you with the cannons, buying Dutch imports instead.'

'The Dutch cannons were the King's choice,' Julian said. 'They're different from any cannons I've seen before. Very long noses.'

Mawde snorted. 'But you had already made cannons so he left you out of pocket. Has he asked you to supply cannonballs?'

'Not yet.'

'There! You see? Every time Treffry could do something good for the people of this village, he chooses an alternative.'

Julian returned a stray tool to its place on a shelf above a workbench. 'And I presume you want to do something about it?'

Mawde tried to calm herself. 'Treffry has a ship

docked at Penryn. I don't know when it's due to sail or if it will be laden or empty. But I know Treffry. He won't want to delay its departure if it will cost him money. I believe he will pressure the captain to sail at the first opportunity.' She glanced towards the nearest window and lowered her voice. 'We could lure that ship to the rocks.'

Julian did not react as eagerly as Mawde had hoped. 'Before we plan anything, we need more information. I'll find out what it's carrying and when it will sail.'

'How?'

Julian smiled. 'Don't you worry about that.' He turned serious again. 'My boat is too small to handle violent weather, Mawde. We need something with a sturdier hull.'

'*Mistress of Carrick*. She's as good as abandoned now, but she would get us across the estuary.' Mawde sensed Julian's hesitation. 'If you're worried that she's not seaworthy, why not see for yourself? Join us for supper later and check her over on your way.'

Julian pulled Mawde into his arms. 'I will do as you ask, Mistress Sherman. I find you most persuasive.'

Julian arrived earlier than expected. 'I had a look at your fishing boat, Mawde. She seems fine to me.'

'That is good news! Thank you, Julian.'

Mamm bustled into the kitchen and welcomed Julian with a smile. 'You're joining us for supper, I hear?'

Julian gave her an apologetic smile. 'Please forgive me, Mistress Wyn, but I regret I must decline.'

'A pity. Can I at least offer you a cup of ale?'

'Not this time. I have important matters to attend to.'

'Very well.' Mamm gave Mawde a knowing smile. 'The

evening has arrived with a chill in the air. I'm going to fetch my shawl.'

Mawde waited for Mamm to close the door behind her. 'Why can't you stay?' she asked, with an urgent whisper. 'We need to discuss our plan.'

'Hush, Mawde, and listen. Tell me, what do you hear?'

Mawde closed her eyes. The fire popped and crackled. She heard Mamm singing as she climbed the stairs. The first raindrops pattered against the windows. Chickens clucked in their pen.

'Mamm, rain and chickens.'

'But no storm.' Julian rested his hands on her shoulders. 'The rain is light, the wind is gentle and the sky will be clear tonight. We must be patient, Mawde. We'll know when the time is right.'

Mawde felt the tension build in her neck and the back of her head. 'It's almost April,' she moaned. 'It could be months before the next storm.'

'In that case, we will wait. And anyway, Treffry's ship will have little of value stowed in the hold. He's sending furniture to his house in Fowey, so we'd risk too much for too little gain, and it's likely we'd be caught.'

'I can't pretend I'm not disappointed.' Mawde sighed. 'Must you leave now?'

'I'm afraid I must. Tithes are due soon and my ledgers are not in order. I must spend the evening reviewing my situation and planning for my future.'

Mawde felt a rising sense of panic. 'Are you thinking of leaving the village?'

'Goodness, no! There's something else I'm considering, but the matter needs more thought.' He kissed Mawde on the forehead. 'I must tear myself away from you now, but I promise that whatever decision I make, you'll be the first to know.'

# CHAPTER FORTY-SEVEN

FORGET-ME-NOTS bloomed in frothy blue swathes. Red campion bobbed in the breeze. The clear skies and calm seas of early summer heralded a mood shift in the village. Wood-crafted toys and cloth poppets sold well at Penryn's market, providing an income for two families and hope for everyone else. Sir Hugh had expanded his flock of sheep but moaned about the slow pace of the spinners. He agreed to sell Mawde the unspun wool and then she purchased five spinning wheels. Village women used Julian's barn, taking turns to use the wheels while others used drop spindles and distaffs. Julian transported the spun wool by boat and sold it to the weavers in Truro. After paying each woman two pennies per day, Mawde was making a profit.

As pleased as she was with her fledgling business, her savings were not growing fast enough. The prior's gold was dwindling fast, and she needed to pay her own bills. She put a purse aside to pay rent for two years but needed more for her plans for the village – and to buy the freshwater boatyard. She still had the jewelled chalice locked away in the chest, but that was for if she grew desperate. Her only option was to bide her time and wait for a storm and a wreck.

Mawde closed her business ledger and stared down at her shoes. The faded leather was badly scuffed and splitting at the seams. The cordwainer was due to make his weekly repayment but Mawde decided to ask him for new shoes instead.

The cordwainer looked overjoyed at Mawde's request for footwear. 'When the other women see your new shoes, they'll all start placing orders.' He beamed at Mawde. 'Praise the Lord, you found a way to help them earn some money.'

Mawde left his house in a cheerful mood, eager to spend time with Julian. She slowed her steps when the forge came into view. Recently, she had dreamed about becoming Julian's wife. Mawde drew to a stop and watched a thin ribbon of blue-grey smoke creep out of the forge chimney. Was that really what she wanted?

Julian appeared in the doorway to the forge and leaned against the doorjamb. He waved when he saw Mawde in the street and beckoned for her to join him. Mawde's pulse quickened at the thought of his arms folding around her and the thrill of his passionate kisses. She returned his wave and hurried towards him.

'Look at this,' Julian said, taking her hand and leading her into the forge. Horseshoes sat in piles of four, crowding a long narrow workbench. Sets of keys, locks and bolts almost filled another. Cannonballs formed a pyramid in one corner of the forge, and Julian's apprentice was huffing and puffing while hammering the handle of a skillet.

'Who ordered all of this?' Mawde asked when the banging of metal on metal ceased.

'The King dismissed my Cornish-made cannons, but

Treffry placed an order for two hundred cannonballs and plenty of ironwork besides.' Julian sent the apprentice to fetch a pitcher of ale. As soon as he was out of earshot he added, 'I'm earning good money now, Mawde, and there's something I want to ask you.'

'Wait.' Mawde pressed her finger to Julian's lips. 'I think I know what you're about to ask, but first, there's something you must tell me. Did you tell the whole truth about how my brother died?'

'A fair question,' Julian replied, looking deep into her eyes. 'I stand by what I've told you.' He repeated the story exactly as before and Mawde felt the regret in his words. 'My dear, sweet love,' Julian said, taking her hands in his. 'If I could relive that day, I would not go near your brother and John would still be alive. Not a day passes without me thinking of him and seeing his lifeless body. I will never forgive myself for my role in his passing.'

He drew away at the sound of footsteps and moved towards the fire. The apprentice arrived with the pitcher of ale and three sturdy cups.

Mawde took a few sips to moisten her dry mouth. 'Julian, can you spare a few minutes to walk with me outdoors?'

He gave the apprentice a few instructions and followed Mawde out of the forge. They walked in silence away from the village, following a path high above the beach. They stopped to sit on a grassy bank facing the ruins of the priory.

Mawde reached for Julian's hand. 'Every day, I pray for forgiveness for sins I've committed. Things I've done and choices I've made that caused other people to suffer. I'm desperate to make amends.'

Julian put his arm around Mawde and drew her closer

to him. She felt him kiss the top of her hat and her tears fell in torrents.

'Hush, dearest,' Julian said, drying her cheeks with his fingers.

'There's more I wish to tell you,' Mawde said, looking at him through misty eyes. 'It's about my life in London.'

'No,' Julian said, raising his palm. 'I've no wish to hear it. The past is done, and we cannot change it, but we can avoid repeating mistakes – God knows we've both made plenty. That's why we understand each other, Mawde, and why we try to put other people's needs before attending to our own.' Julian shifted position and knelt on his good knee. He held Mawde's hand and raised it to his lips. 'My darling Mawde, you have captured my heart and I want you to be my wife.'

Mawde drew her gaze away and stared at the priory ruins. Something that had given sanctuary and hope now lay broken and turning to dust. Mawde loved Julian, of that she was certain. But what if he changed, like Nicholas?

Julian gave her a tender smile. 'It's a big question and I'll not rush you to answer. Take as long as you need.' He pushed himself to standing and looked back towards the village. 'I must return to the forge before my apprentice causes a disaster. Yesterday, he backed into the fire and a flame caught his breeches.'

Mawde smiled at the image of the youth smacking his own backside to put out the flames and sitting in a pail of water.

'That's better,' Julian said, taking her hand and helping her to her feet.

They walked back to St Mawes, their arms interlinked, while Mawde considered her feelings for Julian. They were not the fanciful romantic flushes that servant girls had discussed at Powderham. Her feelings were an intense affection and respect for someone who, like her, understood hardship and the consequences of poor choices.

Julian released her arm as they reached the edge of the village. 'I meant what I said, Mawde. Take as long as you need.'

Mawde watched him stride away with his limping gait. He stopped and turned to look at her before disappearing into the forge.

'Wait!' Mawde gathered her skirts in one hand and ran towards him. She flung her arms around his neck and smothered his face with kisses.

'Mawde!' Julian said with a chuckle. 'Everyone can see.'

'Let them,' she said, kissing him again. 'Soon we'll be man and wife!'

# CHAPTER FORTY-EIGHT

MAWDE OPENED her bedchamber window and took deep breaths of sweet clean air. It was a perfect August morning and a beautiful day for a wedding. Herring gulls soared through the air, gliding and circling beneath an azure blue sky. Wood pigeons cooed from high in the trees and a glossy black chough strutted about, pecking the ground with its orange beak. A delicate breeze carried the sound of waves lapping at the shore and the faint buzzing of a bee on an early morning forage for nectar. Mawde pictured the creature covering itself in pollen, drifting from late pink sea thrift to bright white oxeye daisies.

'You look beautiful, my dear,' Mamm said, coming up behind her. 'Agnes has made a wonderful job of embroidering those sleeves.'

Mawde traced her finger over the neat stitches. Honeysuckle trailed from the shoulder, interspersed with butterflies and bees. Mawde's sky-blue robe draped elegantly over her dove-grey kirtle, and she wore a lace-edged partlet that Mamm had bought for her.

'We should start walking,' Mamm said, taking Mawde's hand. 'You don't want to be rushing or you'll overheat.'

Mawde took a deep breath and linked her arm through Mamm's. Her pulse thundered in her ears, and she feared her heart might burst.

'Mamm?' Mawde's voice wavered. 'Am I doing the right thing by marrying Julian?'

Mamm patted her hand. 'I have no doubts whatsoever. The people of the village love him, and his feelings for you are clear. Happiness has found you at last, my dear, and I am so delighted.'

Mawde pictured Julian waiting for her at the church. Even the thought of him brought a joy she could not put into words.

Agnes was at the foot of the staircase and beamed at Mawde as she descended. 'These are for you,' she said, handing Mawde a neatly tied posy of pink stonecrop flowers interspersed with white campion.

'And this too,' Beth said, stepping forward to fix a bridal veil to Mawde's hair. Beth rested her hand on the swell of her advanced pregnancy. 'This veil has brought happiness to my marriage to Henry. I pray it brings the same good fortune to you and Julian, too.'

'Thank you, dear Beth,' Mawde kissed her friend's cheek. She knew Beth still missed Nicholas, so her blessing warmed Mawde's heart.

'Nicholas is at peace now,' Beth said, as if she had read Mawde's mind. 'He would want you to be happy.'

'Come,' Mamm said, stopping further conversation. 'No more dilly-dallying. It's time to walk to the church.'

When Mawde stepped into the cool shade of the court-yard, Perry approached and bowed. 'Follow me, my lady,' he said, looking smart in his doublet and hose.

Perry led them through the gate and into the lane towards the village.

'Perry, this is the wrong way,' Mawde cried. 'The wedding's at St Just Church!'

'Indeed it is,' Perry replied. 'But you must come this way if you're to arrive on time.'

Mamm took Mawde's arm in hers and patted her on the hand. 'Humour him. I sense you're in for a surprise.'

When they reached the centre of the village, a crowd greeted them in the square. They clapped and cheered as Mawde approached and parted to flank her route. Perry stopped and stepped aside when he reached two horses harnessed to a carriage. He held out his hand to help Mawde step up to her seat. Mamm was next and settled beside her. Agnes and Beth sat opposite. A groom encouraged the horses to move forward, and Perry walked behind the carriage.

Mawde twisted in her seat. 'Perry, thank you for this!'

Perry raised both of his palms. 'Alas, it is not of my doing. Your husband-to-be persuaded Sir Hugh to lend you this carriage.'

'Sir Hugh?'

Perry smiled. 'Indeed.'

The distant sound of pealing bells welcomed them to St Just. The horse and carriage progressed slowly down a steep hill towards the old church. People from St Mawes and St Just had gathered to see the bride and clapped and cheered when Mawde stepped down into their midst.

Julian was standing in the church porch and looked resplendent in a formal gown. He looked more like a gentleman than Nicholas ever had. His shirt was bright white and his doublet embroidered with a pattern that matched Mawde's sleeves. His eyes sparkled when he looked at Mawde and he gave her a loving smile.

Beth and Agnes had decorated the church porch with greenery and flowers. Mawde could smell the light perfumes of lavender and wild rose.

Rector Tregate took his place in front of them and called everyone to silence. He looked from Julian to Mawde and began the wedding service.

'Dearly beloved, we are gathered together here in the sight of God to join together this Man and this Woman in holy Matrimony; which is an honourable estate, instituted of God in Paradise, and into which holy estate these two persons present come now to be joined.' The rector looked beyond Mawde and Julian to the family, friends and villagers jostling for a view behind them. 'If any man can show any just cause why they may not lawfully be joined together, let him now speak, or else hereafter forever hold his peace.'

Mawde could not resist a furtive glance over her shoulder, hoping no one would speak out against her. The rector's brief pause felt like a minute, and Mawde held her breath until he spoke again.

Julian placed a gold wedding band and a sovereign on the rector's Bible. The ring gleamed in a ray of sunlight and Mawde fancied it was God's way of showing approval for her marriage. The rector sprinkled the ring with holy water and gave it back to Julian.

Julian held Mawde's hand and spoke with a confident voice. 'With this ring I thee wed, this gold and silver I thee give, and with my body I thee worship, and with all my worldly goods I thee endow.' He touched Mawde's thumb with the ring. '*In nominee Patris*.' He moved the ring to her forefinger. '*Et Filii*,' and then, touching her middle finger, he said, '*et Spiritus sancti*.' He placed the ring on her fourth finger. 'Amen.'

The rector blessed the newlyweds and led them and the

congregation inside the church. The congregation settled on the pews to celebrate the wedding mass.

The joyful pealing of church bells announced the end of the service.

'I declare I'm the happiest woman alive,' Mawde said, standing on tiptoe to kiss Julian on the lips.

Mawde insisted Mamm, Beth and Agnes join her and Julian in the carriage to return to St Mawes. By the time they reached home, Clare, Jenet and the baker's wife had moved the hall trestle table outside and covered it with roasted geese and capons, fragrant breads and preserved fruits. Smaller trestle tables dotted the courtyard with fresh meat pies and platters laden with slices of ham, pickled vegetables and cheese. At the centre of the courtyard, there was a small table supporting a pyramid of saffron cakes, each one bursting with succulent fruit and smelling of subtle fragrant spices.

'My gift to you,' the baker's wife said, beaming. 'And me 'usband's too.'

The landlord of *The Dolphin* arrived with a cartload of barrels of ale. The next hour passed with joyful chatter, feasting and drinking. Mawde revelled in the attention of the villagers as they took turns to offer their good wishes.

'It took us a while to realise what you've done for all of us,' said the cordwainer's wife. 'We see it now, and we want you to know we're grateful.'

The baker struck up a tune on his fiddle and the court-yard was cleared for an afternoon of dancing to many a merry jig.

As dusk fell, the rector arrived to bless the marital bed.

Mawde's face dropped when she saw him, and she drew Mamm aside. 'I hate the thought of consummating this marriage in the bed I shared with Nicholas.'

Mamm stroked Mawde's cheek. 'Try not to think of him, today of all days.' She waved to Perry, and he hurried across to join them. To everyone, she announced, 'The time has come to take Mawde and Julian to their bedchamber.'

Mawde felt her colour rise.

'Follow me.' Perry marched indoors, leading the procession to the main bedchamber upstairs.

Mawde gasped when she saw the bed. The old bedstead had been taken away and replaced with a four-poster hung with sumptuous green and grey drapes. 'This bed is too grand for us,' Mawde declared, admiring the carvings of leaves and birds on the posts.

'Nonsense,' Mamm replied. 'Lady Trevanion is refurbishing her guest rooms. When she heard about the plans for your wedding, she offered this as a gift.'

Mamm dismissed everyone from the bedchamber except Beth and Agnes. They helped Mawde out of her wedding attire and dressed her in a lace-trimmed chemise. After Mawde settled beneath the coverlet, Mamm called for the men to return. Henry said something that made Julian laugh as he climbed in next to Mawde.

Beth pulled the drapes around the bed and ushered everyone from the room. Julian rolled towards Mawde and drew her into his arms. When Julian lifted the skirt of her chemise, she did the same with his nightshirt. She held her breath in anticipation of their first intimate touch. Julian eased her onto her back and soon they were moving as one.

Afterwards, Mawde lay on her back and stared up at the canopy. Their coupling had been passionate yet tender and full of love. She smiled. At last, she had married a man who loved and respected her. She turned her head expecting to see Julian sleeping, but his eyes were wide open and he was watching her. She rolled towards him and ran her hand over his arm and then his chest. She held his gaze while her hand crept lower. Soon, he was inside her again.

# CHAPTER FORTY-NINE

Beyond the kitchen windows, thick clouds dulled the autumn light. A gust shook the window casements and raindrops pounded the glass. The kitchen door flew open and banged against the wall as Agnes stumbled in from the courtyard.

Mawde pushed the door closed against the resistance of the wind. 'Agnes, you're soaking wet,' she said, watching water drip from her cloak and puddle on the floor. 'Dry yourself by the fire.'

'There's no time,' Agnes said, wheezing and clutching her chest. 'We need Mamm at the farm. Beth's gone into labour.'

Mamm entered the kitchen with her winter cloak in her hands. 'I saw you running along the lane,' she said. 'Is Beth losing a lot of blood?'

Agnes shook her head.

'How long has she been labouring?'

'An hour. Two, at most.'

Mamm wrapped her cape around her. 'Then there's no need to panic.'

'Shall I come too?' Mawde asked.

'No.' Mamm nodded towards the kitchen table, where Mawde was butchering pieces of pork. 'Best not leave that lying around. You carry on and salt it. I'll send for you if we need help.'

'I'll take you to the farm,' Julian said. He donned his favourite cape and a wide-brimmed hat and went outside to prepare his horse and cart.

Mawde watched them depart with her hands resting on her belly. Fortunately, God had blessed her with a husband content to live without children. She turned her attention back to the pork. *I'm probably too old now, anyway.*

Late in the afternoon, Julian returned in a state of excitement.

'What is that smell?' Mawde asked, wrinkling her nose as he passed. 'And what have you done to your cape?'

Julian grinned. 'A fisherman told me to coat it with tar. Said it would keep out wind and rain. Turns out he was right.' He kissed Mawde on her cheek and wafted the cape to make her laugh. 'I've just delivered another of Treffry's orders of cannonballs, knives and swords.' He pulled a purse from inside his jerkin and jangled it in front of Mawde. 'Today's a good payday for us, and not only because of this.'

Mawde raised her eyebrows. 'Tell me more.'

'I will, but first, I need a drink.' He poured himself a cup of small beer and drank it in a few gulps. 'The King's raising an army again,' he said, refilling his cup. 'He's sending soldiers to France. He's ordered Treffry to muster men and send them to Portsmouth immediately.'

'How does that benefit us?'

'Treffry let slip that his men are resisting. He's spent so long at the castle here that he's neglected his businesses and lands. He hasn't paid his men their wages for three or four months, so they're refusing to leave Fowey until they get their money.'

Mawde placed pieces of pork into a barrel. She scooped salt from a large sack and packed it around the meat with her hands. 'Do you think he'll come here demanding our rent even though we're not in arrears.'

'No. He's not hard up for coins, but he is in danger of incurring the King's displeasure, and we both know what that might mean.' Julian mimed a noose around his neck.

Mawde shuddered. 'Don't do that.'

'Forgive me.' Julian turned serious. 'Treffry needs to remedy the situation as soon as he's able, so he's setting sail for Fowey tonight. He was raging when I turned up, and moaning to his steward that the only ship available has an inexperienced captain.' He glanced towards the window, where raindrops were running in rivulets. 'The poor fellow tried to turn him down and declared a storm is brewing, but Treffry promised an extra payment and changed the captain's mind.'

'Treffry won't wait just one night and wait for the storm to pass?'

'It would seem not. He needs to placate his men and return here tomorrow. He has a merchant due to visit from Truro the day after tomorrow. He's offering Treffry the investment of a lifetime, but that ship sails three days from now. Treffry doesn't want to miss his chance but he risks losing everything if he disobeys the King and so he sails tonight.'

Mawde dropped the salt scoop and wiped her hands on her apron. She sat at the table and looked at Julian. 'Will Treffry's ship be carrying money?'

'I'm sure of it.' Julian settled opposite her. 'It's likely he'll have chests holding more coins and gold than most people see in a lifetime.'

Mawde looked through the window at the darkening sky. 'Tonight there will be a full moon.'

'But if the heavy rain persists, clouds will block the light.'

Mawde placed her elbows on the table and interlocked her fingers. 'We have a good income from your earnings, and the farm profits pay Treffry's rent. We have a proportion of the fire dues and my share of the spinners' earnings. The prior's gold won't last long, especially after winter sets in. A significant sum of money would enable us to secure everyone's future in the village.'

'That's right,' Julian said, 'And an opportunity like this one might not come again.'

Mawde rested her forehead on her knuckles. 'Mamm isn't here. Agnes lives on the farm. Perry is tending St Anthony's fire. They'd have no knowledge of what we'd be doing, but what about the watchmen at the castle?'

'They're unlikely to pay us any heed if we go sooner rather than later.' Julian paused. 'If we're going to do this, we should leave before it gets too dangerous.'

Mawde felt a frisson of fear. Was the plan too foolish? Was it worth the risks? 'I'd have enough money to buy the boatyard,' she mused. 'Old Man Ferrers can help me build it up and together we'll reclaim the reputation he once had. He could refurbish the *Mistress of Carrick* and then build more boats so we can grow our fishing fleet.'

'I could build a larger forge,' Julian said, 'and take on two or three apprentices.'

'It's only fair that we benefit too,' Mawde said, 'because we'd be taking the risks. But we would use the money wisely and employ local men and women.' Her thoughts raced as she imagined the possibilities. 'We'd have to proceed slowly though, or people would wonder how we came by the money.'

Julian drummed his palms on the table. 'So, what do you say? Shall we take Treffry's ship? I can make sure his money chests go missing, and I'm sure we'll receive a generous reward for any cargo we rescue for him.'

Mawde considered it for a long moment. 'Yes,' she said, suppressing her doubts. 'We'll do it for the village.'

# CHAPTER FIFTY

THE DAYLIGHT FADED FAST. Gusts of wind lifted roof tiles and rattled them like loose teeth. Mawde pulled on a pair of breeches that had belonged to Nicholas. She checked herself in the mirror and frowned. It would look suspicious for a woman in breeches to appear by a shipwreck. 'But they'll keep me warm,' she said, pulling a kirtle over her head.

The wind whipped at Mawde's skirts and tangled them around her legs. She scurried along the path to the beach, struggling to match Julian's pace.

'It'll be a rough crossing,' Julian shouted against the roar of the wind.

'Do you think the ship will sail?' Mawde yelled as she clambered into a rowing boat.

Julian nodded. 'At high tide. Treffry was desperate.'

Julian rowed to the *Mistress of Carrick* and helped Mawde clamber aboard. 'What's your excuse for being on the wrong side of the water if this goes according to plan?'

'What wreck survivor would ask such a question?' Mawde pulled the hood of her oiled cape over her forehead to shield her face from the rain. 'I'll say I was in the woods gathering rosehips and penny buns when I grew disoriented because of the storm. I'll say a took the wrong path and missed the ferry back to St Mawes.'

Julian pursed his lips. 'I suppose that's just about credible.'

Mawde felt Julian's concern radiating from him. 'What excuse will you give?'

'That's easy.' Julian grinned. 'I'll say I went looking for you. Stay low now, in case anyone sees the boat. They can't know you're aboard.'

As they made their way towards the opposite shore, waves crashed over the hull. Mawde crouched low against the bulwark and hugged her knees to her chest. Despite her layers of clothes, her bones ached with cold. The boat rocked and shuddered, tossed on jagged waves. It rolled steeply to one side and Mawde slid across the deck. Her back struck something hard, and she cried out with pain. She was about to ask Julian to head back towards home when they grounded on a beach.

'It's high tide, Mawde. Now is our chance to back out. Otherwise, the boat will be stranded until the beach floods again.'

Doubts gripped Mawde's mind and tightened around her chest. The sky was quickly turning black and her skirts were wet and heavy. But they would probably never get the same opportunity again. 'We stay,' she shouted to Julian.

Julian dropped the anchor and threw a rope onto the beach. He lowered himself into the shallows and instructed Mawde to do the same. She stared at the black, glistening water and wished she had oiled her boots.

'Climb over the side like I did. I'll catch you and carry you to dry land.'

With grim determination, Mawde did as she was told.

Julian's limp grew more pronounced while he carried her onto the shore.

'We'll need to hurry through the woods,' Mawde said, as he set her on her feet. 'There's a thin sliver of moon to guide us but I don't think it will be there long.'

Mawde hunched forward into the wind, dodging branches and young trees. Mud squelched beneath her feet and she slipped several times. At last, they cleared the tree line and reached the hut near St Anthony's Head.

The shadowy interior smelled musty and damp. A thin ray of moonlight slipped through the roof where a section had collapsed. The pale grey light illuminated a moss-covered wall and a tinderbox on a rickety shelf.

Julian built a small pile of kindling in the middle of the floor while Mawde tried to coax a spark. After a few failed attempts, a thin flame curled up from the wood and the rest of the kindling caught. The light from the fire revealed a log pile in one corner with wood dry enough to burn. Mawde placed two logs over the burning kindling and warmed her hands near the flames. 'This would be romantic if not for the storm raging outside,' she said.

'An idea for another time.' Julian threw another log onto the fire. 'I'll leave you here to dry off while I light another fire.'

Mawde shook her head. 'I'll persuade Perry to let St Anthony's fire go out.'

'I'll do that.'

'No, Julian. I will do it.'

They left the hut together and went their separate ways. Mawde could see the glow of St Anthony's fire and followed a well-worn path towards it.

'Mistress?' Perry's face was pale with shock when Mawde joined him by the fire. 'What are you doing here?'

Not wanting to lie to Perry, Mawde ignored his question. 'No assistant here with you tonight?'

'No, though I sorely need one. I cannot keep the flame alight. I need to fetch dry wood.'

*This is my chance*, Mawde thought. 'Tell me what I need to do while you fetch more logs.'

Perry hesitated.

'Well?'

'Stand where I am now to keep the wind off the fire. I'll return as fast as I can.'

Mawde watched Perry scuttle away and disappear into the gloom. The fire was struggling to take hold with small, flickering flames. Mawde stepped away from the fire to let it take the full brunt of the wind. The rain dampened the feeble flames and sent up acrid smoke. The wind gathered strength and the rain fell in torrents. Mawde trampled on the embers of the fire until they no longer glowed. She knelt on the muddy ground and prayed for God's mercy for her part in making the fire go out.

Perry returned empty-handed. 'It's no good,' he shouted. 'The storm blew the wood store door open. All the logs inside are wet. We'll have to hope the rain eases soon so I can try again to light the fire. Pray God, no ships sail tonight.'

'We'll catch our deaths out here,' Mawde yelled above the gale. 'We should retreat to the workman's hut. There's a low fire burning there, and a small log pile to keep it going.'

Mawde and Perry linked arms as they made their way to the hut, the blustering gale billowing Mawde's skirts and almost lifting her off the ground. After securing the door against the storm, Mawde settled close to the fire. The wind howled and shrieked outside and blasted draughts through the cracks. Mawde watched the flickering flames while fretting about Julian. Had he tumbled on the rocks? Had the waves swept him out to sea? When Perry started to mumble a prayer, Mawde trembled with cold and fear. The terrible risks of her foolhardy mission struck like a blow to her chest. Another poor choice, albeit with good intention, was risking the life of someone she loved.

A different sound carried in the wind. Mawde strained her ears to listen.

'Perry! Do you hear that?' Her throat turned dry. Her heart thumped against her ribs. 'Someone's shouting outside.' Mawde fastened her cloak and ventured out of the hut. A gust of wind almost knocked her off her feet. She grasped the door frame to keep herself upright. The rain had eased and the clouds had parted to uncover a bright full moon. Puddles glinted in the swathes of light falling towards the ground.

More shouts carried on the wind.

'That sounds like Julian,' Perry said. He sprinted towards the tree line.

Mawde followed him into the wood, colliding with low branches and stumbling over roots. Waves smashed against the rocks, thickening the air with sea spray.

Perry came to an abrupt stop and pressed his fist to his mouth. 'Dear Lord, no!'

Mawde followed his gaze and saw a ship foundering on the rocks.

Perry grasped her arm. 'Was your husband on that ship?'

Mawde shook her head.

'So why is he down there now?'

A large fire blazed in a small cave sheltered from the wind. The light from the flames and the moon above illuminated a shipwreck. Mawde made out Julian's form waving from the rocks. 'Hurry!' he shouted. 'Come down to the beach!'

Perry climbed down a bank of rock. Mawde scrambled down after him and stumbled at the bottom. She felt Perry's hand grasp her forearm but she shook him off and shooed him away to go to Julian's aid.

'Light and a rope!' Julian bellowed as he scrambled towards the water. Mawde found two coiled ropes near the fire and a pile of dry branches. She slung a coiled rope over her arm and buckled under its weight. She plunged a branch into the fire, then used it as a torch to guide her across the rocks. She passed the rope to Perry, then held the torch above her head. Julian was lying on a rock, trying to pull something from the waves. She glimpsed the pale face of a man, then his head disappeared beneath the water. Julian had a firm grasp on his wrists and dragged him onto the rocks. The man spluttered and coughed. Mawde heard him gasp for breath. Perry took the man's arm and helped him climb towards Mawde. The man offered Perry profuse words of thanks. Mawde froze. It was Captain Treffry.

'What in God's name—?'

'No time to explain,' Mawde said, gathering her wits. 'Come to the fire and warm yourself.'

Treffry leaned heavily on Mawde's shoulder as he limped up the beach. She settled him on a rocky ledge and gave him her cape. 'Put this on,' she said, before lighting another torch and hurrying back to Julian and Perry.

Julian had tied one end of the rope around his waist. Perry was securing the other end to a tree.

'Julian!' Mawde cried. 'Be careful.'

She held her breath as he lowered himself into the sea and disappeared from view. She gasped with relief when she saw him again, swimming against roiling waves to reach the side of the wreckage. Someone lowered a rope ladder over the side and Julian climbed onto the deck.

Mawde felt a firm hand grasp her elbow. 'Go to Treffry and attend to his injuries as best you can.' Perry took the flaming branch from her. 'I'll help Julian rescue the crew.'

'What about the cargo?' Mawde said, watching a crate crash against a rock.

Perry gave her an odd look. 'Let's not worry about that now. We should attend to the crew instead.'

Mawde sat with Treffry and watched the rescue unfold. Two sailors made it ashore unscathed, then helped Julian and Perry. Progress was slow, but the tide was ebbing, making it easier to access the ship.

'Praise the lord, you've all been spared,' Mawde said, turning to look at Treffry. He placed his palm on the top of his head and grimaced when he pressed. His clothes were ripped and his arm was bleeding from several nasty gashes. Mawde turned away from him to rip strips from her petticoat, hoping he would not see her breeches.

'That should do until I can dress it properly,' she said, after binding the wounds on his arm and another on his leg.

'Indeed,' Treffry replied with an ugly scowl that made Mawde's blood run cold. 'So, tell me, Mistress Sherman, why are you here?'

'Mistress Viker,' Mawde corrected him while trying not to shrivel beneath his stare. 'I was gathering rosehips and mushrooms and missed the last ferry. It must have stopped early because of the storm.' Even to her ears, it sounded like a far-fetched explanation.

'And your husband?'

Mawde shook her head. 'I don't know. I presume he came to find me.'

Treffry harrumphed. 'That explains the fire.'

'What do you mean?'

He pointed at the flames flickering at the mouth of the cave. 'We thought that was St Anthony's fire, so sailed too close to the headland.' He shook his head. 'By the time we realised our mistake, we didn't stand a chance.'

They both fell silent and watched Julian help a crew member climb off the ship.

'I should go and help,' Mawde said, eager to leave Treffry. 'He might be injured.' As she made her way towards the rocks, she saw Perry easing himself along the rope that Julian had secured to the ship. *Someone must be badly hurt*, she thought. Suddenly, a loud crack split the night air. The ship broke into pieces, and the stern fell away. Mawde saw Julian standing on the edge of the wreckage holding the end of a rope. He was leaning forward, peering into the water as if preparing to jump.

'Julian, no!' Mawde's heart rose into her throat.

Julian leapt off the wreck and was consumed by the breakers. Mawde dropped to her knees and clasped a jagged peak of rock. As she stared at the roiling sea, regret engulfed her like a fog. 'It wasn't supposed to be like this,' she murmured. 'Don't let my husband drown.' At last, Julian reappeared. He was swimming on his back and trying to drag a man with him. Perry heaved the man onto the wreckage and then reached down for Julian. Mawde breathed again.

Two uninjured sailors were piling cargo crates on the beach. Another was half-dragging himself across the rocks, unable to take his weight through one of his legs. Mawde moved forward to help him, but her boot slipped on slick wet weed. She tumbled backwards and struck her hip, her back and her head. A searing pain passed through her skull. Everything turned grey. The howling wind faded and then... nothing.

# CHAPTER FIFTY-ONE

IT WAS the smell of smoke that roused her, and the cracks, pops and shifting of wood as it collapsed among the flames. Fire! Mawde tried to sit up and open her eyes, but a sharp pain passed from her head, through her spine and into her legs. She tried to speak, but her throat was dry, and she coughed and choked instead. Her head pounded for several seconds afterwards, as if she'd been hit with a club.

'Help me!' she croaked at last.

'Lord be praised, you've come back to us.'

'Mamm?'

There was a rustle of skirts, the patter of footsteps, and the sound of water being wrung from a cloth. Something cool covered Mawde's forehead. Then she heard Mamm's voice.

'Why did you go foraging when you knew a storm was brewing? And whatever possessed you to try to reach the wreck? Now you have a fever for your trouble and a lump on your head! Your back is black and blue, and as for your ankle... it's three times its normal size!'

Mawde forced her eyelids open. She was lying in her bed. She tried to recall what had happened, but no memories would come.

Mamm fussed around her, rinsing out the facecloth and adjusting the bedcovers. 'You should have a drink,' she said, picking up a spoon and cup.

The cool liquid soaked into Mawde's tongue like water into a sponge. Her mind started clearing. Mamm should be at the farm. Agnes had come for her, gasping and wheezing. Mawde grasped her mother's hand. 'Beth?'

Mamm smiled. 'Safely delivered of another baby girl. Two days old, already!'

'Two days?' Mawde shook her head and grimaced with pain.

Mamm's smile evaporated. 'You had us all worried, Mawde. In all that time, you've barely moved. I wanted to send for the rector, but Julian said no. He was adamant you'd pull through.'

Julian. The mention of his name triggered a vague memory, but Mawde could not drag it to the forefront of her mind.

Mamm sat on a stool and rested her forearms on the bed. 'It was a fearsome storm. It took chunks out of houses and toppled countless trees. Thank God there was a brief lull while you were on that beach, otherwise there's no telling what might have happened to you.' Mamm wiped a tear from her cheek. 'I thought I was going to lose you.'

A storm. The fog in Mawde's mind cleared. A shipwreck on the rocks. She shivered.

'Are you cold, my dear? There is a dreadful draught.' Mamm bustled across the room and fiddled with the window catches. 'This one isn't shutting properly. I'll ask Julian to fix it.' She turned to look at Mawde. 'He's been sick with worry. I should tell him you're awake.'

When Julian entered the bedchamber, his eyes were glistening. 'You were out cold,' he said, smothering Mawde's hand with kisses. 'Even Treffry was worried.'

'Julian, will you help me sit up?'

Julian hooked his arms under hers and lifted her into a sitting position. He plumped three cushions and piled them behind her, then eased her back against them.

Mawde was hurting everywhere. She waited for the pain to subside. 'The crew,' she said. 'Did they all survive?'

Julian lowered his head. 'They did. One sailor's leg was badly injured, but Treffry summoned a surgeon. The surgeon said the leg will never recover, but at least the fellow will live. Other than that, their injuries weren't too serious. Treffry has some nasty gashes, but none of them too deep.'

Mawde closed her eyes. 'Thank God.' She opened them again and shook her head. 'What were we thinking, Julian? To take such risks for the sake of coins?'

'I know.' Julian intertwined his fingers with hers. 'The uninjured sailors helped me salvage the cargo. Between us, we did well. It included three crates of pewter Treffry was sending to Fowey. I hid one below the deck-boards on the *Mistress of Carrick* and returned the other two to Treffry, much to his delight.' Julian tightened his grasp on her fingers. 'He rewarded us handsomely for saving him.' Julian released Mawde's hand and went to the clothes press. He lifted out a large coffer and carried it back to the bed. 'Treffry hit his head on the mast when his ship struck the rocks. He was out cold, face down in the water when I found him. He knows he would have drowned if I'd not risked my life to help him.' Julian opened the coffer and pulled out a leather pouch. 'Look at this, my love.' He tipped the contents onto the bed – shillings, angels and sovereigns. 'These are all the coins you gave him whenever

you paid the rent. He gave them back as our reward.'
Julian placed the coffer on the bed. 'I also salvaged this.'

Mawde stared wide-eyed at the contents of the coffer.
It was almost full of sovereigns.

'It's a lot of money, Mawde. More than I had hoped.'

Mawde saw tears gathering in Julian's eyes. She stroked
the side of his face and heard him catch a sob.

'Why are you so sad? We have come out well from this,
and everyone survived.'

Julian pinched his lips together.

'Julian?' Mawde's voice had turned shrill. 'You told me
yourself that none of the sailors died.'

Julian's tears streamed down his cheeks and dripped
onto the coins. 'It's blood money,' Julian whispered. 'I'm so
sorry, Mawde.'

'What do you mean, blood money?' Mawde noticed
violet shadows hanging beneath his eyes. While she had
slept for two whole days, Julian had not slept at all. 'Tell
me,' she insisted.

Julian's bottom lip quivered. 'Perry.' His face worked
through several expressions of disbelief, anger and
remorse. 'It breaks my heart to tell you that Perry didn't
survive.'

'But I saw him standing beside you! He was with you
on the wreck.'

'Perry lost his footing climbing down to the rocks.'
Julian's Adam's apple wobbled as if he was choking on his
words. 'He fell into the water, and I couldn't see him,
Mawde! I went in after him, but by the time I reached
him…' Julian buried his face in his hands. His body
convulsed with sobs.

Mawde felt a pain in her chest as if her heart had
ripped to shreds. She had made a poor decision again, and
dear, sweet Perry was dead.

# CHAPTER FIFTY-TWO

FOR TWO WEEKS, Mawde stayed in her bedchamber. Her nights were disturbed by nightmares, her days were consumed by grief. Voices shouted in her mind: her father, her cousin, her grandmother, and Queen Anne Boleyn. The only voice she didn't hear was the one which should chide her most. Kind, gentle, loyal Perry. Mawde had made him an unwitting participant and traded his life for coins.

Despite her stubborn silence, Julian sat with her hour after hour. He bathed her face with soft damp linen and held her while she slept. He tried to tempt her appetite with tiny chunks of cheese, sips of fragrant pottage and bread dipped in sweet plum jam. But Mawde refused everything.

One bright November morning, Mawde eased herself off the bed and hobbled to the window. The sun shone like polished steel from behind fractured clouds. The wind had dropped. The sea had calmed, and the estuary was crowded with fishing boats, ships and skiffs. Mawde stared towards the opposite coast and followed it towards St

Anthony's Point. Somewhere out there, hidden by a kink in the coastline, was where Treffry's ship had wrecked, and where Perry had drowned. The weight of guilt pressed down hard and Mawde collapsed to the bedchamber floor. Great sobs wracked her body, and she cried until her tears ran dry. Exhausted, she lay on the rush mats and drifted into a troubled sleep.

'You'll starve to death if you don't eat something.'

'Tamsin?' Mawde opened her eyes to see her cousin offering her a biscuit. 'It wouldn't be a bad thing if I died.' Mawde waved away the offering. She'd had the same conversation with Tamsin many years ago, after her beloved father's fatal accident, for which Mawde still blamed herself. 'I'll be with Da soon,' she said. 'And you and baby John.'

'Don't say that, Mawde. Imagine your ma's distress if you were to pass.'

'She'd be better off without me. So would Julian. Grandmother was right when she said I was cursed.'

'You know as well as I do, Mawde, that's so far from the truth.' Tamsin smiled. 'I know you care about other people and want to help them with their plight. Trouble is, sometimes you try too hard, and that's when you make a poor choice. You'll work it out. I know you will.'

Tamsin's outline faded as if she was drifting away.

'Don't go!' Mawde reached for Tamsin's hand, but all she caught was air.

Mawde felt a pressure on her upper arm. 'Come now, sweeting, you can't stay there.' Julian scooped Mawde up in his arms and lowered her onto the bed. 'You're turning delirious, and I'll wager it's from starvation.'

Mawde looked around the room. 'Tamsin was here.'

Julian kissed the top of her head. 'Tamsin's been gone a long time.'

'I know.' Mawde felt wretched. 'That's also my fault.'

Julian sat beside her and held both her hands. 'No, Mawde. You didn't start the fire, and from what I've heard, even if you had raised the alarm, it was already too late for Tamsin.'

'I wish I could believe that.' Mawde started weeping. 'I'm sorry, Julian. I'm sorry for making you risk your life too.'

'I could have refused.' Julian leaned forward and embraced her. 'We're both guilty, Mawde. I set the fire that lured the ship to the rocks, so Perry's blood is on my hands.' Mawde felt his body twitch and knew he was weeping too.

Julian released her and sat up straight. He dried his tears with his sleeves and took a few deep breaths. 'You cannot let this setback stop you from achieving your plan. Perry would want you to see it through.'

'You're right.' Another wave of sadness engulfed Mawde but she bit back her tears. 'Perry never pitied himself. Not even when the priory closed. He faced every adversity with courage, and from now on, I will do the same.'

'That's the spirit,' Julian said, rising to his feet. 'And I will too.'

Mawde tried to collect her thoughts. 'Julian, what will we do about St Anthony's fire now Perry's no longer here?'

'I already have it in hand. A surprising number of men came forward and offered to take turns. They'll each cover one shift per month. I said we'd pay them from the dues.'

'Thank you. I don't want to see another shipwreck for as long as I live.' Mawde eased herself out of the chair. She removed her sweat-soaked night chemise and rubbed her skin with a clean, coarse cloth. 'Julian, will you ask Clare to bring up a fresh bowl of water?' Mawde wrinkled her nose. 'It's time I had a wash.'

Mawde felt refreshed after washing and dressing. Julian helped her walk down the stairs. She felt lightheaded moving about and asked for a bowl of broth and a small piece of bread. Feeling much better after something to eat, Mawde thought about her home. It was large and austere, with echoes of Nicholas, and not what she wanted at all.

A few days later, Mawde announced to Julian that she was going to see Captain Treffry.

'Shall I go with you?' Julian offered.

Mawde shook her head. She wrapped herself in a thick woollen cloak and pulled the hood over her coif. 'There's something I wish to discuss with him, and I'd rather do so alone.'

Treffry was in the guardhouse and greeted Mawde with a smile. He escorted her to his office and softly closed the door.

'Thank the Lord for mushrooms!' Treffry said, dragging a chair towards the fire.

A breath hitched in Mawde's throat. 'Mushrooms?'

'Yes, mushrooms! If not for you foraging in a storm, your husband would not have searched for you, and I would have perished in the shipwreck.'

Guilt pricked at Mawde's conscience as she settled on a chair. 'Are you fully recovered?'

Treffry sat at his desk and touched the top of his head. 'It's still a little tender there, and my arm is very sore, but I should not complain because at least I didn't drown.' His face dropped. 'I'm sorry about Perry's passing. He was a likeable fellow.'

Mawde pinched her lips together. She still couldn't hear Perry's name without shedding tears.

Treffry rested his forearms on the desk. 'What brings you here today?'

'I wanted to thank you for our reward. It was a generous sum of money.'

Treffry leaned towards her. 'My dear, your husband risked his life. And...' He sighed and looked away.

'I hear King Henry wants your men to fight in France?' Mawde said, eager to change the subject.

Treffry nodded. 'Alas, that is true.'

'Including men from this castle?'

'Unfortunately, yes.'

'So, now is a perfect opportunity to employ local men from the village.'

An amused smile played on Treffry's lips. 'You don't give up, do you?'

'It would help a few families.'

'Mistress Sherman, I—'

'Mistress Viker.'

'Of course, I keep forgetting.' Treffry reddened. 'An unforgivable mistake after your husband saved my life.'

'Yes, he did, didn't he?' Mawde said, warming to her cause.

Treffry fixed his gaze on her. 'Mistress Viker, you have a determination that is lacking in many men.' He raised his hands in a gesture of defeat. 'I concede to your demand.'

Mawde permitted herself to smile. 'You will? They're already accomplished archers from practising at the butts. I believe you'll find the men reliable and eager to learn new skills.'

'I'll take your word for that.' Treffry rose from his seat to throw another log onto the fire. 'I fancy a glass of warm spiced wine. Can I offer you the same?'

'No, but thank you.' A draught trickled under the door and cooled around Mawde's ankles. 'Captain Treffry, it's freezing inside this castle and it's not yet the end of November. Do you intend to winter here, or will you return to your wife in Fowey?'

Treffry stoked the fire with a poker and drew a larger flame. 'Alas, I must remain here as captain of this fortress, while my wife prefers the warmth and comfort of our home in Fowey.'

'Would she like my house?'

'I'm sure she would, but she wouldn't want to impose.'

Mawde rubbed her palms on her skirt. 'I'm suggesting that you buy it.'

Treffry's lips twitched. 'Why would I buy a house for which you already pay me rent?'

Mawde pressed her thighs together to still the trembling in her legs. 'I pay rent for the land, not the fabric of the building. The house was built at Nicholas's expense. I intend to vacate it. If you have no desire for it, then I shall tear down the building and you'll have nothing but a field to rent – assuming you can find a tenant.'

'That's ridiculous!' Treffry scoffed. 'A waste of a good building. Why would you demolish it?'

Mawde held her composure while looking directly at Treffry. 'As the village blacksmith, my husband is used to making new metals from scraps of old. We would salvage anything useful, including bricks, beams and roof tiles. I would not lose the house entirely but rebuild somewhere else – the same way the priory stones built these castle walls.'

Treffry leaned back in his chair with an expression of amusement.

'If you buy the house,' Mawde continued, 'you'll own the building and the land, not to mention a home you can share with your wife. It would be convenient for you seeing as it's near the castle. Will you at least give the proposal some thought?'

'What about the farmland?' Treffry asked.

'I have no desire to continue renting that land,' Mawde said. 'But as it's my cousin who manages the crops, you should consider an arrangement with him.'

Mawde studied the expression on Treffry's face. He appeared to be mulling it over.

'I miss my wife's cheerful countenance,' he said at last. 'And the comfort of my bed.'

'So, the arrangement would suit us both!' Mawde stood and fastened her cloak. 'Having watched the priory crumble, it would be a pity to see another building razed to the ground. My house can be yours in exchange for £25.'

'£25!' Treffry snorted. 'Have you no sense of value?' He opened the door for Mawde and stepped aside for her to pass.

'Think about it,' Mawde said. 'I'll give you one week to decide.'

# CHAPTER FIFTY-THREE

Mawde gradually regained her strength over the following days, but found herself constantly on edge, hoping for news from Treffry.

On the sixth day, Julian arrived home for dinner with an announcement that made her smile. 'Treffry's men left today, including the men from the castle. That means a few more local men will earn a decent wage.' He washed his hands and dried them before serving himself some beef stew. 'I have more good news,' he said between mouthfuls. 'I've taken on a new boy and he's keen to learn my trade. Simon's putting more effort in too, so I can take on more work.' Julian brandished his empty spoon at Mawde. 'Sweeting, you haven't touched your food. Are you feeling ill?'

'No, I'm not unwell.' Mawde dipped a crust of bread into her bowl of stew. The gravy smelled of onions and basil and made her mouth water.

Julian soon finished his and helped himself to more. 'I heard there's to be a new mill adjoining Henry's farm. The miller asked me to make the ironwork needed for the construction. And today I received an order for sconces for the village chapel and St Just Church.' He took a large swig of ale and raised his cup to Mawde. 'Fate is smiling upon us now, my love.'

'Agnes will welcome the news about the new mill,' Mamm said.

Mawde raised an eyebrow. 'Do I sense a proper courtship coming?'

Mamm smiled. 'I hope so.'

A loud knock at the door brought their conversation to a halt. Mawde caught her breath.

'I'll go,' Julian said, rising from his seat.

He returned with a letter in his hand. 'It's for you, Mawde,' he said, handing it over. 'Delivered by Treffry's steward.'

Mawde broke the seal and carefully read the contents. Her eyes settled on the offer of £22. She refolded the letter and beamed at Julian.

'Good news?' he said, returning to his seat.

'The best,' Mawde replied. 'I asked Treffry if he would buy this house, and he has written with an offer we should accept.' Mawde reached across the table and rested her palm over her mother's gnarled hand. 'Mamm, we can move back into the village. You won't have to walk so far, and we'll be closer to our neighbours.' Mawde reached for Julian with her other hand. 'And Julian, you'll be closer to the forge.'

'It'll be a relief for my poor old knees,' Mamm said. 'But where in the village will we live?'

'Don't worry about that, Mamm.' Mawde smiled at her mother and then her husband. 'I'll find our perfect home.'

❀

Mawde scoured the village for houses that might be empty, but every house was occupied, too small or run down.

'Found anything yet?' Julian asked, when she entered the forge with a basket of food for him to break his fast.

'Not yet.' Mawde cut a slice of cheese and passed it to Julian. 'There's a merchant's house that's empty but in a very poor state of repair. No one knows how to contact the owner. I'll have to ask Sir Hugh next time he comes to the manor.' She cut a piece of cheese for herself and savoured the saltiness on her tongue. 'I went to the boatyard,' she said. 'I spoke to Old Man Ferrers, and he agreed to let me invest. He wasn't keen to partner with a woman, but I persuaded him with my terms.'

'You're getting rather good at that,' Julian said, reaching into the basket for slices of dried apple.

'I am.' Mawde cleaned the blade of her knife and stowed it in its sheath. 'Ferrers agreed to employ four men who have carpentry skills. He said he can teach them to adapt their skills to repairing and building boats. He has a nephew who was a boatbuilder, but he left St Mawes to mine tin. We're going to ask if he'll come and run the boat-yard so that Ferrers can retire.' Mawde brushed crumbs from her lap. 'When word spreads that Ferrers' yard is building clinkers and skiffs again, I'm confident they'll be in demand, and we will all do well from it. There are plenty of merchants and investors with an eye for a decent boat.'

'How will you find these merchants?' Julian said. 'They've all left St Mawes.'

Mawde took a piece of apple for herself. 'I see them in Penryn. When I collect the fire dues, there are masters and captains there. More often than not, they moan about their boats, saying they're not built like they used to be. When the first skiff is finished and ready to leave the yard, I'll get someone to sail to Penryn and show off the quality and build. We'll make sure each boat's affordable to an investor with a modest purse. Then, when orders come in, the price to buy will rise.'

Julian gazed at Mawde with a look of wonder. 'My darling wife, where did you find that business mind?'

'I spent a long time observing Nicholas,' Mawde replied. 'His motivations were selfish, whereas I believe there's more to be gained from a balanced partnership.' Mawde rose from her stool and picked up her basket. 'My thoughts are whirling around far too fast. I'm worried I'll forget something important.' She kissed the top of Julian's head. 'I'll go home and pen my thoughts to paper. That way, I'll keep them straight.'

Julian stood and walked her to the door of the forge. 'I didn't take to Nicholas, but at least he was good for something.'

'What do you mean?'

'By leaving you widowed, he fired up your spirit. You *will* improve this village.'

Mawde stepped outside and gazed at what had once been the priory. 'I have to,' she whispered. 'I owe that much to Perry.'

Early the next morning, Mawde walked into the village and passed Julian's forge. She followed the bend in the road and stopped outside a large cottage. She turned to admire its view over the harbour, village and estuary. St Mawes Castle shimmered in the distance, its whitewashed walls glistening in the cool silvery sunlight. To Mawde's left was the bend of the coastline where it met the Percuil River.

Across the water, men were at work, turning the ruins of the priory into a grand new manor.

Mawde straightened her hat, adjusted her jacket and approached the cottage door. Her first knock went unanswered and so she knocked again.

A voice called out from somewhere inside, but the words were indistinct. A few moments later, the door opened.

'My dear, it's a pleasure to see you.' A hunched old woman stepped aside and beckoned for Mawde to enter.

Mawde stepped into a large room that spanned the width of the building. The furniture looked immaculate and smelled of beeswax and lavender. Half of the room served as a dining area, the other half as a parlour. Three walls had been whitewashed; the other was covered with a mural.

'May I?' Mawde asked, pointing to the wall. 'I'd love to have a closer look.'

'Please dear, be my guest. It's there to be admired.'

Mawde studied the details of the painting: every house in the village, the strip farms, the sea and the harbour. It was enclosed by a colourful border of different species of fish.

The woman jabbed her finger at the image of a field beside Mawde's house. 'I need someone talented to add the castle here. Only then will that section be complete.'

'It reminds me of how the village looked when I was a child,' Mawde said, picking out the field containing the ruins of her home. A lump rose in her throat. She moved towards another section of the mural. 'Tell me about the boats.'

The woman pointed to the largest boat depicted in the picture. 'This one was my father's. When he died, my husband took it over.' She pointed to another boat. 'This was the next one my husband acquired. He fished from dawn until midday and then worked every afternoon in the priory kitchen garden.' She had a faraway look in her eyes. 'My husband was a good man. He never shied away from work and saved hard for our future.' The woman pointed to the third boat. 'What do you see here?'

Mawde stepped closer to examine the boat. 'It's my *Mistress of Carrick*!'

'Aye, that it is. I sold her when my husband died, but her new owner lacked the vigour for a life of fishing. It's no wonder he fell into debt.'

'Old Man Ferrers is going to refurbish her for me. I'll soon have her fishing again. He said you still own your other two boats but might consider selling them.'

The old woman gave Mawde a sad smile. 'They're no good to me now. The men who used to fish for me now work at the castle, and I'm too old to find new skippers. I always thought my son would fish, but he abandoned nets for cannons. He left St Mawes to seek adventure and joined the King's navy. He's on a ship called *Mary Rose*. God willing, he'll survive any battles at sea and we'll see each other again.'

'Did you give all three of your boats names?'

'But of course! One is called *Marion*, after my husband's grandmother. The other is *Genevieve*.'

*Marion. Like Maid Marion and Robin Hood,* Mawde thought. 'Genevieve, after the French Saint?' she asked.

The woman shook her head. 'My name is Genevieve. It actually means 'white wave'. My husband thought it an appropriate name for a boat destined to fish in all weathers.'

Mawde's pulse quickened. 'Will you sell your boats to me?'

The woman turned towards the mural. 'That depends on what you would pay.'

'Will you accept fifteen sovereigns for both? I can give you the money today.'

When the woman turned back towards Mawde, her eyes looked hard and flinty. 'Fifteen sovereigns aren't enough. But I will accept twenty.'

'Your boats are decaying on a beach. I will pay you seventeen.'

'They're not decaying yet.' The woman's eyes softened again. 'I'll not try to push your offer higher. I accept they both need work.'

'Thank you,' Mawde said, handing over a leather purse containing the precise sum she had hoped to pay.

The woman took the purse and tied it to her belt. 'Now the boats are no longer my responsibility, I will join my sister in Tregony. She's a widow too now, and we'll enjoy each other's company.'

'Won't you persuade her to move in here with you?'

The old woman laughed. 'Goodness, no! Not only is my sister as stubborn as a mule, but she has four beautiful grandchildren. Nothing will drag her away from them.'

Mawde looked around the room. It was a reasonable size yet cosy. It was the type of house she had imagined might one day be her home. 'What will become of this cottage?'

The woman placed her palm on the wall. 'Many years ago, the lord of the manor granted this cottage as a gift to his long-serving steward. That steward was my grandfather. It will break my heart to leave this house, but the time has come for me to move away.'

'I would like to buy it.'

The woman considered Mawde. Her demeanour turned shrewd again.

'Thirty sovereigns.'

More than Treffry would pay for Mawde's larger house, although he already owned the land. 'I'm sorry,' Mawde said. 'I cannot pay that. It's much too large a sum.'

'Make me an offer.'

Mawde looked more closely at all four walls. The plaster had cracked in places and one wall was stained with damp. 'How many bedchambers?'

'Two, and space to add more rooms at the back if you are so inclined.'

Mawde stared at the mottled glass windows, uncertain how to proceed.

'Tell me, dear, what can you afford to pay?'

Mawde's spirits lifted. The woman was eager to sell.

'I used a hefty portion of my savings to buy your boats. It doesn't leave me with much.' It left her with plenty locked in her coffer, but she could not risk disclosing her wealth. 'I will offer you twenty sovereigns. That's more than I paid for your boats. The boats will earn back my investment whereas this house will not.'

'It's not enough,' the woman said.

'I understand.' Mawde smiled politely and thanked the woman for her time. After stepping outdoors, Mawde said, 'I wish you success with finding a buyer and I hope your move to Tregony goes well.'

Mawde was almost at the end of the path when the woman called out to her. 'Mistress Viker! I accept your offer.'

Mawde let out a gasp of joy. Butterflies danced her stomach.

'There's something you must do when this house becomes yours.'

'What's that?' Mawde asked, stepping back towards the woman.

'I know you're gifted with using your hands, and creative like your dear father. Whatever alterations you make to this house, promise you'll update the mural?'

Mawde smiled. 'I will.' She promised herself and the old woman it would be one of the first things she did.

# CHAPTER FIFTY-FOUR

THE RENOVATIONS STARTED IN WINTER. The damp wall, soft with rot, was demolished and rebuilt. The builders replastered every wall except for the one with the mural. They added a new wing to the rear of the house with a bedchamber, kitchen, storeroom and still room in it. Meanwhile, Mawde kept her promise to the old woman by adding the castle to the mural and altering the shape of her home.

Mawde had never slept so well as she did during those winter months. It was as if God had forgiven her sins and rewarded her commitment to the village. She had instilled a sense of confidence in every man and woman.

Sir Hugh had a flock of three hundred sheep when shearing time arrived. Mawde worked alongside the village women washing the fleeces, combing and carding. She bought more spinning wheels for the women and persuaded Sir Hugh to pay them for piecework.

Treffry was as good as his word and employed local men for his castle militia. Other men fished, farmed strips of land, or worked as carpenters and builders. Mawde was met with smiles wherever she went, and the people hailed her as the wise woman of the village.

The building work on Mawde's cottage finished in mid-July. The builders loaded their tools into a cart and Mawde settled her bill.

'What will you do now?' Mawde asked the man who had been in charge of her renovations.

'We've a merchant's house to rebuild.' He pointed towards a three-storey house crumbling near the quay. 'There's a fellow in Truro who owns that house and he's bought the one next door. Wants them knocked into one large house for him and his family to move into. Trades in cotton and silk, he does. Says he wants to live nearer his ships. It's what we need here, people with money, so let's hope more follow his example.'

Mawde bade him a farewell and hurried into her cottage. It would soon be noon and Julian would arrive with the first cartload of furniture. Mawde swept the floors and scrubbed the windows, removing every speck of dirt. As she emptied her pail of water and vinegar, she saw Julian leading his horse and cart. Cousin Henry followed behind with his largest horse-drawn wagon.

'Thought Julian might like an extra pair of hands,' Henry said, after helping Mamm down from the wagon. 'There's plenty of furniture to load and unload.'

By dusk, furniture filled the rooms and the cottage felt like home. From her windows, Mawde could see the house she had left behind and felt not a hint of sadness. The stone walls were cold and austere, and so characteristic of Nicholas.

Julian slipped his arms around her waist and nuzzled her neck. 'Happy?' he asked.

'Couldn't be happier,' Mawde replied.

As the summer days lengthened, Julian worked later, often not returning home until after Mawde had retired to bed.

'I'm worried about you,' Mawde said late one evening, gazing at the bowl in front of him. He had swallowed only a few mouthfuls of pottage and a single mouthful of bread.

Julian let out a yawn. 'I confess I'd rather sleep than eat. My order book is filling fast. Even with Simon and my new assistant, I can't keep up with demand. Phillip's a competent blacksmith but he's not as fast as me.'

Mawde stood behind him and massaged his shoulders. He carried the smell of smoke on his skin and the masculine tang of hard work. Julian closed his eyes and Mawde felt him relax beneath her touch.

'Did you know Sir Hugh now favours St Mawes above his other manors?' Julian said. Mawde pressed harder on his taut neck muscles. Julian groaned with pleasure. 'His entertaining season is well under way. Turns out his guests like my work.' Julian turned his head to look at Mawde. 'Sweeting, we are inundated with orders. His guests want ornamental locks, buckles and clothes pins. And we can barely meet the demand for boot scrapers, armour and pots. I'll have to employ another blacksmith if my days continue like this.'

Mawde felt his shoulders tense. 'Julian, what is it?'

Julian reached for one of her hands and pulled her towards his lap. 'Is your Mamm in bed?'

'Yes, and no doubt fast asleep. She tires so easily these days.' Mawde stroked the lines that had deepened by his eyes. 'Something's on your mind, I can tell.'

'I've been thinking about the pewter we kept from Treffry's ship. I should melt it down and reuse it. That and anything else you have from the old prior's grave. I worry about keeping stolen goods in the house. I'd sleep easier at night if I turned them into something unrecognisable.'

'You worry too much. There's little of the priory treasure left.' Mawde tapped the bunch of keys tied around her waist. 'No one but me opens the coffers.'

'I know, but even so…'

Mawde stroked the furrows in his brow. 'Put those thoughts out of your mind.' She slipped off his lap and held out her hand. 'Let us retire to bed. I've never seen you look this tired, and I want you to sleep well.'

Julian held her hand and looked at her with smouldering eyes. 'I will happily retire to bed, but not to go to sleep.'

Mawde gave him a coquettish smile. 'As you wish,' she said.

# CHAPTER FIFTY-FIVE

ONE HOT JULY DAY, Mawde was feeling listless. Even the slightest task drained all her energy. She settled on a shaded patch of grass, hoping she would cool quickly. She listened to the clang of metal on metal ringing out from Julian's forge.

'I don't know how Julian can bear it with the fires going,' Mamm said, handing a cup of ale to Mawde.

'He has Treffry to thank for that.' Mawde took a few sips of the cool liquid. 'Julian wanted to finish early today, but Treffry sent an urgent order for pewter. He has a party of dignitaries arriving tomorrow and needs cups, plates and spoons.'

Mawde drank more of her ale and rose to her feet. 'Thank you, Mamm. I feel better already. I'll bake today's bread.'

Sometime later, a furious banging on the front door caused Mawde to drop a lump of dough. 'Who could that be?' she said, wiping flour from her hands. The visitor pounded a second time and harder than before. Mawde's stomach flipped as she pulled open the door. Julian's apprentice was standing on the doorstep. His chest was heaving and sweat soaked his brow.

'Simon?'

'Mistress, come quickly!'

Mawde raised her hands to her cheeks. 'Your master, is he hurt?'

'No, mistress, but come now! Treffry's men came to arrest him.'

Mawde's legs wobbled like unset custard as she tried to keep pace with the apprentice, but by the time they reached the forge, Julian was gone.

'They took him to the castle, mistress,' the assistant blacksmith said.

Mawde hurried out of the forge and ran along the street. Her shift clung to her back and hair clung to her face. She passed the house that had been her home with barely a fleeting glance and stopped at the castle guardhouse, gasping for breath.

'My husband,' she said, leaning forward and grasping her side, trying to ease a stitch. 'Where have they taken him?'

The guard opened the gate for her. 'The dungeon,' he said. 'Turn right before the footbridge, down the path and then turn left.'

Mawde raised her hand to thank him and careered down the slope. She stopped at the top of a flight of stone stairs and willed her heart to slow and ease the thundering in her head. When she opened her eyes, Treffry was at the bottom of the steps, giving her a steely stare.

'This way,' he said.

'What is he accused of?' Mawde asked, clinging to the wall as she descended.

'He can tell you himself.' Treffry took a torch from an iron holder and escorted Mawde along a gloomy corridor, his footsteps loud and echoing. He stopped outside the furthest cell and handed her the torch. The smell of burning pig fat caught the back of Mawde's throat.

'You can have a few moments with him,' Treffry said, unlocking the cell door.

Mawde peered inside the cell. Julian was crouching in a corner with his head buried in his hands. He was rocking back and forth. 'I'm sorry,' he whimpered. 'I'm so sorry. This is all my fault.'

The cell door screeched as Mawde pushed it open. She stepped inside and placed the torch in a bracket on the wall. The small space reeked of damp and the stench of bodily waste. A rat lay rotting by the door with flies crawling over its carcass. A large cockroach emerged from a hole in the floor and scuttled over to join the feast. Mawde shuddered and moved towards Julian, dragging her skirt through the filth.

'Why has Treffry brought you here?' she asked, knowing all too well they had both done things for which they could be locked up.

'Phillip told Treffry I had his pewter.'

'How did he find out? Surely you never discussed it?'

'No! When Treffry asked for new pewterware, I thought it was the perfect chance to melt the pewter from the wreck. I told you I was worried about keeping it at home.'

'You did.' Mawde felt for the keys she wore at her waist. 'How did you get to it?'

Julian looked away. 'Three nights ago, while you were sleeping, I took your keys to open the chest. I was going to tell you after I melted it down and had coins for the metal instead. Because we live so close to the forge, I could take the pewter there unseen. I wanted to avoid this very situation.' He turned back to look at Mawde. 'My love, I got it so wrong. I hid all the pewter under some sacks in the corner where only I work. The next day, it was so hot, I said we should finish early. But I lingered behind the other two, saying I'd damp down the fires. But that wasn't my intention at all.'

Julian fell silent as sobs built in his throat. Mawde sat down beside him. The cold and damp of the stone floor seeped through her skirts.

'Time's almost up!' Treffry's voice boomed along the corridor and ricocheted off the walls.

'What happened, Julian?' she asked gently.

Julian dried his eyes. 'I started melting the salvaged pewter and mixing it with metal scraps. I'd even poured three new plates, then Phillip came looking for his belt.' Julian looked wretched. He ran his hands through his hair. 'There was nothing I could do. I had a pile of Treffry's pewter plates on the workbench, ready to melt them down. Each one bore Treffry's initials and his family crest. If they had all looked new, I might have got away with it. But most of them were dented and scratched from a battering during the wreck. Phillip made nothing of it, though. He acted like he hadn't noticed. We spoke of several other matters before he left, and I thought I'd got away with it.'

'You think he told Treffry?' Mawde asked.

Julian glanced towards the door and tilted his head as if listening for footsteps. 'Must have come straight to him.' The cockroach scuttled between them. Julian clamped it in his hand and hurled it against the wall. 'No doubt Treffry gave him a handsome reward.'

The sound of approaching footsteps filled Mawde with dread. 'What can I do to get you out of here?'

Julian hung his head. 'Alas, my love, there is no hope, and my time is almost done. Your chest contained a gold chalice, and I took it to remove the stones. Treffry found it.

Such a piece can only have come from a religious house, and therefore belongs to the King. I refused to say how I came by it, and sweeting, you must never let on. They will hang me for stealing from King Henry, for that is what they'll say I have done. But if giving my life saves yours, I am more than ready to die.'

Julian rose to his feet, rattling the chains secured around his ankles. As he helped Mawde to stand, she flung her arms around him.

Julian clung to her. 'Promise you'll continue helping the people of St Mawes.'

'No!'

'Please, Mawde, you must if we're to give my fate a purpose. Mine and Perry's.'

Treffry loomed in the doorway. 'That's it. Time to go.'

Julian pulled Mawde towards him and kissed her passionately. 'Let me go with good grace,' he whispered.

Mawde felt Treffry's hand on her arm and tried to shrug it off. But Treffry tightened his grip and manhandled her out of the cell. He slammed the door and turned the key. Mawde grasped the metal bars, unwilling to let Julian out of her sight. But Treffry was too strong for Mawde, and her fingers slipped.

'Julian!'

Julian tried to walk towards the door, but the shackles held him back. 'Go in peace, my love.'

A wave of nausea gripped Mawde. Bile burned at the back of her throat. She forced herself to swallow the liquid that rose into her mouth.

'I'm carrying your child,' she said, as her fingers separated from the bars.

A look of delight settled on Julian's face. 'We are truly blessed!'

Treffry tugged Mawde's arm. His fingers tightened like a vice.

'One more minute, please!' she cried.

Treffry tutted and muttered under his breath.

'The name of our child, Julian. You must choose the name.'

Julian did not hesitate to give Mawde his answer. 'If it's a boy, you must name him Perry. Florence, for a little girl. God has blessed us with His gift, my love. Through our child, my spirit will live on. Go now, I beg you.'

The strain showed on Julian's face despite his brave smile.

Mawde tried to swallow her sorrow. 'I love you.'

Julian placed his palm on his chest. 'With all my heart, Mawde, I love you too.'

'Let's go.' Treffry pulled Mawde towards the steep steps and the blinding sunlight.

# CHAPTER FIFTY-SIX

JULIAN WAS TAKEN to the August assizes in Launceston and found guilty of three crimes: stealing gold from King Henry VIII, causing loss of life by wrecking a ship, and stealing Treffry's cargo. He was executed four days later.

For weeks, Mawde moved about in a daze, unable to process what had happened. By night, she dreamed about his hanging and his twitching legs refusing to still. By day, his absence was a physical pain that gnawed away at her heart. Often, she thought she glimpsed his shadow or heard the creak of his leather jerkin. Then she'd remember that Julian was gone and would grieve all over again.

But then, one day in early October, Mawde's pregnancy quickened. The delicate flutter within her womb was like a soft nudge from Julian. Their child needed her to gather her wits if Julian's death was to mean something. It was time for Mawde to resume her campaign to secure the future of the village – and the future of her and Julian's child.

Mawde settled at the dining room table and studied the entries in her ledgers – one was for the household accounts, the other for her business ventures. She was receiving income from renting the forge to an eager young blacksmith. She made a small sum from each of her boats, the fire dues and the loan repayments. But it wasn't enough. One day, the loans would all be repaid, and most of the money for the fire dues paid men to work the nightly shifts. She had plenty of coins locked away in her coffers waiting for the right investments, schemes that would pay her for her trouble while benefitting local people. It was time to call a village meeting.

At twilight the following day, Mawde draped a shawl across her shoulders and secured it with Julian's brooch. She joined a throng of men and women entering the chapel. Mawde made her way through the assembled crowd to stand beside the rector. The rector called the chapel to silence, and all eyes turned towards Mawde. Gone were her nerves from those earlier days when she had addressed hostile villagers. Instead, she smiled at friendly faces watching her from the pews.

'The last year or two has seen a change in fortune for many of you,' she said. 'Two families have regular trade in Penryn selling wooden crafts and toys. The builders and carpenters are working on houses for merchants keen to live in our village. We have two new boats fishing our waters, and the boatyard has taken on more men. These are a few examples of how our village is recovering from the dark days that descended upon us when the priory closed.' Her words were met with eager nods and murmurings of agreement. 'Our weekly markets are still paltry affairs compared to how they once were,' she said. 'I propose we work on this and hold a monthly market fair. We want outsiders to come with money. Do you all agree?'

Her words prompted eager applause and a hubbub of

excited chatter. She waited for the noise to subside and raised her hand to call them to silence.

'I propose we hold the first of these fairs early next spring and run them until the end of the summer. If they are as successful as I hope, we will repeat them the following year. We need to make them worthy of people travelling here by boat. That means we need quality goods to sell, so visitors spread the word.'

The reaction of the villagers was better than she had hoped. The chapel buzzed with optimism.

'Every stall holder must have their turn at enjoying a prime position. I therefore propose we confirm each person's pitch before each market day.' Curious faces greeted Mawde's suggestion.

The cordwainer asked, 'How would that work?'

'It will need careful planning,' Mawde said. 'I'm willing to take that on. I was thinking of using a rotation system such as my cousin uses for his crops. In other words, if you have a pitch assigned that's not as desirable as you hoped, do not be disappointed because your turn for the best pitch will come. Every market day, your location will move one pitch along from the last.'

A heckle of dissent came from somewhere in the middle of the room.

'Of course,' Mawde continued, 'it's up to you to sell quality goods to build your own reputations. That way, customers will seek you out no matter where your stall is located. We are a small but growing village. When I was a child, stalls lined the street. I say they should do so again and fill the village square.'

'What's in it for you?' shouted a man from the back of the room.

'A share of profits from my family's stall.' Mawde smiled. 'You've tried our biscuits, sweetmeats and my sister's honey. The more we all try to make this a success, the more each family benefits – mine and yours included.'

'Fair enough,' the man replied, appearing a little chastened.

'Consider this too,' Mawde said. 'We should provide entertainment. When people arrive on the boats, they'll hear music playing from the market. They will hear the hum of merry voices and they'll certainly smell our food. We can have hog roasts, pies, pancakes and bread, and our baker's delicious saffron cakes.'

The baker preened in the middle pew and waved his hand at Mawde.

'Our fishing families can sell smoked mackerel, fresh whiting, turbot and lobsters. We'll have dancing, tournaments and activities for children with storytellers, races and games. Our market will be more than a collection of stalls. It will be a celebration of the spirit of our village.'

Mawde glanced at the rector. He gave an approving smile. Mawde closed her eyes and imagined Julian was with her. He would have been so proud! She placed her palm over her belly. She was doing this for him and their child.

'So, what do you say?' she said, looking from one person to another. 'Shall we create a market that's the talk of the Duchy and make customers eager to come time and again?'

'Aye!' shouted the baker, punching the air with his fist.

'Aye!' shouted the cordwainer, rubbing his palms together with glee.

'Ayes' echoed around the chapel. Mawde called the villagers to order again.

'I propose we start our monthly market fair on the third Tuesday of March. Anyone wishing to run a stall, come to see me at my house. Meanwhile, share the news of our plans. Fishermen, spread the word in Penryn when unloading your catches. Carpenters, builders, tell your customers when you work in other villages. This will only be successful if everyone plays a part.' Men and women murmured their agreement. 'This is not just a small village in Cornwall,' Mawde added. 'This is the village of St Mawes!'

Men and women stood and cheered. Mawde's spirits soared. She had done so much wrong in the past but now she was making amends by instilling confidence and trust. She looked at the image of Saint Maudez offering wisdom to his students and thanked God for guiding her to follow the saint's example. At last she had a found a way to atone for all of her sins.

'There's one more thing,' Mawde said, pulling attention back towards her. 'Every year, pilchards pass our coastline, but we don't take advantage of their numbers. I say it's time we used our fleet to land them on our shore. We will gut them, salt them and sell them on, but I'll need all the women on the beaches. It's unpleasant work but will reward us well. Tell me now, are you willing?'

'Aye,' Beth shouted from the back of the room, smiling warmly at Mawde.

'Aye,' Agnes cried, following Beth's example. She flushed deep red to the roots of her hair when the miller's son grasped her hand.

'Aye,' came the shouts from more of the women.

'Then let's do it,' Mawde said, raising her voice, 'for each other and St Mawes!'

# CHAPTER FIFTY-SEVEN

MAWDE WAS PAINTING sea creatures on the bottom corner of her mural. Yellow whelks nestled between orange starfish, and a playful dolphin leapt over a seal. A knock at the door made her jump and drop her paintbrush. She retrieved her brush and wiped it on a cloth before going to the door to greet her visitor.

A young man stood on her path. He removed his hat and stammered his greeting. 'Good morrow.' He fanned his florid face with his hat. 'Are you Mistress Viker?'

'Yes, I am she.' She caught the young man glancing at her hands. 'I was painting,' she said, rubbing a stubborn patch of orange staining the base of her thumb.

The young man's Adam's apple bobbed up and down. 'Forgive me for showing up unannounced, but they speak highly of you in the village.' He glanced back at the street before looking anxiously at Mawde. 'I wish to borrow money.'

Mawde stood aside and beckoned him indoors. 'This is not a conversation to have on the doorstep.'

She registered his surprise as he admired the painting

on the wall. She pointed to her latest additions. 'I was painting a starfish when you knocked. Please, have a seat.'

The young man perched on the settle.

'I don't recall seeing you in the village,' Mawde said as she sat on her cushioned chair.

'No, mistress. We were living in Truro, where we worked as weavers.' His eyes filled with sadness. 'My mother died and we moved here to live with my aunt.'

She gave the young man a moment to compose himself, and then asked, 'Where is your aunt's house?'

'Near the quay,' he replied.

'One of the merchant's houses?' Mawde asked.

The young man shook his head. 'A little further along from those and nothing quite as grand.'

Mawde studied her visitor with his earnest expression and clean-shaven face. His shoes shone with polish and he was wearing a doublet of good-quality wool. 'Tell me why you're seeking a loan.'

'My father's not as young as he was,' he replied, 'but he still knows how to weave. With the loan, we can buy a loom and weave here in St Mawes.'

'I see. Why didn't your father come with you today?'

The young man twisted his cap in his hand. 'He's a proud man, mistress. He doesn't like the idea of borrowing.'

Mawde gave a rueful smile. 'That, I understand. Is he still a member of the guild?'

'He is, and I hope to join the guild myself. I've spent most of my life learning the craft.'

'Who will I be lending the money to, you or your father?'

The man's cheeks turned florid. 'I'll take responsibility for the loan. My ambition is greater than my father's. He has no desire to weave these days, but he's willing to oversee me.' He sat up straighter. 'Soon, I'm to marry, and I wish to support my wife from my own weaving business.'

Mawde admired the young man's ambition. 'Do you have other weavers in the family?'

'Oh yes! A cousin the same age as me. I hope to lure him here to work with me.'

Mawde recognised the determination in his eyes. 'In that case,' she said, 'I will give you the money, but enough for two looms, not one.'

The young man looked puzzled. 'Why two? I can only operate one at a time.'

Mawde smiled. 'I believe one loom will prove insufficient,' she said. 'Our spinners already make a large quantity of yarn, and I will persuade Sir Hugh to sell some of it to me. I'll also buy fleeces direct from my cousin and pay the spinners for piecework. Do not underestimate how busy you'll be with your looms.' She smiled. 'We'll need an arrangement with the Penryn fullers to dye your cloth before we sell it. I think we can organise everything between us, don't you?'

The young man nodded eagerly. 'Yes, Mistress Viker, thank you. But what will be the terms of the loan?'

Mawde leaned towards the hearth and added a log to the fire. 'I have no intention of putting you in debt.' Disappointment shadowed the young man's face. 'However,' Mawde continued, 'I will pay for two new looms, and we'll run the business as a partnership. I will receive one third of the profits after costs and tithes have been met. You will keep the rest. If the village continues to grow, as I expect it will, our venture will expand and so will our profits. Tell me, what do you think of these terms?'

A broad smile appeared on the young man's face. 'I like them very much.'

'Good. I will have a deed drawn up for both of us to sign.'

Mawde rose to see the young man out. 'Wait!' she said. 'I forgot to ask your name.'

'I'm Simon,' he replied. 'Simon Harvey.'

'My father's name was Simon,' Mawde said wistfully. 'It must be a good omen.'

# CHAPTER FIFTY-EIGHT

THE THIRD TUESDAY of March arrived, with white clouds dotting the sky. Boats jostled on the shimmering water, and the village was abuzz. Hot pies scented the air, chased by the smell of roasting pig. Fiddles played merry tunes and travelling minstrels entertained.

Every stall was surrounded with visitors eager to spend their money. Men bartered over the blacksmith's tools while women bought brooches and pins. The baker cooked fresh pancakes while his wife sold saffron cakes and pies. A fisherman's wife sold whiting fritters while her husband filleted fish.

Mawde soon had a gaggle of women poring over her goods. They bought her comfits, jellies and preserves, lavender bags and scented oils. Soon, Mawde had sold every item and asked Agnes to pack up her stall while she wandered through the market to admire the other stalls. Everyone had worked hard to make quality goods to sell. Mawde bought a rattle shaped like a dolphin for her baby, due the following month.

She heard a group of dejected men grumbling by the

sea wall. She slowed her steps to hear their words and felt obliged to interrupt.

'Forgive me for eavesdropping,' she said, 'but did I hear you say you have no work?'

'Aye, that's right,' one man said, 'thanks to Sir Hugh.'

'How so?' Mawde asked.

'He's cutting back on farming to buy yet more sheep for wool. He doesn't need us to work his land so we might try our luck with tin. Trouble is, we'd have to leave the village and there ain't no guarantee we'd get work in tinning.'

The other men mumbled their agreement.

'Maybe I can help,' Mawde said. 'Perhaps offer something better.'

'Like what?' said the oldest of the men. His top lip had a scar on one side which made him look mean and surly.

'Are you willing to learn new skills?' Mawde asked. 'And work hard for a decent living?'

'Of course.'

'Perhaps more importantly,' she said, 'are you willing to work for a woman?'

All four men exchanged glances.

'Aye,' they said in unison.

'Good. I own a small fishing fleet and will soon have two new boats. They're in the yard at Freshwater and will be ready in four to six weeks. Until then, make yourselves available to my crews. They'll help you find your sea legs and teach you all you need to know. How does that sound to you?'

The eldest man whisked the cap from his head and scrunched it in his hands. 'That's kind of ye, and I thank ye. I will not let ye down.'

The other men echoed his sentiment and Mawde left them in happier moods.

By mid-afternoon, the stalls had been cleared and trading gave way to dancing. The villagers lavished Mawde with praise, and she revelled in their attention. She wished she could stay and dance with them, but she was tired, and her back was aching. Instead, she went home with Mamm at dusk and settled early for the night. She closed her eyes and imagined Julian lying beside her in the bed with his body pressed against hers and his breath warming her cheek. She placed her palms on her belly and pretended her hands were his. Julian's child wriggled and kicked, and Mawde knew his spirit lived.

# EPILOGUE

*Five months later*

THE SUN SANK SLOWLY towards the horizon, painting the sea with liquid gold. A gentle breeze rustled leaves in the trees, and beach asters bobbed in the soft light. Boats danced around their moorings as the tide reached its peak and turned. Delicate waves lapped at the shore, exposing shingle and patches of sand. A cormorant dived for its supper and a herring gull circled above.

The baby fussed in Mawde's arms and brandished a tiny fist.

'Are you hungry again, little one?' Mawde lifted her partlet and loosened the lace of her bodice. The baby opened her rosebud mouth and suckled at Mawde's breast. 'Your da would have adored you. Although he can't be with us now, we'll always have his love.' The baby paused her suckling and fixed her deep blue eyes on Mawde. 'One day, I'll tell you his story,' Mawde said. 'And one day, I'll tell you mine.'

The baby finished feeding, and Mawde gently rubbed

her back. She smiled at her daughter's gurgling and noisy, inelegant burps. When the baby settled and her eyelids drooped, Mawde stood and rocked her to sleep.

The balmy summer evening cast a calm over St Mawes. The castle glimmered in the distance, guarding the Carrick Roads. The village streets were quieter now that village men manned the garrison, but their houses glowed with whitewashed walls and new shutters at the windows.

Village businesses were thriving, including Weaver Simon's. He had soon earned a reputation for the quality of his fine-weave cloth for Sunday doublets and kirtles and his sturdier weaves for work clothes. The builders and carpenters had full order books thanks to merchants eager for waterfront homes. Even Sir Hugh paid attention to Mawde's business ideas and praised her proposals for catching pilchards. He paid for a large salting shed to be built on the quay and donated it to the village.

Mawde looked for her fishing boats at anchor in the harbour. One by one, she identified them and softly spoke their names. '*Mistress of Carrick*, there you are. I see you *Marion* and *Genevie*ve. *Spirit of Tamsin*, you work hard. You too, dear *Peregrine*.'

The air turned cool as the sun sank lower, dipping beneath the horizon. The baby stirred in Mawde's arms, and opened her curious eyes. Mawde felt a surge of love as she watched her baby look around. Her eyes roved towards the harbour and then she smiled at Mawde.

'God forgave me,' Mawde said, stroking the baby's forehead. 'He freed me from my nightmares and gave me a wonderful gift.' She adjusted the baby's blanket to protect her from the chill. 'My darling girl, I promise you that I will love you forever. You're the light that brightens my world, my Florence Juliana.'

THANK YOU FOR READING THIS BOOK.

I hope you enjoyed reading this tale about Mawde. If you did, and you can spare a minute or two, it would mean the world to me if you would leave an honest review on your favourite bookstore's website.

You might enjoy my other books:

*The Second Mrs Thistlewood*

The Roseland Collection
*Mawde of Roseland*
*Mistress of Carrick*

The Mayflower Collection
*Winds of Change*
*Running With The Wind*
*The Winter Years*

**Have you joined the
Allium Books Readers Club?**

Members receive a monthly newsletter, advance notification of my new releases and a FREE downloadable short story. There's no catch to joining, and I'll never pass on your information to third parties. You can unsubscribe at any time. If you'd like to know more about this club and my other published books, please visit my website at www.dionnehaynes.com.

# SELECT BIBLIOGRAPHY

If you would like to learn more about the Tudor era, here is a small selection of excellent non-fiction books:

*How To Be A Tudor* by Ruth Goodman

*Woodsmoke And Sage* by Amy Licence

*Eating With The Tudors* by Brigitte Webster

*The Private Lives Of The Tudors* by Tracy Borman

*The Tudor Housewife* by Alison Sim

*The Lives Of Tudor Women* by Elizabeth Norton

# ACKNOWLEDGMENTS

My sincere thanks go to Liz Monument (lizmonument.com) for her excellent editing feedback, Beverley Sykes (superscriptproofreading.co.uk) for her attention to detail and exceptional proofreading service, and Dee Dee (deedeebookcovers) for the beautiful book cover design.

As always, I'm grateful for the support and encouragement from my family and friends, and especially my husband – for listening to my ramblings, making countless cups of tea, recovering my lost computer files, and for always being there.

And finally, I'd like to thank you for choosing to read this book.

Printed in Great Britain
by Amazon

46977225R00192